On the Level

A Mystery of Romance, Suspense, and
Home Improvement

David Edgar Cournoyer

Long Island Sound Press

Published in Colchester, Connecticut by
Long Island Sound Press

Author's Note: Although the geography and architecture of the borough of Groton City, Connecticut inspired the setting for this novel, the story is a work of fiction. Names, characters, incidents, and places mentioned within are either products of the author's imagination or used fictitiously. All characters are fictional and any similarity to persons living or dead is purely coincidental.

Cover art and cover design by Marissa Stanton.

ISBN: 978-0-9888926-0-6

For Gloria

Acknowledgements

Many people have inspired and supported the creation of this book. Although any remaining deficiencies are my responsibility, I wish to acknowledge several people who have helped to improve the quality of this book.

Thank you to writing coach Elizabeth Lyon and mystery novelist Carolyn J. Rose for knowing the guidance I needed and providing it with respect, thoughtfulness, and patience.

Thank you to Dr. Martin Bloom for providing a critique of an early draft. Sandy Planeta, Beverly Popowich, and the members of The Write Stuff also have been wonderfully encouraging of my efforts to write fiction. Special thanks are due to Suzy Cordatos and Kristi Rhodes who invited me into their critique group, inspired me to try the novel form, and provided critical feedback about my efforts.

Thanks also are due to Groton Bank Historical Association for providing a web site that facilitated my research, and Association President Tom Althuis who greatly increased my knowledge of the architectural heritage of the community that inspired this story.

Thank you to the many people who helped with the research and provided feedback. Richard and Pamela Young of Omega ReMax Realty of Manchester New Hampshire advised me on matters of real estate practice and were encouraging all along.

I am also grateful to Andrew J. Cournoyer, my son and business partner, for his inspiration and several plot ideas.

Finally, thank you to Gloria, who makes the sun come up for me every day. You have always been my strongest source of support and inspiration. Your presence made even the difficult portions of this journey fun.

David Edgar Cournoyer, March, 2013

Chapter 1

Joe Simpson's last minutes were filled with ocean breezes, the calls of herring gulls, and the smell of newly mowed grass. A younger man might have survived the two-story fall but Joe hit the ground like a crab dropped on the rocks. Vital fluids seeped from his bone-punctured organs. Joe had traded in secrets for nearly eighty years before discovering one that got him killed. As his life-force ebbed, Joe was satisfied that the fatal secret wouldn't die with him. Franklin Breault, his clever protégé, was about to receive a legacy he couldn't refuse. Joe's last thought was that this gift was as dangerous as handing Franklin a running chainsaw.

* * *

The letter that unraveled my life arrived the same Tuesday that Joe Simpson died. As he lie on the lawn in front of his Greek Revival home beside Long Island Sound, one of my parents had visited the mailbox in front of our raised ranch, retrieved the envelope and left it in my apartment. I appreciated all the little things they did, but living in their basement sometimes made me feel like I had never grown up.

I tore open the flap and pulled out the mist-soaked contents. The envelope contained a bill of sale. The property offered was a rundown Queen Anne Victorian. The price was one dollar and a commitment to restore it under Joe's supervision.

Joe Simpson, Ph.D., B.Arch., had purchased the Queen Anne from the town as a ruin. By offering it to me, he would preserve another piece of fast-disappearing history. The project would provide the internship I needed to complete my education so I could get a real job and move out of my parents' basement. The bill of sale should have been like a winning lottery ticket. As it turned out, it was more like a call to jury duty.

It was no accident that Joe hadn't signed the form. The lack of a signature was a summons. As much as I loved the old man, he was the most controlling person I knew. He insisted on selecting subcontractors, suppliers, and the mortgage originator. I had resisted, wanting to run my own project. I was angry that he hadn't signed, and angry at his efforts to control me. I didn't know that it was already too late for us to work out our differences.

Four days later, on the Friday morning of Joe's funeral, I stood in front of the Queen Anne. The decaying beauty loomed against a gray sky in an old neighborhood called Groton Bank. It was peaceful, if not quiet. The New York to Boston Amtrak train issued a shrill warning as it approached Mystic Station across town. On the far side of the river the Block Island ferry announced its departure with a ground-shaking blast. Cars swished past on the riverfront, rumbling along sections of Thames Street made of stamped concrete grooved to look like brick. I was sick with the feelings of loss and guilt. I was angry that Joe had dangled a new life in front of me and then took it with him to the grave.

My girlfriend, Linda, was waiting back at the funeral home. She hadn't bought the explanation that I was checking on the house for Joe's widow. Linda had given me a knowing look and said it was okay that I needed some time alone before saying a public goodbye to Joe. I felt a little bad about trying to deceive her. Generally I stick to the truth. Honesty often caused trouble but facts were easier to keep track of than lies.

"Damn it!" I punched the steering wheel and climbed out of the truck. I wouldn't blame Joe's widow if she chose not to honor his verbal offer. She hadn't made her intentions regarding the Queen Anne clear yet and I was desperate to know her plan.

Without this project I couldn't qualify for a license as a preservation architect. Worse, this happened as payments on a mountain of student loan debt came due. I couldn't talk to Linda about my fears because she didn't share my love of Victorian homes. Linda would be happier if I got a safe job designing kitchens and bathrooms for wealthy summer residents.

The old Queen Anne looked like a cursed and neglected fairytale castle, desperate for a modern Prince Charming with a tool box. A crooked center chimney loomed over the house with a drunken tilt. A conical roof shaped like a sorcerer's hat capped a turret-tower built into one corner of the building. Sun and ice had curled and cracked the shingles across the undulating roof. Splintered plywood covered several broken windows and rot had destroyed sections of gingerbread trim. Rain and mildew had painted black streaks down the gray horizontal cedar siding, like icing on a decaying cake.

Whipped by the wind, a tree limb slapped against the old house with a loud crack. The landscaping was closing in on the structure. The Queen Anne needed work soon or there would be nothing to restore. Once the neglect progressed too far, the structural integrity would be lost and the building would fail. For an instant I had the heretical notion that the house might have passed that point, but quickly repressed the thought. Joe once said that any building still standing could be saved. Besides, my passion to restore this house was only partially about advancing my career. In addition to the thrill of owning a true Victorian, this was the house I wanted to share with Linda as my wife.

I slid out of my truck and strolled to the back to inspect the foundation wall. Smells of mold and rot swirled. A month ago a late summer tropical storm had torn off the copper gutters. Since then the water had collected against the foundation and bowed in the basement wall. I headed for the back entrance to check for any new damage.

Nineteenth-century masons had built the foundation from stone blocks, but a more recent owner had added a basement hatchway built of concrete. I reached for the handle of the coffin-shaped metal door that covered the opening. The cover creaked as it rose, releasing a cloud of musty air. I stepped in and started down the rough stairs.

I was about half way down when I heard a soft mechanical click. As I turned back toward the hatch cover, the sky darkened and a weight slammed down on my head. A sharp pain registered, and my cheek felt wet.

Blood. My legs gave out and I tumbled into darkness.

I must have faded in and out of consciousness several times. When things cleared up a bit I was surprised to see Joe standing over me removing the bill of sale from my pocket. He was tall and had lost some weight.

A hand reached toward me and a voice whispered. "Forget about this house. It's beyond saving."

I must have been hallucinating, but at the time it felt pretty real.

The image faded and was replaced by a throbbing headache. My face was mashed into wet sand. The copper taste of blood was on my tongue. My whole body ached and my clothes were damp. The stench of wet, moldy air cleared my head a little. I pushed up to a sitting position. The fuzziness receded at about the same speed as my old pickup truck straining on a steep hill. Light filtered around the partially closed hatch cover.

Shaking, I turned and climbed the first step. In the distance an ambulance wailed. I reached overhead and pushed on the metal hatch cover. The effort caused my temples to pound as fireworks erupted behind my eyes.

I sat down on the stairs to regroup.

Damn, that hurts. What was I doing in an abandoned building without a hardhat? You'd think I would have been more careful after Joe's death less than a week ago. He had always admonished me to tend to safety first. "What an idiot," I mumbled.

I stood again and pushed. The hatch swung open with a

head-splitting shriek. I climbed another step and came level with the wedges that should have kept the heavy metal door propped open. I leaned on the frame waiting for my eyes to regain their focus.

The door mechanism was covered with rust. Apparently the corroded stops hadn't engaged properly. Blood on the metal plate confirmed that the hatch cover had hit my head. I climbed out and let the damn thing slam shut, waves of nausea rippling through my gut.

The bang on the head suddenly made me feel breakable. What a house of cards life is for a handyman. Most days I didn't think about how fragile my situation was, but a broken arm or a twisted ankle could make it impossible to work. No work meant no money and ultimatums from angry creditors and my impatient girlfriend. My new career as an architect was supposed to provide a buffer from all that, but I couldn't get my license until I completed one more internship.

I staggered back to the truck with my feet dragging. The chimes in the clock tower at the First Church rang. I had missed the memorial service! Joe might not notice, but Linda was waiting for me at the funeral home and she was probably furious.

Linda Kisslovich was standing in front of the Groton City House of Rest when I arrived. Despite the years we'd been dating, I still got a little flutter in my gut when I saw her. Ash brown hair cascaded in curls around her shoulders. Black stockings highlighted her curvy legs. Red shoes with five-inch heels decorated her feet. A short black silk dress topped by a shiny red raincoat covered the rest of her. Not traditional funeral clothes, but in her red and black outfit, she looked hot enough to peel the paint off the white-washed clapboards behind her.

A little tension in her cheekbones and tightness around her eyes told me she was annoyed, but when she saw me her expression changed to concern. She pulled open the truck door, her eyes large with worry. "Jesus, Frankie, you're hurt. There's blood all over your face."

She climbed in and extracted the tube of all-purpose chlorine wipes she had insisted I keep in the truck. She took my face in her hands and gently caressed the blood and dirt away from my cheek with a moist towel smelling of bleach.

I liked her touch, although the chlorine stung when she found the cut on my head. For all Linda's grousing about my lack of financial success, I knew she cared about me. More than anything else in the world, I wanted to rehab the old Queen Anne and move into the renovated home with Linda. The tender way she blotted the blood from my face temporarily took my mind off how little progress I was making with all that.

I had difficulty turning my thoughts into words. "I banged my head."

Linda inspected my eyes. "You should go to the hospital."

"I can make it to the cemetery."

Linda treated me to a wry smile. "Hospital first, cemetery only as a last resort."

If she was joking I couldn't look that bad. "When did the hearse leave?"

"Five minutes ago. Can we really make it?"

"Watch me."

I turned the truck inland. We raced north, beside the mile-wide mouth of the Thames River where it pushed into Long Island Sound. Traffic flowed steadily along the spider web of city streets filled with early twentieth century two-story homes. I headed back toward the Queen Anne, passing the shipyard and dozens of little white bungalows competing for river views. We turned inland at Arnold Street at the southern end of the Groton Bank Historic District. The older homes on Arnold were mostly built after the Civil War, whereas the homes on the granite ridge behind them dated all the way back to the Revolution.

The old Victorians always made me think of my cabinetmaker Grandpa Breault. I still remembered the feel of newly milled trim, the smells of his shop, and the satisfaction of working with my hands. After Grandpa died, Joe had showed me how to look at

6

classic homes with an architect's eye. It was like having x-ray vision. I understood the techniques needed to build houses and the art and imagination that made them beautiful and functional.

Linda kept blotting my face with the wipes, her concern slowly yielding to impatience. "I don't see why it was so important for you to go rummaging around in that ruin today. Old Victorians are death traps."

By the time we reached the hill above the cemetery, I smelled like a lifeguard at the Y.

"Frankie, do you really want to do this? You're the color of old plaster."

"I'm okay." My head hurt, but I was determined to make Joe's burial. I pulled the truck in the driveway of the Queen Anne for the second time that day. Linda stuck a couple of adhesive bandages on my scalp and covered the makeshift repair with a baseball cap she found behind the seat.

Raindrops started to fall so I scooped a battered golf umbrella out of the junk behind the seat and stepped around to the passenger side. With one arm supporting the umbrella and the other around Linda's trim waist, we slid down the steep sidewalk. At the bottom of the hill we crossed Mitchell Street and scurried through the massive stone arches that frame the entrance to the Colonel Ledyard Cemetery.

My statuesque mother towered above the crowd. With her hair combed into a silvery sphere, she looked like a giant dandelion gone to seed. Dad stood beside her with baggy clothes and thin, gray hair like a deflated senior citizen blow-up doll.

We squeezed through the crowd and reached my parents. They exchanged hugs with Linda and raised their eyebrows with loving disapproval at my dirty clothes, ball cap, and ripped umbrella. Mom reached in her pocket and removed a small envelope.

"Where have you been? Nora Simpson left this. She wants to talk to you."

"Thanks Mom." I allowed myself a moment of optimism.

Maybe Nora wanted to go through with the deal for the Queen Anne. There would be problems. I'd need a new supervisor for the internship and Nora might impose new conditions. But her summons meant there was a chance I could make this work. I found myself sweating and breathing hard. I wanted to talk to her right away.

Mom placed the envelope on my outstretched palm. I closed my fingers over the top. Something about the line of fingertips along the sharp edge triggered a memory. I struggled to recall where I'd seen this before. I remembered seeing a row of fat fingertips out of the corner of my eye, just before everything faded to black. The fingers in my memory weren't curled around an envelope but the edge of the hatch door of the Queen Anne.

My aching head fizzled like a high voltage transformer in the rain. I realized that the fingers pointed the wrong way. They weren't mine. Someone had been pushing the hatch cover from the outside as it crashed down on my head!

Chapter 2

The September rainstorm that had been inching in from the ocean blew into the cemetery and replaced the salty mist with fat raindrops. The pea-sized orbs drummed with audible force on the polished coffin suspended above Joe Simpson's final resting place. Like marbles in a grim pinball game the drops rolled along grooves in the lacquer finish and dripped into the pit. Wind gusts whipped the branches of the oak trees and the green leaves quivered under the onslaught. The temperature cooled quickly and Linda began to shiver as we waited for the service to begin.

I shivered too, for a different reason. Someone had deliberately slammed that hatch cover on my head. Who would do that? All I wanted was to be sure the building was okay, return to the funeral home, say goodbye to Joe, and get on with my life. Was that too much to ask?

The confusion must have shown on my face. Linda reached up and touched my forehead, her eyes narrowed. "Frankie, what's wrong? You look like a decorator caught using last year's fabrics." Since high school, she'd talked like that to me, using her own quirky language drawn from her fascination with decorating, reminding us of our goal to be a top renovation team.

I pulled Linda away from the sea of umbrellas. My eyes cut to the hundred or so people clustered around the casket, temporarily forgetting my grief. I wondered if my assailant lurked somewhere in the crowd. No other vehicles were parked on the street during my earlier visit to the Queen Anne. Whoever hit me may have come from the cemetery. I leaned near Linda's ear. "I remember what happened at the house. Someone deliberately hit me with the hatch door."

Linda turned whitewash pale. "Why would anyone do that?"

"That's what I've been trying to figure out."

The funeral home staff finished arranging the scene and the first of several ministers started to speak. We moved back toward the crowd. Linda stepped gingerly across the soft ground trying to avoid digging in her spiky heels. I didn't hear a word that was said. Scenes from my life in which Joe participated kept playing in my head like movie trailers. I hadn't appreciated him nearly enough.

The air smelled of ozone as the rain poured down in silver spears. The mourners sent longing glances toward their cars as the clergy vied to outdo each other in their praise of Joe. A rip in my umbrella let a stream of water fall on my shoulder. Regrets washed through me as chilling as the rain. I shuddered and shifted the leak away. Memories of my anger about the missing signature and the apparition in the basement caused me to pat down the pocket where I had placed the unsigned bill of sale. The crackle that I anticipated didn't come. I jammed my hand inside and clawed around the pocket. The form wasn't there. I must have dropped it in the Queen Anne's basement. The document was worthless without a signature. Why would anyone want that?

A group of men on the opposite side of the casket, wearing dark suits, expensive raincoats and blank expressions, caught my attention. Developers. Joe's single-minded pursuit of preservation had deprived many in that crowd of land they wished to exploit. No doubt, if the developers had their way, Joe's motto, Preservation Before Profit, would have been carved into his chest with a dull knife.

I nudged Linda and spoke in her ear. "See those guys? They're here only to make sure he's dead."

Linda pushed on my hand to tilt the umbrella and studied the crowd. Her eyes opened wide and her mouth formed a shocked circle. "Frankie! I'm sure they're here out of respect."

The service ended and the crowd began to file by a coffin that seemed too small to contain such a valuable man. Linda and I took our turn in line, said a silent farewell, and moved a short way off. When the procession ended, the clergy spoke quietly to Nora Simpson and then joined the crowd as it flowed toward the cars. Linda and I held back and watched the funeral director and his assistant lower the casket. Joe disappeared from the surface of the earth.

My heart ached. Through blurred eyes I looked up at a ring of restored Victorians surrounding the cemetery. They were a testament to Joe's preservation efforts.

Linda followed my gaze. "I wonder how Joe got the owners to fix up all those old houses."

"I don't know." I pictured the stern, hawk-faced Joe. Mixed feelings about him twisted my gut again. He never asked, he ordered, and he always seemed to get his way. He had been supportive, smart, and helpful, but also demanding, arrogant, and controlling. I wondered how he had approached the many homeowners he persuaded to renovate.

Linda peered intently at me. "Frankie, are you feeling well enough to go to the reception at the Branford House? You could drop me off and your parents will take me home if you're not up to it."

Mom and Dad liked Linda. She had literally been the kid next door when we were growing up, a curly haired little charmer. When we had grown and became romantically involved in high school, they'd gone out of their way to make her feel she was part of the family. I think that they longed for the day that she would become the daughter they never had.

We joined the crowd headed toward the exit. "Is everything all right, Frankie?" Linda asked again when I didn't respond to her question about the reception.

"Sorry. Yeah, we can go. I want to talk with Nora, unless we catch her at the car."

Linda lifted her delicate chin in a defensive gesture. "I hope it doesn't seem insensitive but I need to drum up some work at the reception."

Linda provided the drive in our business partnership. Her warmth, creativity, and good looks were great business tools. Women respected her genuine concern and artistic talent and men, including me, found her irresistible on many levels. She was also the most determined person I'd ever met. At eighteen she had a major row with her parents and they'd kicked her out. She'd scratched out an existence at first by cleaning homes and later designing makeovers of summer cottages with me as a business partner. The rest of the world saw Linda as a confident designer, but I knew the insecure young girl driven by fear of poverty who lurked below the surface.

"Good idea. Joe's friends own big Victorians and they always need work."

Linda put on the impatient face she produced whenever I mentioned my preference for historic renovation. She nodded toward the cluster of developers I had pointed out earlier. "I hope those builders will be at the reception. Maybe one of them will need a decorator to stage some model homes."

I loved Linda, but her attitude toward real estate development couldn't have been more different from mine. She saw new buildings as blank canvases where she could create beautiful interior spaces. I saw the cheap developments as artless boxes with plastic exteriors ruining neighborhoods where Joe had so vigorously defended the grace and beauty of traditional styles.

I turned toward her. "We're doing all right without them."

Linda raised her face, took my arm and breathed deeply. "Frankie, we're barely getting by."

This was an old argument so I didn't reply. Instead I distracted myself by checking out the crowd. Out on the street, the mourners who had departed first were nosing into the constant traffic on Mitchell Street. Inside the cemetery most people were studying the walkways, trying to avoid the fat, wriggling earthworms fleeing the wet lawn. Several of the men in the contractor crowd were directing hungry gazes at Linda. I was a little uncomfortable with their stares. Those guys generally got whatever they wanted. I hoped that none of them would decide that Linda was an accessory that they had to have.

An umbrella broke away from the stream of contractors flowing toward the parking lot and angled toward us. I couldn't see the face of the owner, but I didn't need to. The pinstriped suit and shiny shoes were as distinctive as the color coding of cheap power tools. "Come on, Linda. Let's go. Bobby Lester is on his way over."

Linda pulled back, displaying an interest in my archrival that I didn't appreciate. "Frankie, don't be that way. He used to be our friend."

I tried unsuccessfully to keep the irritation out of my voice. "He isn't my friend now and I don't want to talk to him."

An inch shorter than my six feet, Bobby was dressed sharply in a black raincoat over a suit that had managed to stay pressed despite the rain. His straight black hair showed signs of an expensive cut, probably at a price tag as high as the cost of the new truck battery I needed. Bobby had been after Linda since our days in school. He tipped his umbrella to get a better view.

"Wow, Linda, lookin' good!"

Linda beamed, obviously enjoying the compliment from her former boyfriend. Bobby didn't say anything for a few seconds while he studied her from head to toe. His eyes lingered at points that would have invited a sexual harassment complaint from a more easily offended woman. Linda flashed her boys-will-be-boys crooked smile and let him stare. I stepped forward intending to punch the leering expression off his face but Linda extended a restraining arm and faced Bobby. "I hear you have a new car."

Bobby's grin displayed teeth too perfect not to be caps. "Want to see it?" He took a remote control from his pocket, pointed it toward the street and pressed. Lights flashed and the engine rumbled on a sleek, space-gray BMW convertible.

Linda rewarded Bobby's show with a smile. "Your law practice must be doing pretty well."

Bobby pocketed the remote and put a hand on Linda's arm. "Want a ride?"

Linda held my arm tightly to let me know that punching his face was not okay. "Thanks but Frankie is taking me to the reception and his truck is parked up the road."

I gave Bobby a look that would have melted an iceberg. He removed his hand from Linda's arm. He had a look on his face as if he'd stepped in something disgusting. "So, Franklin, you're still driving that wreck?"

"At least I paid for mine with honest money. Did you buy that BMW with the money your Dad stole from my family?" Bobby's stepdad, Robert Caspar, had organized a big condominium development called Washington Way. My dad and his friends had invested heavily. Caspar and the money had disappeared without a trace. Part of what we lost was my college fund.

Bobby reddened. "It's leased. And no court of law has ever convicted Dad."

"Disappearing is a pretty convenient way to avoid prosecution."

Bobby's face tightened. His jaw clenched and his eyes had compressed to slits when he turned back to Linda. "Maybe some other time." He speared me with his eyes and tramped toward the exit, bowed by anger and humiliation.

Linda's eyes blazed into mine. "Why are you such a jerk around Bobby? I know your history, but he has feelings too." Linda moved to the far side of the umbrella.

I watched the BMW burn up the street. "Sorry. I don't know why he makes me crazy." I reflected that these were my second and third lies of the day. I wasn't sorry and I did know why I hated him. Everything Bobby had was purchased with money stolen from my dad. He wanted Linda too, and if I didn't get my career going soon I was afraid he might get her.

Linda signaled forgiveness by letting me take her arm. We

14

moved with the crowd toward the cemetery gates. Before we reached the exit another umbrella, this one bearing the colors of a local real estate franchise, blocked our path. Steve Smith, a real estate agent who sent Linda and me a lot of work, peeked out from under the soggy canopy. Steve was among the most successful brokers reselling limited, valuable, coastal properties.

"Hi. You two need a ride?"

"Thanks but we're parked up the street." I nodded toward the group Steve had left. "I'm surprised that so many builders and developers came to Joe's funeral."

Two men wandered up and joined Steve. I recognized Steve's companions and we nodded greetings. Victor Bennett, a powerfully built six-foot-five-inch demolition contractor, hadn't changed from blue jeans and muddy work boots. I wondered if the mud had come from the yard of the Queen Anne. The second man, Tony Gorky, a stout mortgage broker in a wrinkled gray suit, carried most of his bulk around his middle. Tony could do a lot of damage with a hatch cover if he wanted to. Mud covered his shoes too. I surveyed the crowd at lawn level. Nearly everyone had muddy shoes.

"We all knew Joe. He was the godfather of historic preservation. I don't know about the others but Victor, Tony, and I are here to observe the end of an era." Steve's voice had a hint of irony, like he was celebrating the end, not the era.

Victor and Tony turned to leave but Steve hesitated. "Joe was your mentor, wasn't he?"

"Yeah, he helped me choose courses and internships. Why?"

"Do you think you'll inherit his library?"

"He planned to give me his books on architecture but that's all."

"Well, if Nora lets you look at any of his other stuff, maybe you could help me. I heard Joe was researching a history of the neighborhood. It has been rumored that he profiled lots of guys, including the three of us, in his notes. If you find anything like that we'd really like to have those files."

"Why don't you ask Nora?"

"Look, Franklin, I have to be honest. Joe and I weren't all that tight and Nora knows it. All I'm asking is that if you find anything about local builders, you know, guys like Victor, Tony, and me, let me see the papers first. We'd like to know what Joe thought of us, him being such a great man."

I would have guessed that Steve didn't care much what anyone thought about him unless he could take it to the bank. He said that bit about Joe being a great man with a straight face, but Joe's preservation agenda had been bad for real estate sales. I doubted that developers like Victor and Tony thought of Joe as a great man either. Still, Linda and I needed Steve's business and what harm could it do? "Sure Steve. If I see anything like that I'll be sure you have the first look."

"Great!" Steve focused on Linda. "I may have a new project for you and Franklin."

Linda snapped to attention. She turned on the charm and leaned far enough into Steve's personal space that his wife would have been forced to defend it if she had been present. A mere foot away, she licked her lips. "We love to work for you, Steve. What do you need?"

Steve grinned back and made no effort to move away. "The developers of a new condo project need a designer and stager for some model units. I could put in a good word."

Steve continued addressing Linda but deliberately turned and made eye contact with me. "I'll talk to you after Franklin gets back to me about those papers."

Linda turned her face at the last second to take his good-bye kiss on her cheek. Steve returned to his Hummer with Victor and Tony in tow.

I knew why she did it, but her flirting bothered me. "I thought you were going to plant one on his lips," I complained.

She gave me an exasperated look. "Don't be jealous. He's married, old enough to be my father, and has known me since I was a child."

The way Linda used her charm to manipulate men brought a problem in our relationship into focus. She was the perfect girlfriend. She had a body that would stop traffic, and she was often warm and considerate. She was an amazing designer, clever and creative. My enthusiasm for those sides of her made me resist the fact that some of her characteristics drove me crazy, not in a good way—like her flirting, her disdain for my career choices, and her attempts to remake me in her image of an ideal boyfriend.

A little voice in my head said I would need to take her off the pedestal on which I'd put her and deal with our issues. I had a bad feeling that if I didn't find a way to work this stuff out it would be our undoing.

Linda and I made the steep climb up Arnold Street to my truck. The heavy rain had created a pond in the front yard of the Queen Anne that extended all the way to a debris-covered storm drain in the street. If that water continued to back up it was going to fill the basement again.

Linda touched my shoulder and interrupted my trance. "Frankie, can you help? The door is stuck again, the water is rising, and I don't want my dress wet too."

Water damage seemed unlikely since her long legs held the hem of the short dress well above the level of a hundred-year flood. But I did wrestle the balky handle of the passenger side door open in time to save her shoes from the increased flow. Water continued to back up as the debris further clogged the drain.

"I've got to clear that junk." I grabbed an empty five-gallon bucket and a shovel from the truck and scooped up the muck. I hoisted the bucket and shovel into the truck bed.

The reception was being held a couple of miles away on Avery Point, a peninsula that extended a half mile into Long Island Sound. The crowd had already filled the parking lots so I improvised a space beneath a massive copper beech tree a short walk from our destination. Branford House, a hundred-year-old, thirty-one-room, Tudor-Style granite mansion, rose above a sea of lawn. Linda stared at the magnificent stonework on the building. The blocks were cut from granite the same color as the rocks scattered beside the ocean. "Wow, they built with stones from the ledge. That's magnificent."

Her enthusiasm made me smile. "I thought you didn't like old buildings,"

"It's rundown ones I don't like. This place is to die for."

We stepped into the two-story foyer of the ballroom. A large crowd of guests had already arrived and scattered in small groups below the intricate carved wood panels that adorned the walls. I recognized a cluster of wealthy owners of classic Victorians, members of the historical society, holding court in a corner. A sprinkling of local politicians vied for the attention of the mayor. Shipyard workers, scientists from the pharmaceutical labs, and clusters of college students and retail store workers sampled from a buffet table. Joe's friendships had transcended most of the social boundaries of our southeastern Connecticut home.

The background noise was intense, fueled by hundreds of conversations and dress shoes snapping against the white marble floors. Linda and I approached the reception table and signed the guest book. She handed me her shiny raincoat and whispered. "I'm going to try to scare up some work for us. Why don't you go find a men's room and finish cleaning up?"

It took a lot of scrubbing. The soap they put in men's rooms of fancy halls is useless against serious dirt. I got my hands clean, but my headache was getting worse. I dried my hands, and was about to start a search for Nora Simpson when the door opened with a crash.

A man my age propelling an orange sport wheelchair rolled in. Sandwiched between his sandy hair and powerful shoulders, Eric Freelove wore a big grin. He checked out the mud stains on my clothes. "Hi, Franklin. Linda told me you'd still be here. She said the only way to clean you up would be to run you through a car wash."

"Hi, Wheels. Yeah, I fell down some cellar stairs."

"Balance problems? Yoga's good for that. You should drop in at the gym for Amy's class." Eric Freelove and his wife, Amy, owned a fitness center on Main Street. Joe had helped them find a building and arranged for a mortgage.

"Maybe later. Right now I need to find Nora Simpson."

I entered the ballroom. A wall of French doors bordered a flagstone-covered patio and courtyard with the ocean beyond. The rain pounded against the glass, filling the gutters and scouring the paving tiles in the gardens and walkways. Nature was putting on quite a show and I couldn't resist the urge to stop and watch it.

"Hey, Bro, figuring out how to improve the drainage?" asked a brown-skinned man taller than me. He bumped my shoulder with a bony fist the color of a cinnamon stick.

"And you're probably designing a fuel cell that runs on rainwater." Albert Henley, electronic genius, had been my best friend since elementary school. He called me "Bro" as sort of an ethnic joke since that old street form of address was also the correct way to pronounce my family name. "How are things at Silicon Shack?"

Albert snorted. "Selling electronics to mediocre brains with credit cards is like pointing a remote control." After earning a degree in computer science and engineering, Albert found a job selling electronics retail. I wasn't surprised that he was good at sales. He had been talking me into doing what he wanted since we were kids.

"I'm looking for Nora. Have you seen her?"

"The widow Simpson is greeting people at the other end of the hall. I'm surprised to see you here, Bro. Crowds aren't your thing."

"Yeah, well, this is for Joe. And I need to talk to Nora."

"You gonna try to talk her about the old Victorian on Arnold?"

"I'm hoping she'll honor Joe's promise to sell it to me. You still willing to help with the electrical?"

"Sure, but that place is over a hundred years old so you know what we'll find: knob and tube wiring, sixty-amp service, basically a complete re-wire job."

Albert was right. As much as I loved the design and carpentry of Victorians, the electrical, plumbing, and heating systems were usually awful. I preferred renovation with modern electrical and mechanical systems as long as they didn't defile the architectural purity of the structure. The buildings I renovated would have the best of the old and new. "If I make a deal with Nora, can you look it over next week?"

Albert agreed and I headed to the other side of the hall. When I arrived the chairs were empty. From another guest I learned that Nora had complained she was ill. Her sister had driven her home minutes earlier.

With my main purpose for attending the reception frustrated, I searched for and found Linda. Before I could drag her away, she introduced me to a couple my parents' age. "Franklin is my partner and the best handyman in town. He specializes in historical renovations." She bestowed a sweet, slightly ironic smile on me. "Frankie, the Petersons are New Yorkers. They want us to remodel their Victorian summer home on Long Point."

The four of us discussed commuting on coastal route 95 and the good life in the path of salt spray while Mr. Peterson checked out Linda appreciatively whenever Mrs. Peterson wasn't watching.

By the time the Petersons rejoined a larger group of New York vacationers I wasn't feeling so good. "Can we leave?"

Linda surveyed the crowd for additional potential employers. Steve Smith was talking to Bobby Lester. "I want to follow up on those condo designs Steve mentioned. Get the truck and I'll be out in ten minutes."

I trudged to the truck, feeling worse with every step, and climbed in. I hoped it was Steve and not Bobby who Linda had stayed to talk with. As I prepared to head back to pick her up, I remembered Nora's note. I pulled the envelope out and ripped it open. Joe's widow had printed six words on the card: *Joe's death was not an accident!*

Chapter 3

Nora's message confirmed a thought that had been rattling around the fringes of my consciousness. I don't know if the bump on the head or the words she wrote were to blame, but suddenly I felt nauseated.

As Linda reached for the door handle, my head throbbed like someone was trying to drive a sixteen-penny nail through it. I don't know if it was the note or the bang on the head, but I opened the door, leaned out, and threw up. Before I could catch my breath Linda switched from decorating diva to ambulance driver. She came to my side of the truck, sidestepped the mess, gently nudged me into the passenger seat, and got behind the wheel.

"Come on Frankie. No arguments this time. We're going to get you checked out." She spoke in a firm, take-charge voice, but a little quiver at the end belied her concern.

Friday was usually date day for Linda and me, but instead of going home to change for a night out she kicked off her shoes and drove me to the hospital. The emergency room visit lasted five hours. Linda stayed with me while the doctors poked, scanned, and finally put a couple of staples in my head. The discharge nurse advised me to pick up some acetaminophen, warned me off alcohol and strenuous activity for a couple of weeks, and suggested that I wear my hard hat next time I crawled around in a ruin. I left with a bill the size of the GNP of a third world country, grateful for my student health insurance.

Linda drove me to my apartment and tucked me into bed. She picked up her coat, stepped next to the bed and ran her fingers through my hair. "I'm going now. I'll I ask your mother to check on you later."

We had talked about living together but her condo was too small and she didn't want to live in my parents' basement. More than anything at that point I wanted her to stay. I was seldom injured and the experience left me feeling vulnerable.

"It's not a good idea to leave a guy with a concussion alone." I wouldn't turn down a little sympathy romance either, although the pain would probably wreak havoc with my libido.

Linda bent down and placed a soft kiss on my lips, knowing what I had in mind. "I'd better go. I have a design to prepare and you're banned from strenuous activity."

Saturday morning I awoke to a ringing phone, a headache, and a tender scalp. It was Linda checking on me and repeating the order to avoid heavy work for a while. That worked for me. I called Nora Simpson, hoping to discuss that note and maybe to cut a new deal for the Queen Anne. She invited me to come over as soon as possible.

The Simpsons' Greek Revival stood on Groton Bank in the historic district. Even in the fall, the weekend traffic was heavy. I avoided the major routes and in minutes was outside the white, square two-story structure Joe and Nora had lived in for a half century. I parked on the street and stepped out. Classical columns flanked the pediment-capped entry porch containing the front door. Pairs of double-hung windows were stacked symmetrically across the face of the home. But the roof and a window set in a large triangular dormer called a cross gable caught my attention. The papers said Joe had been painting attic window trim when he slipped and fell. Why was eighty-year-old Joe painting in September? It had been a wet, cold month and Joe would have known that the paint wouldn't set up properly. And why was he out on the roof when the trim could be reached from inside?

Something in that story stunk worse than the boxwood

hedges beside me. Boxwoods have all the charm of a neglected litter box. Still looking up at the window, I turned the corner. Without warning I bumped into something that felt like a rubber mountain. I bounced off and sprawled out on the grass.

I blew a leaf out of my mouth and studied the lawn from ant level. The grass was littered with leaves that were getting a head start on the fall molt. I was lying close to the spot where Joe had landed, which felt very creepy. Even more unsettling was the pair of boots inches away from my face. I lifted my eyes and saw that they were attached to Victor Bennett, the demolition contractor I'd seen at the funeral.

I jumped to my feet. "What are you doing here?"

Victor's eyes reflected surprise and something else, maybe discomfort at being caught in Joe's yard. "Watch where you're going." He snarled and stomped toward the street.

I watched his retreating back, wondering why he had been behind the house. It wasn't only his size that gave me the chills. His guilty expression said he was up to something.

Nora came to the door in time to see me brushing the grass off my clothes. Her spare frame was covered by a dress of a dark color that created an indefinable but definite impression it had been bought before I was born. I could smell fabric softener and moth balls. As she shuffled forward, she bent slightly from the waist as if her spine refused to completely straighten. Her initial expression was as bleak as the weathered gray steps. When she recognized me a flash of welcome replaced her tired expression.

"Thanks for coming, Franklin."

Nora nodded toward the bandage on my head. "What happened to you?"

"It's just a bump." I picked at grass on my sleeve, unable to meet her eyes. Words that would describe what Joe had meant to me wouldn't come. Embarrassment over my decision to approach her about the Queen Anne so soon after Joe's death left me tongue-tied. I settled on a predictable phrase. "I'm so sorry about Joe. I miss him already."

Nora was expert at dealing with the awkwardness of condolence and took my fumbling attempt in stride. "So do I, Franklin. Come in and have some tea." As we turned Nora's gaze landed on Victor climbing into his truck out on the street. Her eyes narrowed. "I'm surprised to see that man again. I thought Joe had run him off for good."

"Do you know Victor Bennett?"

She nodded. "Yes. He's an overstuffed, steroid-fueled, house killer."

It hurt my sore head, but I laughed at Nora's perfect characterization of Bennett. "Do you know why he's hanging around here?"

"He works for the people who want to build the condominiums on the hill behind the house. He says he's looking for a way to get access to the property."

"What does that have to do with you and Joe?"

"Victor said his employers wanted to buy that old Queen Anne on Arnold. He was insistent and Joe finally got angry and ordered him off the property."

I swallowed hard. Joe had bought that building hoping that I would restore it. Did that action have anything to do with his death?

Nora stepped into the house, beckoning me to follow. We entered a great room created when the original living and dining rooms were opened up to the eat-in kitchen in the rear. Dozens of mismatched plates sparkled under clear plastic wrap on the worn laminate kitchen counter.

Nora gestured toward the plates. "The neighbors have brought enough pastry to open a bakery." We spent the next half hour drinking hot tea, eating day-old muffins, and catching up on news of Groton City. I tried to steer the conversation toward the Queen Anne, but Nora wanted to talk about Joe. "The police found a paint spill in the attic and decided that he was doing the trim outside the window. I don't believe it. He didn't say anything to me about painting."

I swirled my spoon through the tea. Nora was right. The paint on the house, including the window trim, looked fine. "So what do you think happened?"

She glanced up toward to the top floors. "I was out when he fell. All morning Joe had been searching for something in the record room in the attic. All his fussing was driving me crazy, so I left to run some errands." She stood up and began covering the food and moving the plates from the table to the counter. "Before I left he called someone. I heard him say that he wouldn't let whoever it was get away with it again."

"Do you know who he was talking to or what he meant?"

Nora dropped her gaze, shook her head. When she looked up there were tears of determination in her eyes. "Franklin, I want you to find out who killed Joe and why."

I wasn't prepared for that. "Isn't investigating murder a job for the police?"

Nora's chin quivered. "They think it was an accident."

"If the police didn't find anything what could I do? I'm not a detective."

"Franklin, Joe once said to me that one of the reasons you are so good at renovation is your ability to see the causes behind things."

"I can fix water leaks but that doesn't mean I can investigate a murder."

"Joe had faith in you and so do I." Nora locked her eyes on mine. "I know what Joe offered you. If you'll help, I'll honor that agreement and get one of Joe's architect friends to supervise the renovation so you can use it as your internship."

My heart echoed in my ears like a hammer drill in barrel. There was hope for my license after all. With the internship out of the way, I could move into the Queen Anne. With a house and license I would ask Linda to marry me. This time she might agree.

The flash of excitement passed quickly. I wasn't a detective. How would I explain to Linda why, instead of working, I was investigating a murder that may not have happened? Besides, if someone murdered Joe, did I really want to get mixed up with whoever did it?

None of those objections mattered. I was in the minute that Nora asked. What could it hurt to ask a few questions? I wasn't working anyway. "Okay, I'll try but I don't know where to start. Everyone liked Joe. Who would want to hurt him?"

Nora's eyes bored into mine. "Don't patronize me. I know what kind of man my husband was. He could be ruthless when he wanted something. Any number of the people in this town that he stepped on could be carrying a grudge."

I hadn't thought about enemies. Joe's bullying was bound to have generated some. But murder? No one had tried to kill him before this. Something must have changed, something worth killing over. "Did anything happen recently that might have made one of those enemies desperate enough to resort to murder?"

"Not that I know of, but for a guy who isn't a detective you've found a good place to start the investigation."

Chapter 4

The collision with Bennett had already given me a close-up view of the lawn, so I chose to start my investigation in the attic. Nora pointed to a beige six-panel door that had been painted in so many different shades over the years that the cracks contained a rainbow of colors. I twisted the black enamel knob and entered a column of cool, stale air.

A run of twenty steps led to the second floor landing. Twenty more steps and I reached the attic. Wide unpainted pine boards, topped by a century and a half of ground-in dust, covered the floor. A galaxy of dust particles sparkled in rays of light streaming through a tall window.

Piles of junk serving as walls divided the attic into three areas, a wide central corridor that stretched from the stairway to the front of the house, and two rooms, one on each side. The room to the left was filled with castoff furniture, lamps, luggage, and pictures that my frugal mentor had kept on the theory that today's junk is tomorrow's antique.

The room at the right held shelves and boxes of books and file folders. Joe's archives. I had told him that these records could be converted to digital formats, but he insisted that print spoke to him in ways that electronic records didn't.

I crossed the corridor toward the arched window in the alcove created by the cross gable. Suddenly it was difficult to breath and my feet felt like I was slogging through thick mud. Joe, a man who'd been an anchor in my life, had fallen, or been pushed, through that window. I ached to think that I'd never see him again, never have his guidance. What made his death even more difficult to accept was Nora's idea that someone might have killed him.

A breeze penetrated the vents and raised enough dust to make my skin itch and the hair on my neck to rise. Sensing a presence, I plucked an orphaned piece of baluster out of the debris and held the stick in my fist like a club. I slipped into the maze created by the piles of junk. Dust muffled my footsteps and rose in fuzzy clouds. A door closed on the floors below and my heart beat loudly. Shadows stretched behind every stack but didn't move, nothing in the room broke the silence, and the powdery haze settled.

A movement registered on the corner of my eye. I turned in time to see the slipcover on an upholstered wing back chair ripple. I moved quickly around the chair, the baluster raised to strike. A writhing black cylinder about four feet long burst from under the chair and streaked between my boots.

I slammed the wooden stick down sharply, breaking it and missing the undulating tail of a squirming black snake. I whirled and threw the half stick still in my hand toward the fleeing reptile as it disappeared into a hole in the baseboard.

I shouldn't have been surprised. Snakes are common in attics and basements of old buildings. Black snakes are harmless and an ecologically better approach to mouse control than poisons or traps, but encountering one felt nasty.

I returned to the arched double-hung window. I knelt down, lifted the sash a few inches from the low sill, and glanced out. A narrow section of roof with a shallow pitch stretched between the window and the gutter. Time and weather had curled and cracked the asphalt shingles. Someone had tramped across them recently and left a ragged line of crushed edges that disappeared out of my line of sight.

I pushed the heavy lower sash to the top of the jambs and crawled out on the roof. Once outside I followed the trail of footprints a short way. I stood with my back to the attic window studying the tracks. I took the tape off my belt and measured a print, twelve inches. A big man had stomped here.

Crack! Wham!

I felt as well as heard the sound cut across the neighborhood and echo back. I dived to the roof and sprawled out on the shingles, an arm wrapped across my head to protect the stitches. My heart was pounding and the blood felt like fire racing through my veins. *Was that a gunshot?*

I rolled on my side and discovered I was on the gutter, my head dangling into the space two stories above the lawn. I broke out in a cold sweat. This wasn't far from where Joe had gone over the edge. I waited for his killer to finish me off too.

After clinging to the roof for a long time during which nothing happened, I rolled over and checked out the street. A car passed heading toward the river, but didn't look suspicious. I relaxed. If an attack was going to come, it would have happened already.

I pushed, got back on my feet, and returned to the window. The upper sash had fallen and was now firmly closed. I peered inside. I saw my reflection and a dim view of the interior of the attic but no sign of the killer I half expected to see. Another glance at the rooftops around the neighborhood didn't turn up any suspicious characters with a rifle or shotgun. Perhaps I'd overreacted a bit.

The falling window had made the noise, and it had fallen because the sash cords holding the counter weights had broken a long time ago. The pocket pieces were split where the falling weights had hit them. Only the friction of the warped frame had held the sash up. Most likely the wind or settling of the house had triggered the fall. I had mistaken the impact of the lower sash against the sill for a gunshot.

"Geez, Franklin, why are you so jittery?" I hadn't been this jumpy since the first time I'd faced a building inspector.

I tried to open the sash with my fingertips but I couldn't get a good grip. I wondered if this happened to Joe too. I stepped carefully to the edge of the roof and looked down. One story below, the top of the entry porch offered a tempting route of escape, but only a fool would jump or try to climb down. I felt the cell phone in my pocket. I could always call Nora and ask her to come up. Joe had a cell phone. If he'd been stuck, he would have called someone.

I forced myself to relax and look around the roof before calling Nora. Newspaper accounts said Joe had fallen close to the entry porch but the path of crushed shingles I had spotted earlier went in another direction. I decided to follow the trail.

I traced the footprints to a heap of leaves so large that they spilled into a nearby gutter. Leaf-clogged gutters were trouble. They tended to cause ice dams that ripped shingles from the roof and caused water damage inside.

To help Nora avoid leaks, I scooped up an armful of fragrant, decaying vegetation and tossed it over the edge. Under the second armful, I discovered something that might explain why Joe had climbed out on the roof. A padded waterproof envelope was nestled below the soggy leaves.

I picked up the packet. The fresh printing suggested that it hadn't been outside long. There was no way that this got on the roof by accident. Inside the envelope was a clipping from a magazine. One side showed three men in front of a shiny billboard, and a fourth man standing a short distance behind them, obscured by glare.

I turned the print over. The reverse side contained pieces of two columns of print. Nothing on either side of the clipping hinted at its importance or the identity of someone who would want it enough to kill for it. But if Joe hid the envelope on the roof he must have been expecting someone to try to retrieve it.

I returned to the window and worked at opening the sash. I removed the tape measure I always keep on my belt. I placed it against the glazing bar and pushed upwards with the heel of my hand. The glass bowed and the glazing cracked but the sash moved up enough for me to get my fingers under it.

I pushed the window open and slid inside. I noticed something that I had missed earlier. A few feet away from the window was a large puddle of a milky white liquid on the attic floorboards. It looked like paint. There was no can around.

I dropped to the floor and touched the puddle with my finger. The paint smeared. Why would it still be wet? And why was it so far from the window Joe was painting?

I remembered something I'd seen in the junk room. Three bulging paint cans sat near a dust free circle of flooring, probably marking where a fourth can had rested. I picked up one of the remaining cans. The label identified the contents as oil based paint produced by a manufacturer no longer in business. The distorted can suggested that the contents had been around long enough to freeze. One season of freezing would destroy the ability of paint to dry and this can was old enough to have frozen many times.

The hairs on the back of my neck began to tingle again. Joe wouldn't paint with this stuff. Why would he have removed a gallon? And where was the missing can?

I crossed to the record room. Cartons filled the shelves along the walls. Someone had pulled down several boxes and stacked them on a wooden table. The lidless boxes contained an assortment of odd-sized newspaper clippings, photos and magazines. I used the camera on my cell phone to record the scene. Someone had stacked the lids in the corner. I counted covers and boxes and ended up with one extra lid. A box was missing. What was in it? Questions continued to pile up.

Nothing else caught my interest so I headed back down toward the kitchen. The state of the boxes in the records room matched Nora's story about Joe searching for something. Apparently he had found it and hidden it on the roof. What was so important about the faded photograph? Was Joe's killer one of the persons in the picture? Then there was the spilled paint, not paint that anyone who knew building would have used. Why was it so far from the window and where were the brushes and rags? Although I still had no evidence that someone had pushed Joe, his death didn't look to me like a DIY accident.

By the time I reached the kitchen Nora had finished tidying up and sat at the table waiting for me.

"How did your investigation go?"

"Don't get upset, but I came across a big black snake."

Nora chuckled. "So that is what the banging was about. I hope you didn't hurt Harvey."

"You've named it?"

"Joe did. Harvey was the name of my first boyfriend. Years ago Joe gave up trying to catch the snake and let him terrorize the mice."

"What size shoe did Joe wear?" I asked.

"Ten and a half. Why do you ask?"

"I found some pretty big footprints on the roof."

"Officer Williams could have made those prints. His boots could double as snow shoes. What else did you find?"

"Nothing conclusive, but something didn't feel right up there." I explained about the frozen paint and the spill. Nora agreed that Joe had been too smart to use old paint. I told her about the clipping hidden on the roof. I took the square of paper from my pocket. "Do you recognize any of these people or the setting?"

Nora stood up and retrieved a pair of glasses from the counter and took the picture. She turned it over and studied the back. She pointed to the nearly featureless faces. "The setting looks familiar but the faces are too washed out to recognize. But I've seen this place before. It might have been the groundbreaking for that Washington Way development. That'd make this picture ten years old."

So maybe the men in the picture were the original partners. That would mean Victor Bennett, Steve Smith, and Tony Gorky. I wondered if number four could have been Robert Caspar, already preparing his disappearing act. As I headed for the door a thought popped into my head. "Did Joe ever tell you how the Queen Anne got so run-down?"

Nora leaned against the counter searching her memory. "The owner abandoned it and then the town took it. Joe paid the taxes and bought it from the city a few months ago."

Joe's purchase of the house a few months ago may be the change in the status quo that I was looking for. Could the purchase of the Queen Anne have upset the equilibrium and provided a motivation for murder?

Nora looked tired so I decided to save any other questions for another time. "I'll call you when I find out anything."

"I'm moving in with my sister in Ledyard, but you can reach me here for a couple of weeks. Joe and I planned to finish our days together in this neighborhood, but. . ."

Nora couldn't finish the sentence. She stood in the worn Victorian kitchen with tears of grief running down the deep furrows of her cheeks. She put her hands on my shoulders, leaned her head on my chest and cried. Raw, angry sobs vibrated through her.

I'm not much of a hugger, but I wrapped my arms around her and held on, trying unsuccessfully not to add my tears. My loss was not as great as hers, but painful enough.

Finally Nora's shaking subsided and she took a ragged breath. She patted my arm, stepped back. We wiped our eyes. I flashed ahead to the inevitable day that I too would be grieving the death of the love of my life. As a blueprint for the universe, it sucks, but it's the way things seem to work. I didn't know if discovering who murdered Joe would make his death hurt less, but I was determined to try.

Chapter 5

I retrieved a fat carpenter's pencil from the truck's glove box, tore off the flap of a box of nails and wrote down the questions I had produced so far. The list filled the little cardboard square. The trip to the attic raised more questions than answers.

I needed someone who could help with answers. For that I needed an expert on all things Groton City, someone with her finger on its pulse and her nose in everyone's business. Fortunately I knew such a person and she worked a couple of blocks away.

When not helping patrons, Librarian Julia Judge knitted nonstop and gobbled up mystery novels and local gossip like a wood chipper eats brush. Julia knew more about Groton City than anyone in town, making her the perfect ally for a fledgling detective.

The air inside the gray granite portico of the library smelled of aging books and ink from the stacks of glossy magazines and newspapers arrayed inside the door. "Franklin Breault," Julia called in a loud voice when she spotted me from across the room.

The heads of senior citizens bobbed up from behind computers like pets who had heard their master open a box of treats. Julia waved me over to her desk. As I neared, she tossed her knitting into a drawer, sprinted around the desk, and gave me a big motherly hug. She released me and stepped back with her hands on her hips. "Wow, you're all grown up." Her expression said she was probably trying to figure out how a puny little kid turned into a lean, six-foot tall, twenty-five-year-old.

"Hi Mrs. Judge," I said with less volume but equal affection.

A copy of *Architectural Process* on her desk brought me back to the days when I had preferred tools and wood to deciphering the printed page. Sensing my disinterest in reading, Julia had steered me toward books filled with fantastic illustrations of architectural and engineering marvels. Learning to read the brief captions seemed like a small price to pay for unlocking the secrets between the covers. By the time I graduated to build-it-yourself books at age seven, she had turned me into a reader. Julia's interest and patient support led me to a love of books and a lasting affection for her.

"What's happening with your architecture license? I heard you finished school and that you and Joe had planned to renovate that old Queen Anne on Arnold Street for your final internship."

I picked up the glossy magazine on Julia's desk. The cover showed her next to a vintage salt box from the colonial period. As president of the historical society, she fought to preserve historical architecture as hard as Joe had. "Joe's death complicated things but Nora has offered the Queen Anne to me and help finding a supervisor for my internship."

Julia picked up a framed newspaper column from her desk. Joe's picture and his obituary from the *Groton City Times* stared back from behind the glass. "Like a lot of people, I miss Joe. No one did more to preserve the architectural treasures around Groton Bank." A tear escaped as she cradled the picture in her arms and sank into the desk chair.

I hesitated for a moment, not wanting to intrude on her grief. Her friendship with Joe made her a strong potential ally. Did she share Nora's suspicion that someone murdered Joe? "Nora doesn't believe he fell while painting. She asked me to check into his death." I explained about the paint can, the footprints on the roof, and the clipping.

Julia looked at the picture quickly, like she had seen it before. She got up, marched to the periodical rack, and searched the stack of pamphlets "This picture was on the front page of an old economic development brochure. I'm sure we have one but I don't see it here."

While Julia searched I picked up a newspaper with the headline: *Local Activist Dies After Fall*. She saw what I was reading, leaned toward me, and spoke in a low voice. "The TV and papers describe his death as an accident, but I have heard things. Nora has good reason to question the official explanation."

I glanced around the room to see if any of the other patrons heard us speaking. I stepped closer. "What have you heard?"

She directed me toward a chair, flopped back down in her own, rolled over to the computer and pecked out a string of rapid keystrokes while she continued talking. "The State Police investigate all unattended deaths in Groton City. The detective who did the investigation came in here earlier checking out Carolyn J. Rose's *Through a Yellow Wood*. He loves to see how mystery writers treat police procedure. I asked him about Joe's death. He said it looked accidental but a few inconsistencies in the scene need explanation."

"Did he say what discrepancies?"

"He thought that someone had contaminated the crime scene. The window to the roof was closed when the police arrived and no one knows who closed it. They took a dented paint can away in case it's needed later."

The hair on my neck began to stiffen. If Joe had placed the paint can on the window sill to prop open the sash and it had fallen, it should have remained there until the police arrived. Someone, maybe the killer, moved it after Joe had gone outside.

"Couldn't Joe have spilled the paint and left the can inside when he climbed out?"

"I guess."

"Did the detective say if the police lab has tested the paint can?"

"They haven't. They probably took it in the off chance that they find a suspect and then they'll check for fingerprints."

"You mean they aren't going to check for prints anyway?"

"No, and given the backlog at the crime lab, it would take a change in the police opinion about this being an accident to initiate any tests." Julia clicked a few more keys.

"Julia, what about motive? Joe's purchase of the Queen Anne on Arnold is the only recent event I know of that was out of the ordinary. Could the developers who were trying to buy it have killed him?"

"I don't know what the old house could have to do with it. That place was abandoned years ago, about when Washington Way failed."

Could history be repeating itself? "Nora said Victor Bennett was trying to buy the Queen Anne from Joe to secure a right of way for a new development. Maybe I should look into the new condominium project."

Julia tapped a few commands into a search engine. The results displayed list style. An eight-year-old story described Washington Way and the disappearance of Robert Caspar and the money. The second story she wanted me to see concerned a new project called Monument Condominiums. She clicked on that one and the story flashed onto the screen. A picture of Joe Simpson and a crowd of protesters in front of the wild patch of land behind the Queen Anne headed the column. "Victor is probably talking about this project."

Julia clicked on a related story. Developers hiding behind an anonymous LLC had filed for a permit to build 200 condominiums on a tract of undeveloped land behind the Queen Anne. I knew from Nora about the development, but I was surprised to read that zoning approval had been given contingent on addition of an access road to the plans. Conventional wisdom was that that land was unbuildable due to being landlocked with inadequate access to a public road. "You think these people had something to do with his death?"

"The Monument Condominiums project probably involves hundreds of millions of dollars of new business. That means lots of behind-the-scenes influence selling. Joe and the historical society actively opposed the project but some of our usual allies sat this one out for unknown reasons. Joe battling developers is nothing new. One of the backers could have had a grudge but something had to be different about this development in order to make it worth risking murder."

Lots of money equals motive. I had moved deeper into the investigation. "Bennett was involved in Washington Way. Do you think the same investors are behind the new project?"

Julia rapidly tapped out a string of commands. She clicked on the Monument Parcel on a map. Lists of files appeared. She clicked on an entry, an application for a residential development. The text appeared on the screen. "Take a look at the application for a permit."

I scanned the form looking for familiar names. "I'll be damned." Robert Lester, Esq., had signed the application for the applicant, Monument Condominiums, LLC.

Julia rippled her fingers across the computer keyboard. A different signature page appeared. "Bobby's stepdad, Robert Caspar, signed the application for Washington Way years earlier."

"The LLC makes it difficult to identify the owners behind the project. Only one partner need sign the application in this state." Julia connected to the tax department and downloaded a property description. Land records weren't any help. "It says the Singer estate owns the land. I bet the LLC has an option to buy contingent on zoning approval for the plan."

Bobby Lester's involvement had me on edge. "Does the application mention anyone else?"

Before Julia could reply I got a reminder of how life in a small town resembles living in a ten-gallon fish tank. Bobby Lester strode in the front doors and headed right for us. He wore a blue pinstripe suit that looked like a duplicate of the outfit he wore to the funeral, less the raincoat and umbrella.

"Say the devil's name and hear his tail swish," muttered Julia as he approached. I couldn't control a smirk brought to my face by her quaint expression.

Bobby produced a strained smile. "Hello, Julia. I hope this person isn't wasting my tax dollars by monopolizing your time."

"Hello Bobby. Since when do you pay taxes? Isn't your name on the delinquent tax list?" Aided by citizens willing to turn in their neighbors for failure to pay taxes, the Groton City tax collector published a list of delinquent taxpayers in the local paper once a year. I was not currently on the list but last year a grouchy neighbor reported that I restored furniture in my dad's barn, so now I had to inventory my tools and supplies yearly and write a check to the tax collector. Rumor had it that a member of the historical society had blown the whistle on Bobby for maintaining an office in his home without paying taxes on the furnishings.

A scowl appeared on Bobby's face. "I've appealed."

Julia smiled politely. "May I help you, Attorney Lester?"

"Don't trouble yourself. I need a copy of some documents and the library is closer than my office. I can find the copy machine." Bobby boldly stepped around Julia's desk and peered at the zoning application on the computer screen. He smirked. "Looking for work Franklin? Maybe I could get you a job as a day laborer."

"You know that expression about a cold day in hell? Well it will never get cold enough for me to work for you."

Bobby flicked a speck of lint off his sleeve. He opened his eyes wide in an apparent attempt to look innocent. "That's not what your partner says. Linda approached me at the funeral yesterday to express her interest in bidding on some projects. This morning she submitted a proposal to stage the interior of our model condo units. So you may end up working for us."

He must have noticed my jaw drop because with a laugh he turned on the heel of one handmade leather shoe and strolled in the direction of the copiers.

I loosened my hands which had been clenched into fists.

Linda, not Bobby, should have told me about the bid. The last thing I wanted was her mixed up with him or the developers. Joe's opposition to their condominium project may have resulted in his death. Even if that wasn't the reason, with Joe gone local developers were likely to declare open season on Victorians. Linda's business with Bobby wasn't going to help our relationship either.

Julia watched Bobby's departure with an expression of distaste. "Linda would be wise to avoid him. His most recent ex-wife serves on the library board. According to her he's auditioning for wife number three." Julia got a thoughtful look. "Are things okay with you and Miss Kisslovich?"

I liked Julia but I knew better than to leak relationship information to her. I redirected the conversation back to the condo project. "Nora said that the developers have their sights on other houses in her neighborhood. Have you heard anything?"

Julia extracted a bottle of waterless hand cleaner and scrubbed her hands as if banishing the bad karma Bobby carried in. "Developers have lusted after those river views as far back as I can remember. If the developers could have bought a house to tear down they would have put in a road to the back lots years ago, but no one would sell."

"Why?" I asked. "The developers would probably pay plenty to get a way in. I'm surprised that no one has sold."

"Homes in that neighborhood never come up on the open market. Private arrangements are always made."

"So why do these developers think someone will sell them a right-of-way now?"

Julia looked over the top of her glasses. "You are asking the wrong question. You should ask why in the past homes never came on the open market."

I looked at the picture of Joe on Julia's desk and thought I knew the answer. "Okay, why?"

Julia looked around, then leaned in to me and whispered. "Because Joe wouldn't let them. He always found the leverage to persuade the owners to let him find a buyer before resorting to an open market."

"How did he do that?"

Julia shrugged. "You probably don't want to know."

It wasn't difficult to imagine Joe using a little arm twisting to convince owners of Victorian homes to let him arrange the sales. Years ago he caught Bobby and me drinking when we were underage. He offered not to report us if we would change our ways. That particular action didn't differ from what most adults do to kids, but Julia had hinted that Bobby and I weren't the only persons on whom Joe exercised his wiles.

Persuasion usually involves either a carrot or a stick. Had Joe persuaded owners to let him use his network of connections to get the best price for them? Or did he prefer the stick, a threat of some sort like he used on Bobby and me? I had a bad feeling where this insight could lead my investigation. If Joe had used threats, the roster of persons who wanted him dead was going to be longer than the punch list for the repairs to the Queen Anne.

Chapter 6

I turned the truck in the direction of Arnold Street. If his purchase of the Queen Anne had something to do with Joe's death, maybe the hit on my head was related too. I might find some clues by returning to the scene. I pulled into the Gas Mart around the corner to fuel up first. A midnight blue van stood at the pumps. I wandered over to the window, and peeked in. "Hi, Wheels."

Eric and I bumped fists. "Franklin, you left the reception before we got to show you our new van. Whatdya think?"

"Wow, does it come with its own gas pump?"

"I wish. It's a nine-passenger. Even with the wheelchair lift it'll hold six comfortably."

Eric's wife, Amy, was in the passenger seat, but I didn't see her daughter. "Who's minding Megan and the gym?"

Amy flipped her long black hair off her shoulder. I remembered the gesture from our days in school. A smile creased her generous mouth. She clearly was enjoying the rare day off from work and child care. "We left our helper in charge and Megan's in daycare. We're looking for a house."

"It sounds like all those real estate shows on TV finally got to you. If you need accessibility upgrades let me know."

I had become an expert at universal design thanks to my

friend's disability. For friends I did the upgrades at cost of materials only. The skills I had mastered along the way helped my remodeling for elderly homeowners, so I recouped any losses that way.

Eric had other news. "If you do restore that Queen Anne on Arnold we may be neighbors. We're considering a unit in the condo complex that developers plan to build on the Monument Parcel behind the Queen Anne."

That got my attention. "What do you know about those condominiums?"

Amy poked her head around Eric. "Steve Smith talked to us about it when he stopped in at the gym. The facilities sounded great and some of the units will be fully accessible."

I wondered how involved in the development Steve was. "I don't know how they're going to build. They don't have an acceptable right-of-way to any town road."

Amy leaned over to answer. "Steve said that they plan to build a road near the Queen Anne."

Suddenly I didn't like what I was hearing. The Queen Anne sat in the middle of a fifty-foot-wide lot. The developers didn't want a road near the Queen Anne but through it. Another uneasy thought crept in. I didn't want my friend to get burned if the project failed. "Hold on to your money, Eric. I have a bad feeling about that development."

"What's going on?" Amy asked.

"It's just a feeling. Can you wait until I dig a little deeper before giving them any money?"

Eric shrugged his powerful shoulders. "Sure. But they didn't want money, only an application expressing interest. Thanks for the warning. Let us know what you find out."

After filling the tank and surrendering a small fortune with my credit card, I left my two friends. The drive to the Queen Anne took me past row upon row of soulless early twentieth-century Victorian knockoffs that lacked the ornamentation of their nineteenth-century predecessors. Careless owners had butchered the few true Victorians in the neighborhood almost beyond recognition. The dream I shared with Joe was to restore these to the distinct beauty with which they were built. I didn't want the dream to die with him, but didn't have any idea how to make it happen on my own.

Joe's Queen Anne sat on the corner of Arnold and Smith Streets at the lower slopes of a steep hill leading up to Groton Bank and Monument Park. I had about as much objectivity about that house as an old flame. From the day that Joe had planted the idea that I could design a restoration plan for this building and make it my own, I completely lost my heart to it. I didn't see the sagging porch. My mind had already straightened it. Instead of worrying about how to waterproof the valleys and seams created by the multiple roof pitches, I saw the exuberant, soaring lines. Smooth fresh boards replaced the rough and splintered siding. I could practically see Linda waving from the tall windows in the turret room with odors of mold and mildew replaced by the fresh scent of baking bread.

I was angry that developers hoped to destroy the house. Linda and I were going to have a serious talk about Monument Condominiums. She was about to drag us into a business deal with the devil, or at the very least, developers who planned to take advantage of Joe's death to launch an assault on classic homes. I hadn't tied the developers to Joe's death yet, but I had a lot of unanswered questions about Steve and Victor and what they knew about it. And then there was Bobby. I couldn't tell which worried me more, that he was dragging Linda into a shady condominium development, or his continuing romantic interest in her.

I stepped out for a closer look at the house. As I moved down the driveway the sound of a straining motor came from the wooded area behind the house. Flashes of white between the tree trunks came from a moving vehicle. A few seconds later a dusty pickup emerged moving toward Smith Street. Lumber, shovels and buckets bounced around in the bed of the truck. The driver slowed only slightly as the vehicle clawed its way back toward

Smith Street. The truck struck the edge of the pavement and launched an orange five-gallon bucket into the air. It flipped and rolled down the slope, scattering its contents among the vines. I stepped into the street and waved my arms to signal the driver, but the muddy license plate disappeared behind a flurry of gravel.

A deep gully between the Queen Anne and the narrow strip of park land between the home and the Monument Parcel had swallowed up the bucket. On the theory that the contents might give me an idea what was going on, I slid down the slope in a shower of stones. The plastic container was decorated on one side with the logo of a big box building supply store. A few minutes rummaging through the brush turned up typical construction stuff: string, a tape measure, red flags, a small sledge hammer, and a couple of bungee cords. I placed the items in the bucket and attempted to climb the steep gully. The loose stone took back a half step for every one forward.

I fought my way about halfway up the hillside before I heard the sound of a vehicle sliding to a stop on the gravel above me. I could see the top of the cab from my position. A door slammed and a head appeared above the ridge followed seconds later by the body of Victor Bennett. Outlined by the sky he looked like an angry giant, but I wasn't worried. Victor wasn't especially friendly but I was sure he was harmless.

The big man stalked toward the ravine, shoulders rounded forward, hands clenched in fists. Black eyes darted intently over the ground and a scowl creased his face. He spotted me, leaned over the edge of the ravine and growled. He pointed to the bucket in my hand. "What the hell are you doing with my stuff?"

I scrambled a little closer to the top of the gully. "I dug them out of the brush where you dropped them. If you hadn't burned out of here so fast you would have seen me signal you to stop." A little embarrassed by the anger in my voice, I tried to show my good intentions by holding out the bucket.

Bennett leaned down and snatched the handle from my outstretched hand. The move took me by surprise and I nearly lost my balance on the steep slope. As I fought to keep my face out of the dirt, he glanced into the bucket and stirred up the contents with a hand the size of a dinner plate. His expression reminded me of a dog defending a bone. He leaned forward. "Is this all?"

The menace in his expression caused me to take a step backwards. Too late I remembered that the ground sloped down sharply behind me. I'd stepped into nothingness. My arms flew up, hands grabbing air. I fell backwards into the thorny ravine. My back slammed into the leaves and my legs rose up. I somersaulted backwards a couple of times. Trees flashed by as I tried to protect my head. My shoulder grazed a small maple and a tangle of vines. I finally stopped on top of a pile of leaves that had collected at the bottom of the ravine.

I lay stunned and winded, but at least I'd avoided another blow to my head. I stood and dusted off my clothes.

I felt pretty foolish for letting Bennett startle me into falling. The pulse in my neck beat like a jack hammer and I had a powerful urge to break something. I scraped a couple of decaying leaves from my hair and slapped the remaining twigs off my clothes. Closing in on a serious rage, I dug my toes in and scrambled up the slope below him.

"Look, Bennett, if it wasn't for me you'd be dragging your fat ass in the brush looking for that stuff yourself. Now, get the hell out of my way. I'm coming up."

The anger in my voice must have penetrated the brain behind the thick skull because he backed away from the edge. With his size he could have thrashed me, but I was too angry to think about that at the time. When he spoke, he almost sounded apologetic.

"Hey, cool off. What's with that temper of yours? I lost some other stuff that I thought was in the bucket. I must have dropped it somewhere else."

Bennett rearranged the corners of his mouth in an expression intended as a smile, but it didn't work. He stretched a hand out. "Let me help you out of there." It sounded like an order. His powerful hand clamped on my upper arm and I felt bones crunch under his vise-like grip. His squeeze felt more like a warning than a helping hand, but he lifted me out of the trench.

Bennett gestured toward the Monument Parcel. "The owners of this land asked me to keep an eye out for trespassers."

Thanks to Julia I knew that the recently deceased owners weren't talking to anyone. The developers, not the owners, had hired Bennett. I doubted that he had any authority. Besides, the Monument Parcel didn't start for a hundred feet. The bucket had fallen on park land. I decided not to press the point. "If you don't want trespassing you should post it. That way people won't bother you by trying to help."

Victor's lemon-sucking expression let me know he heard the sarcasm. "OK, get over it. It's for your safety. I'm doing the site preparation for a big condo development. There's so much ledge that we're going to need explosives to break it up." He ran his thick tongue over his lips as if anticipating the pleasure of the blast. His eyes cut to the Queen Anne. "Of course a demolition excavator could level a dilapidated wood frame house like that in ten minutes without explosives."

The thought of the jaws of a giant machine crushing my precious Queen Anne was infuriating. Nora was right. Bennett was a house killer. But he wasn't getting the Queen Anne. "Keep away from that house. I'm going to restore it."

Bennett let out a grating sound that was his version of a laugh. "Nature will finish it off before you start. All I'll need to do is scoop up the pieces and haul them away."

I remembered the picture from Joe's roof. Was Bennett one of the figures in the picture of the ground-breaking ceremony for Washington Way? Ignoring the rule about poking snakes with a stick, I jabbed at him. His reaction was worth it. "I know what really happened to Washington Way."

The veins on Bennett's neck bulged. His face turned a deeper shade of scarlet than I thought possible. The mixture of anger and fear on his face said that the name Washington Way scored a hit. "How could you know about that? That happened while you were still a kid." He squinted, as if he had figured it out. "It's Joe's files, isn't it? You have the files."

The look in his eyes when he mentioned Joe's files frightened me. Had I gone too far? Victor Bennett was a big, loud guy who liked to push people around, but I had thought him harmless. Now he looked dangerous. I may have been foolish to pretend I knew things I didn't.

When I didn't reply he took a deep breath. Bennett's voice rose up an octave and his expression bordered on panic. "Look, I swear I didn't take that money. It was Caspar. What do you want? The same deal as Joe?"

I shrugged which Victor seemed to take as agreement.

"Okay, I'll call you when something comes up." He hurried back to his truck, slammed the bucket in the bed and drove off.

What was that all about? Joe must have used something related to Washington Way to motivate Victor. But I had no idea what that was and what Victor was pressured to do.

Victor had said he was looking for something that wasn't among the tools I had retrieved, so I resumed my search. The outline of a large boot print stamped in the mud where Victor had stood caught my eye. I pulled out my tape. Size twelve, the same as the marks on Joe's roof.

Another half hour of searching the brush turned up a single prize, the bill of sale for the Queen Anne I'd been carrying in my pocket the day I fell down the stair. I wondered how it got here. Did I drop it when I returned to the truck, or did Bennett have it in his bucket? Was he the person who hit me with the hatch cover? He clearly wanted to keep me out of the area. I doubted that the executor of the Singer estate would allow blasting before the purchase of the property was completed, so what was Bennett really doing on the parcel? I intended to take a closer look, but I would bring an ally with me.

I reached for my cell phone but it was already ringing. It was Nora and she sounded frightened. "Franklin, can you come back? Someone broke into Joe's archives."

Chapter 7

I hurried back to my truck to check out the scene. The call to Albert would wait, but I did want him to help me check out the Monument Parcel.

Nora had been out when the break-in occurred. She had noticed some litter on the back stair and the rear door of the kitchen had been forced in. This time she dredged up enough strength to make it up to the attic. The room that had been filled with neatly organized file boxes was now ankle deep with the contents.

"Why would anyone want this stuff?" Nora asked.

I'd seen Victor in the Simpson's back yard earlier, but that was before I checked the attic and everything had been okay then. It couldn't have been him, unless he came back.

"Was anything taken?" I asked.

Nora didn't know, but invited me inside to look around. I objected. "That might not be a good idea. I may destroy clues the police need."

Nora gave me a sour look. "They couldn't find a horse if it was still in the barn. They can't investigate a murder properly, so why would I have any confidence in their ability to discover who broke into my home? I'm not calling them."

I thought her criticism a little harsh and her stubbornness unproductive. Like everyone else, the police had limited resources. They had to work with what they had and prioritize. I could see that an ambiguous death might not get their full attention. I didn't want to contaminate the scene and make the case harder to solve, but Nora was probably right about the lack of interest.

Someone had searched the room thoroughly. No drawer, box or shelf had been left intact. I picked up a handful of trash: old newspapers, magazines and photos.

Nora shook her head in disbelief. "What could they have been looking for?"

"Whatever it was, the intruder didn't find it."

"How do you know?" Nora asked.

"If they had found it they would have stopped searching and left something untouched. Everything has been searched, so I guess whatever the burglar wanted wasn't here."

Nora looked thoughtful. "Something that should have been here but wasn't. I might know what it was. Joe moved a few things to the trunk of his car a few days ago."

We traipsed back downstairs and outside to a plain, all-function and no-frills carriage shed that had been converted into a garage. Nora motioned for me to open the rolling barn-style door. Joe's dusty old Volvo sat like a faithful dog awaiting a master who would never return. She unlocked the trunk. "Bring out that box."

I reached in and dragged out a heavy cardboard box with no lid. At one time it had held reams of copier paper. Nora closed the trunk and motioned for me to set the carton on it. She gestured to a neatly packed row of file folders, notebooks and glossy coffee-table books featuring Victorian homes.

"What's all this?"

"I found this in the trunk this morning. Joe must have removed the contents in a hurry—there's no lid, but a note on one of the books says it's for you. Maybe you can figure out why he wanted you to see all this."

After one more unsuccessful attempt to get Nora to report the break-in to the police, I tucked the carton behind the seat of my pickup and returned home.

A quick look revealed the contents of the box to be file folders similar to those from the records room in the attic, and odd-sized papers. The books on architecture probably came from Joe's office. I sat in the truck looking over the contents before I remembered to call Linda to see when she wanted to be picked up for dinner. Besides making up for the date I missed yesterday while at the emergency room, dinner would be a good time to clear up a few things between us. I'd tell her about my decision to investigate Joe's death and plans for the Queen Anne. If that went okay I'd explain my reservations about the Monument Condominium project and convince her to withdraw her bid.

Linda's studio was located in a little strip mall on a back street parallel to coastal Route 1. Most of the little storefronts at the rear of a large parking lot were brightly lit, except for several vacant spaces displaying dark interiors and for rent signs. Businesses needing lots of foot traffic tended not to do well on this back street but Linda knew this was a great spot for her. She had taken over the lease of a tiny photographer's studio. She appreciated the good light from the south-facing wall of windows. The studio was in the same mall as the post office, making the location easy for clients to find.

Linda was standing on the sidewalk dressed in her office best when I arrived. I didn't know what to call her look but to me she resembled a French pastry, all sweet and frilly and delicious. We drove to a little pizza joint on the waterfront and sat at a table next to picture windows looking out on the Thames River. Waves created by the wake of boats splashed into the rocks below the building. The sun sparkled on the water behind Linda, but the brightest light in the room radiated from her face.

Linda ordered a crisp white wine for her and a soft drink for me. I appreciated her concern for my doctor's no-alcohol order, but bristled at the unspoken assumption that I needed her to force me to do the right thing. We tried making small talk, but like many long-term couples we kept returning to silences when not talking about practical matters. I sensed that we had something to say to each other, something we were avoiding. When the wine had loosened her up, Linda launched into a discussion of fabrics and designs as she discreetly scanned the room for potential clients. By the time the meal concluded, I had given up trying to make casual conversation and asked about any new jobs in the pipeline.

Linda treated me to a smile with the brilliance of an electric arc welder and revealed the source of her good humor. "I may have wrapped up the deal with a couple of very connected new clients. I spent the day working on some design ideas that are coming along great." Linda stared out over the river with the dreamy look she got when lost in the world of colors and shapes.

I reached out and took her hand. "Great news. I know they're going to love your plans. Speaking about new projects, I've a couple of things to talk about."

Linda's face changed subtly when I mentioned the L word. I'm pretty sure she didn't hear any of the rest. She still wore the radiant, satisfied smile, but her eyes had gone soft and large and her lips parted and slightly puckered. She lowered her gaze from the horizon and looked at me. "Frankie, I'd like to stay over at your apartment tonight. We can talk then."

The suggestion that we spend the night together didn't surprise me. All through the meal I saw signals of her arousal. Business may have caused her sudden romantic turn but I would join in gladly. I called for the check and we stepped out onto a faux brick street under the glow of neon disguised as gas lights.

The weather front that had provided the rain at Joe's funeral yesterday was still hanging around. Drops began to slap against the windows toward the end of our meal and a deluge hit us before we reached the truck. Once inside, I struggled with the levers and pounded on the dash in an effort to get the heater working. Linda shivered with cold all the way back to my parents' house but continued to smile a sweet, anticipatory smile.

"Sorry about the heater. Sure you don't want to go back to your place and get some dry clothes?" I asked.

"It's OK, Frankie. I can dry my clothes here."

I climbed out, crossed to her side, jiggled the door, made a mental note to fix the latch, and let her out. Linda twisted her legs toward the sidewalk and slid down. Her dress rode up revealing an impressive length of thigh. My pulse continued to accelerate even as she stood and the damp fabric dropped back to a slightly less obscene level. We crossed the flagstone walk to the front door. Linda held my arm as we climbed the stairs and stepped inside the foyer.

She kissed me and ran her fingers through my hair, below the bandage on my head. "You've had a rough week. I plan to take your mind off all that." She stepped out of her wet shoes and left them in the hall. She opened the door to the lower level and sauntered down the stairs to my apartment.

I struggled with my wet laces, kicked off the boots and followed her down a few moments later. Linda wasn't in the red-and-white nineteen fifties style kitchen, but she had left a trail of clothes for me to follow. Her raincoat lay across the laminate breakfast bar. In the living room her skirt and blouse covered the glass-topped coffee table. I picked them up and crossed to my bedroom where she had draped her sheer stockings around the door knob. The last few lacy bits of Linda's outfit were on the bedroom floor next to the bed.

It didn't strain my detective skills to find her. Linda emerged from the bathroom wrapped in a fluffy white towel with mischief in her eyes. She sauntered to the bed, pulled back the covers, and slipped between the dark silk sheets. When the covers reached her chin, she slipped the towel out and dropped it on the floor. "Come and warm me up."

The trail of soggy clothes and her little show were having the desired effect. I put her clothes on the chair, removed my own, and joined her.

After Joe's funeral and the bump on the head, I didn't expect much success as a lover, but I had underestimated Linda. Before long the familiar sensation of her soft lips, caressing hands and smooth skin had crowded out all thoughts except of her. Linda proved that an aroused girlfriend can make a guy forget nearly everything else.

Our lovemaking marathon continued into the evening hours until we fell asleep. Before I knew it Sunday morning was streaming through the windows and we still hadn't had our talk. I felt a sharp pain in my ribs.

"Are you okay, Frankie?" Linda rolled over, glided a bare arm across my midsection, shook out a mass of ash brown curls, and laid her chin on my chest.

"I was okay until you jabbed me," I complained rubbing my side. "We really need to talk about this hitting and jabbing." I had never seen direct evidence of anything kinky but sometimes I wondered about an S & M perversion.

"Don't be such a baby. I only poked you. You were talking in your sleep."

The details of the dream faded quickly, but the emotions lingered. "I was running in thick mud, trying to reach Joe. I didn't make it." It wasn't the vision of the body on the ground that left me so unsettled but the unmistakable feeling that something I had done caused him to fall.

Linda scooted up and kissed me. "The news said Joe died accidentally. What could you have done?"

"Maybe he wouldn't have fallen if I'd been helping him."

"That reminds me, what did Nora Simpson want?"

I really didn't want to drag out the bad feeling by talking about Nora. I wanted to forget the dream and the sense of guilt about what happened to Joe.

I took Linda in my arms and held her close. I pressed my lips into the hollow of her neck, tasting the saltiness of her, nuzzling against her warm skin. I spoke into the hollow above her collar bone. "How would you like to take a drive up the coast this afternoon, and spend a couple of days hiking on deserted beaches? The forecasters called for clearing in the east and the rates are pretty low on Cape Cod on the off season."

Linda rolled her eyes in disbelief, as if I had proposed putting aluminum siding on an authentic Revolutionary War-era saltbox. "We can't. I'm choosing fabrics and colors to make over a cottage on Long Point and you need to check for code violations. I promised the owners your inspection report and my proposal first thing on Friday."

I leaned back and stared at her. "When did you plan to tell me about this?"

Linda smiled a self-satisfied smile. "What do you think we were celebrating all night? I closed the deal yesterday afternoon." She bounced on the bed with enthusiasm. I managed a smile but groaned inwardly.

"Can't you ask them to wait a few days?" I had hoped to explain my promise to investigate Joe's death and my continued interest in restoring the Queen Anne in a romantic setting. I'd missed my chance last night and now I wasn't sure the time was right.

Linda sighed, pushed herself up on her elbow and studied me. She looked unsure about why I had objected to the new project but also determined not to allow her ambition to be blocked by whatever it was. "Frankie, get serious. The Petersons know everyone on the coast and I'm the first designer they talked to. I need to impress them. We're not going anywhere until we get that contract."

With the discussion over, Linda reached over me toward the end table. Her naked breasts brushed my chest, but seduction wasn't on her mind as she retrieved the remote and flicked it at the TV.

That happened a lot. Warmth and passions dominated for a while, then I said something that displeased her, and wham, she lost all interest. I really was sick of the way she could turn her interest in me off. The power of that thought shocked me. I had never stopped loving her, but I had started to question if I wanted a life with a woman who was cold and focused whenever she had enough of me.

Light from the flat-panel TV flashed like headlights sweeping between guardrails as Linda channel surfed. She stopped on the home improvement channel. She fluffed up a pillow behind her back and modestly tucked the sheet under her armpits. "Let's look at the *Old Home* show. That program always makes you feel better." I guess she did recognize my down mood. The idea of a home repair program as therapy was a good idea.

The show on the screen featured a couple describing the restoration of their nineteenth-century, Victorian home. A camera zoomed in on the impressive décolletage of the show's host standing in front of the home. Linda looked at me with a wry expression. "Look, Frankie, it's your mistress."

Her guess about my attraction to the pretty actress surprised me. I replied carefully. "For a woman over thirty she looks pretty good, but I never seriously considered a relationship with her."

Linda looked at me with a crooked little smile and poked my ribs again. "Not the woman, Frankie. Look behind her. See the house? It looks a lot like the old Queen Anne that Joe tried to get you to fix up. Only this one isn't a dump."

She gestured toward the middle-aged owners. The woman wore designer clothes and the man a private label golf shirt. They had on an air of wealth and proud smiles, like they had adopted a stray puppy and called in an expensive trainer to make it over in their image. "They may have the money, but they've no idea what goes into a restoration. It's not that Victorians aren't beautiful, but old buildings can take over your life."

That last comment required that I come to the defense of classical architecture. "Don't be too hard on Victorians; you have a lot in common with them." I leaned on my elbow and caressed her curves. "You both have great profiles and everything is in perfect proportion." I placed a row of light kisses along her neck and decided not to mention another trait Linda and Victorian homes have in common. They both tend toward high maintenance.

Linda looked brightly around the room. I knew she was proud

of how her design had transformed my apartment. "Frankie, you're a flatterer. I know you're crazy about Victorians, but I like modern styles. Look what we've done to this place."

I followed her gaze. The clean lines and bold colors of Linda's nineteen-fifty style makeover reminded me of everything right and everything wrong in my relationship with her. The bright colors and bold shapes of mid-century modern style were a rejection of the soft colors and complex detail work of Victorian and Craftsman styles. Linda saw all the classical styles as old fashioned and constrained. Sometimes I thought that she saw me the same way, a quaint, out-of-date boyfriend resisting a much-needed makeover.

Linda stretched and scissored her legs. Her foot snagged the sheets and pulled them down. "I caught my ankle bracelet. Can you unhook it?"

I had given the bracelet to her when we were too young to do more than think about going to bed together. I put my hand flat on her stomach, reached under the sheet and slowly ran my fingers across the smooth skin of her thigh and leg until I reached her ankle. I unfastened the defective chain and let the smooth links caress her as I dragged it out. She noted my efforts at seduction with a raised eyebrow.

"Can you fix it? That piece means a lot to me."

I examined the chain and resisted the urge to search for some pliers. I placed it on the table. "It needs a new clasp. I'll take it to a jeweler tomorrow."

"Thanks, Frankie." Linda brushed a lock of straight black hair off my forehead, one of the signs that she was turned on again. I pressed against her, pushed back the curls framing her delicate face, tasted her lips, and calculated that I might have one more performance in me.

Linda was well into the spirit of things when the shrill ringing of a phone erupted on the nightstand next to the bed. Caught up in the intensifying passion, I ignored the sound, intending to let the machine answer.

"Franklin, it's Nora."

I groped for the handset to interrupt the message. I pressed the buttons, frantic to mute the speaker. "Nora?"

Nora kept talking as if she didn't hear me. "I can't tell you how much I appreciate you looking into Joe's death. I talked to my lawyer and Joe's partner, and you can start the restoration of the Queen Anne as an internship as soon as you are ready."

That pretty much let the cat out of the bag, so I finally found the answer button, thanked Nora, hung up, flopped down on my back, and waited for the fireworks.

Linda levered up on her elbow and looked down at me with an expression of surprise and disappointment she usually reserved for her cat when it peed on the rug.

"Frankie, what was that all about? I can't believe that you still plan to renovate that old house. And you're investigating Joe's death?"

"Nora thinks someone pushed Joe. I agreed to look into it. She offered me the Queen Anne including supervision for the internship."

"Why didn't you talk to me about this first?"

"I couldn't wait. Evidence tends to disappear quickly and the Queen Anne will collapse if I don't fix it soon."

Linda slid her legs off the bed and stood. The mirrors on opposite sides of the room multiplied her image and suddenly rows of gorgeous, naked, angry copies of Linda glared at me. I would have been outnumbered with only one of her.

Linda leaned forward, her expression incredulous. "Frankie, I don't know what's dumber—you playing detective or bankrupting us trying to restore a crumbling old house. Bobby said you would pull something like this."

Bringing the name of my nemesis into a bedroom quarrel wasn't one of Linda's best moves. I felt the pulse pounding behind the stitches in my head. "Let's talk about Bobby. When did you plan to tell me that you submitted a bid to decorate those condominiums he represents?"

"Frankie, we need his business. We're barely surviving. A lucrative contract like that could save us. How will we ever get ahead if we don't go after the big-money jobs?"

That argument spelled trouble. For Linda, failure to get ahead was more serious than infidelity. "I want answers to some questions about Joe's death and one of Bobby's clients may be involved."

Linda ignored my complaint. "How will you earn a living if all your time is going into repairing that old wreck?"

"The internship Nora is offering me is the chance of a lifetime. The Queen Anne will be a great place to live and show our clients that we're a serious restoration team."

Linda looked like she had been sucking lemons. "It's like your degree. You'll never get it done and you'll expect me to wait while you indulge in your architectural fantasies." The army of mirrored Linda's stood there glaring, hands on her hips. Her perfect breasts quivered with each shallow breath.

My temper flared. Linda didn't appreciate all the struggles and sacrifices I had made to finish school and keep our business afloat. While she flitted around in frilly clothes buttering up clients, I banged nails, lugged furniture, and did the work that got us paid. At least that's how it felt at that moment. I fought to keep down the bitterness that rose up in my throat. "That's not fair. I need only a few internship hours to get my license."

The conclusion of the nearly eight years it took to complete architectural school should have pleased Linda but instead she dismissed my efforts. "You don't get it." Linda's brow furrowed; her eyes compressed to slits as she stood facing me. "This isn't about you, Franklin Breault. Do you think I want to spend my life redecorating moldy antiques? What about my dreams?"

I got out of bed and started dressing, no longer clear what we were arguing about. I studied her, but her beauty did nothing for me at that moment. I gazed at the rain-streaked window thinking how much I wanted to escape the house and her. "Damn it, Kissy, why can't you try to understand? I need to find out what really happened to Joe. And restoration of classic homes like the Queen Anne is my life."

"If you start working on that wreck you'll be stuck living here for years." She gave me a cold stare. "And don't call me Kissy. My name is Linda. I'm not a child anymore, which is more than I can say for you."

She gestured at the apartment. "How do you expect anyone to take me seriously with a loser boyfriend who lives in his parents' basement?"

That explained the source of her anger. I wasn't an asset to her career. I turned back toward the bed seething with anger. If I had been a little less angry I probably would have reacted to the regret in her eyes for the loser remark, but I was lost in the moment. "Loser? Damn it, Linda, do you think that you're better than me because my parents offered me a place to live and yours didn't? I'm tired of your bullying and name calling every time I don't do things your way."

Linda glared at me, temporarily speechless. The pain on her face showed the memory of her feelings of betrayal when her parents had banned her over their suspicion that she had aborted their grandchild. She had lost our baby naturally, but they wouldn't listen.

She also seemed surprised at my accusation of her bullying. She took a deep breath and lowered her voice. "I didn't mean that the way it came out. And it's not true that we always do things my way! I care about our future."

Unfortunately, the angry guy I had suppressed for too long was firmly in control of my mouth. Instead of recognizing her efforts to calm things down, I lashed out. "I've had enough of you pushing me around. Keep away from Bobby and the Monument Condominiums. There's something rotten going on there and I'm going to stop them."

I paused for a breath, my chest heaving and the blood rushing in my ears. "If you think I'm a loser for caring about historical restoration, you've got the wrong boyfriend."

Linda's eyes opened wide at my declaration of independence. "You're twisting everything around." Her voice quivered, her eyes filled with hot tears, as she attempted to defend herself. "Besides, if you can commit to playing detective without telling me, then I can make business deals without your permission."

I noticed that I'd put on my shirt inside out. That made me furious. I tore it off and reversed it. "Nora promised me the Queen Anne. I'm going to restore it, get my license, and start my career as an architect. And you don't get a veto."

I may have been too upset to get my clothes on right but I'd got my balls back and it felt good.

Linda's mouth dropped. She shook her head as if trying to rid it of my words. She stalked toward the bathroom, pausing only to snatch her clothes along the way. One flush and several minutes later, she emerged clothed in yesterday's outfit, carrying a bag bulging with toiletries she had left in my bathroom. "Fix your damn house if that's what you want to do with your life, but I can't take this anymore." Tears streaked her cheeks. She stalked across the living room.

I watched her pause in the kitchen and grab the keys to my truck. The door leading to the stairs at the back of the kitchen cracked against the stop. Seconds later the mirrors over the bar rattled as Linda slammed the heavy door front door. The power steering and wheels squealed as she pushed my truck to the limit.

I should have gone after her, but at that moment, having a warm body to hold didn't seem worth the aggravation.

Chapter 8

It didn't take long for me to realize that I could have handled the argument with Linda a whole lot better. I wasn't wrong to want to follow my dreams, but I lashed out at Linda because of guilt that I couldn't live up to her version of our life. She realized she had pushed me too far and tried to cool things off, but I was too angry to turn back. Damn that temper of mine.

After a shower I picked up a spare set of keys. I headed upstairs to see if Dad could drive me over to Linda's condo to retrieve my truck. I also wanted to show him the picture I found on Joe's roof. Maybe Dad could identify the people.

At the top of the stairs I turned toward the rear of the house and entered the kitchen. The smell of a hot pan and burning sauce drifted on the air. I paused at the stove, stirred the sauce, and turned down the heat. Sounds of the TV in the next room told me why Dad had deserted his post.

I entered the living room in time to see him bang on the armrest of his recliner and scold the screen. "$350,000? You're dreaming! Not a penny over twenty-nine five, you morons!" My dad, retired real estate salesman Gary Breault, shouted at the host of one of his favorite shows, *How Much For That House?* Despite the early hour, he wore an open-collar white shirt, dress pants, sport coat, and wingtips. The clothes drooped off his thin five-foot-ten-inch frame. I approached him and placed a hand on his shoulder.

Dad jumped at my touch. When he recognized me he reached up and patted my hand. "Hi, Frank. I thought I heard you go out. You sounded in a hurry."

"You heard Linda leave. She wasn't in a hurry, she was angry."

Dad twisted around and studied my face. "If you don't mind my saying so, you and Linda have a lot of arguments. I'm not sure if the front door can stand more exits like that. Is everything all right between you two?"

One of the downsides of living in my parents' basement is that Mom and Dad often got selective information about my relationship with Linda. The sounds of our arguments probably carried upstairs pretty clearly, but the bed sat on a concrete slab so my parents probably didn't know about the great makeup sex that usually followed a quarrel. That was something for which I was doubly grateful.

It seemed unlikely that the squabble we had would lead to great sex. This was the first time that Linda and I acknowledged that we had been pulling in different directions for some time. I wasn't sure we could get back from the positions we had staked out. In the interest of avoiding too much information I decided not to go into any of that with Dad. "You know Linda. She has a temper like a firecracker."

"Sure, but you also know that her feelings are easily hurt." Dad had been fond of Linda since she was a child. She grew up in a household of screamers, and as a kid she had wandered over to our house many evenings to avoid the drama. I knew that Mom and Dad were hoping to welcome her as their daughter-in-law some day.

I followed Dad's gaze as he turned back toward the TV. "Hey, how did you get that show? What happened to *Rehab For Resale*?" I asked. I like Home TV almost as much as Dad and had memorized the schedule.

Dad shifted in the chair and the frame of his recliner wobbled. "That friend of yours, Albert the electronic genius, showed me

how to get these shows whenever I want them. DVR he called it."
He pressed the button temporarily displaying the digital video
recorder menu. "He says it will work in Florida too."

I retrieved a wrench from a drawer in the end table and
dropped to the floor. The carpet smelled of dust and mildew.
Mom's cleaning standards had slipped. "Why Florida? Are you
and Mom going on a vacation?"

The screen changed and Dad's gaze flicked back to the
program. A pair of homeowners had tried unsuccessfully to
unload a dirty home in poor repair. The real estate actress
delivered her assessment of the intelligence and taste of the
owners while the couple looked on through a remote video link. I
thought the scolding was rude and unnecessary. Dad laughed.
"You tell them, cutie!" He leaned forward and looked down at me
on the floor. "I've lost count of the number of stubborn, lazy
sellers who needed that discussion. I was only trying to help them
get a good deal, but they wouldn't listen."

Apparently, Dad and I shared a family trait—feeling
misunderstood and unappreciated.

A bolt that had fallen out of the frame peeked out of the dust
beneath the recliner. I picked it up and replaced it in its slot.
"What are you and Mom doing today?"

Dad pulled out a newspaper and waved it my way as I groped
the shag carpet looking for the missing nut. "See this? The Nash
family home on Meridian Street is up for sale. We're going to the
open house today. Your mom says I'm on probation."

I was glad that Dad was getting out and not spending all his
time in that chair. Open houses were major social events for
Groton City seniors and a great way to find out who is trading up,
moving out, or on to their eternal reward. Florida is a common
interim destination for seniors. Why had Dad mentioned the
sunshine state? I found the nut, threaded it on the bolt, tightened
it, and slid out. "Give the chair a try."

Dad worked the mechanism a few times. "Thanks. I thought
that felt loose."

"I could use your help prospecting for some new jobs. What are you doing after the open house?"

"Your mom and I signed up for the historical home tour around Groton Bank that kicks off later this afternoon. Maybe we can work on your project tomorrow."

Dad's reference to the neighborhood that Joe Simpson worked so tirelessly to protect reminded me of the nightmare. "Dad, I dreamt about Joe Simpson last night. I can't shake the feeling that he couldn't have died that way."

The program ended. Dad turned off the TV and swiveled the chair in my direction. "And you won't give yourself a moment's peace until you work out how everything adds up. You should talk to Nora. Maybe she can set your mind at ease."

I wasn't sure how much of my discussion with Nora I wanted to share with Dad. "I already did. She promised to honor Joe's offer of the old Queen Anne and to find me a supervisor."

"That's great." Dad pushed the footrest in and stood up. We headed back to the kitchen.

"Dad, can you give me a ride over to Linda's? I need to pick up my truck."

"Sorry, Mom has the car. You could wait but I don't expect her soon. She saw your truck and figured that with you home she could take her time. You know how she worries about me."

Mom had reason to worry. Dad was mostly okay but every now and then he did something that made Mom and me think that he was a few nails short of a full box. Like the time he forgot to open the door before backing out of the garage, or the times he had broken off the car mirrors on drive-through banks. Sometimes he got lost doing errands and came home hours late. Recently he and a couple of his cronies got thrown out of an open house. Dad and his friend had posed as brokers and lost a sale for the real agent. An unpleasant shouting match that cleared the house had ensued. "Dad, what was that scene at the last open house about?"

"I did not make a scene. They were cheating the widow. The

lot alone was worth more than the agent was asking. He was giving a sweetheart deal to a friend."

"Dad, did you know the owners of that home?"

"Glen and I used to have coffee before he died. I couldn't see his widow taken by a crooked agent because she was too trusting to fire him."

That explained it. Dad was attempting to protect the widow, and also grieve for the loss of his friend and his career as a real estate agent. My guess was that desire to help, not dementia, caused his temporary poor judgment.

Dad appeared to lose interest in the open house debacle and returned to our earlier conversation. "What were you and Linda fighting about, if you don't mind my asking?"

I opened the refrigerator door and searched for a soft drink, as much to buy time as to quench my thirst. "Want something?" Dad shook his head and waited for me to continue. I opted for a simplified explanation. "Linda flipped out when I wouldn't let her talk me out of renovating the old Queen Anne. The whole idea of a career in restoration architecture sounds risky to her. She wants me to design kitchens."

I could see on his face that Dad knew he shouldn't interfere but couldn't help himself. "You and Kissy have always had different thoughts about careers, but I thought you had worked all that out."

"She really doesn't like the name Kissy or me at the moment. I think she finally figured out that she's a granite countertop kind of girl dating a laminate guy."

"Too bad. Your mom and I pictured you two married and with babies."

Could that have been the dream Linda alluded to? Our history made the subject of babies uncomfortable. "I'm not sure about that ever happening. Maybe I'll join a monastery, one that needs a handyman, faith optional."

Dad's face brightened as if he had a new thought. "I know what's going on with you two: remodeling stress. I've seen it hundreds of times. A nice couple buys a handyman special as their first home and moves in. The renovation runs into problems and so does the relationship. Some shrink in New Hampshire wrote a book about it."

"But Dad, we haven't bought the house yet. We don't even live together."

Dad considered this for a while. He stood, opened the fridge, and took out the drink he had refused a minute ago, popped the top, and joined me at the table. "OK, anticipatory remodeling stress then. Whatever you call it, your plans to buy a place and move in together required you and Linda to confront weaknesses in your relationship and it scared the hell out of you."

Wow. For a guy who couldn't seem to remember events from one day to the next he had Linda and me figured out. "This has been building for a long time, Dad. I can repair that old house, but fixing Linda and me takes skills I don't have."

"That's because you're a lot handier with tools than people. It's probably genetic. Most of the Breault men were like you, builders and tradesmen, and mostly with low social skills. My dad could build anything but rarely even talked to his family." He pointed toward his chest with a thumb. "I'm the only one who preferred the people side of the home industry."

The reference to my crusty Grandpa Breault brought back fond memories. As a child I had spent countless hours in his workshop with the scent of wood dust in my nose. Grandpa had lavished the attention on me that he couldn't express to his own son. He always found some way to make me feel welcome and needed. He showed me how to use a chisel to shape a piece of trim destined to replace a section that had succumbed to rot on his Victorian farmhouse. I had cried uncontrollably at his funeral and still missed him twenty years later.

Thoughts of my absent grandparent reminded me of the picture I had found on Joe's roof. I removed it from my jacket pocket and handed it to Dad.

"Do you recognize the person in the background?"

Dad squinted at the faded copy. "I remember when this was taken for the newspaper. These three are Steve Smith, Victor Bennett, and Tony Gorky."

"Do you see that fourth guy standing in the glare? Could it be Robert Caspar?"

Dad tilted the photo toward the light. "Nope, too tall. Besides, Caspar probably took the picture. He loved his camera." Dad studied the picture carefully. "See the way the face is blurred? I think he was turning away. This guy didn't want to be in the picture."

I took the photo back. Dad could be right. "What can you tell me about Washington Way?"

"What's to tell about? Those stinkers conned all of us. We lost everything."

"You mean Caspar conned you."

"He got blamed, but if all the records and money hadn't disappeared, Victor Bennett, Tony Gorky, and your friend Steve Smith would probably have gone to jail."

Dad hadn't mentioned Steve's involvement before. "How did they get off?"

"They claimed that Caspar duped them like the rest of us. No one could disprove their story and they produced unpaid invoices that showed they lost a bundle too. But I think that they were in on it. Caspar double-crossed them but that doesn't make them less guilty."

"I've never heard any of this before. They all seem honest enough."

"They appear to have gone straight since then. Maybe I was wrong. It's not often that criminals reform on their own."

"Dad, about Florida? Are you taking a vacation?"

He studied the calendar on the wall before looking directly at me. "We should probably wait and discuss this over dinner, but I'll tell you. Your mother and I intend to sell this house and move into our condo in Naples. I want something with less maintenance in a warmer place."

"Why haven't we talked about this before?"

"We were waiting for you and Linda to have your own place. Don't let your mother know I mentioned this, she wants us to tell you together."

I had a million questions but agreed to wait. "I'll sure miss you guys. Are you okay?"

"For now yes, but not forever. You know that."

We sat in silence for a few minutes, remembering the good times, dreading what would come.

I decided that Linda had held my truck hostage long enough."Will you be okay if I ask Albert to give me a ride to get the truck?"

"Sure, Frank, go on. I'll look at reruns of *The Building Inspector*."

I took out my cell phone and speed dialed Albert Henley, who lived a few miles away on Hamilton Street. "Hey, it's Franklin. Can you pick me up at my Dad's and drive me over to Linda's condo? She's got my truck."

"Yeah, I know. She's on the phone with Marti. I hear you guys had another fight."

Albert's long-time live-in girlfriend, Marti, and Linda were best friends. "Yeah, she's pretty steamed with me. Can you pick me up?"

"See you in about fifteen minutes."

While I waited, I told Dad about the investigation. "There is something besides the Queen Anne that has Linda angry. Nora Simpson doesn't believe the explanation that Joe's death was accidental. She thinks someone murdered him. She asked me to look into it and I agreed."

Dad turned pale. "Be careful. There are things going on in Groton City that you don't want to get caught up in. Not everyone in this town is on the level."

Chapter 9

Albert still hadn't arrived and I had a question about the angry phone call Nora had overheard Joe make the morning he died. I called Nora and caught her before she entered church for Sunday noon service. I asked if she still had Joe's phone. "Will you see if it still has the number of the person who he called the morning he died?" She promised to check after she returned home.

Although the doctors suggested that I take it easy for a few weeks, that didn't pay the bills, including theirs. I resolved to get my truck back and then spend the rest of the day in the shed behind Dad's house finishing a furniture restoration job that would bring in some much-needed cash. I also wanted go through the box of papers Nora gave me, but they were still in the truck.

Albert and I drove to the side of town where Linda had her condo. We progressed into a labyrinth of little side streets with houses every seventy-five feet. Unlike the mansions on Groton Bank, many of these little homes were in serious need of repair. I recognized the Victorian influence on many of the buildings, such as a turret-like corner room on one house or lavish bargeboard trim on the eves of another, but these buildings were the discount-store versions of the homes built up on the Groton Banks by wealthy ships' captains and factory owners. We turned down a street of five identical Victorian-inspired bungalows and pulled up in front of a large, plain condominium complex built in the seventies. Like an invasive plant, the huge, two-story, vinyl-sided box with rows of identical doors and dormers sprawled over fifteen acres of what had been a quiet neighborhood.

Albert located my truck in a visitor's parking space and stopped behind it. I climbed out and approached the driver's side. Linda had locked the door and left the keys dangling in the ignition switch. I returned to Albert, opened the passenger door, and leaned in. "Linda locked the keys inside to let me know she doesn't want to talk to me now."

"Wow, that's cold. You gonna break in?"

"It's okay. She knew I'd bring an extra set."

Albert shook his head. "Sounds like you two have had this dance before. I would think that two people who know each other that well could find ways not to piss off each other."

"Next thing you're going to tell me is not to sweat the small stuff." I knew he wanted to help but my relationship with Linda defied simple solutions.

I shut his car door, pulled out the spare keys from my pocket, unlocked the truck, and climbed inside. The problem with Linda wasn't the small stuff. Our fights were about big things, like would I give up my dreams so that she could have hers. Linda would be happy to design interiors of new construction but I wanted a different kind of business. Did I love her enough to give up my dream? Did she love me enough to let me follow mine? Why did relationships have to be so damn complicated? I didn't know what to do. Maybe Dad was right about the Breault preference for technical problems over social ones.

I put the window down and called to Albert. "If the truck starts I'll head back home to work in the shop. Thanks, man."

The motor turned over slowly, but caught. Albert waved and headed toward his home. He was right about Linda and me. We knew each other well enough to really hurt when we fought. Whatever the future held, we needed to find a way to disagree without lashing out.

Back at home I had placed the box of papers on the breakfast bar when the landline rang. I expected it to be Nora telling me she had Joe's phone, but instead Julia Judge's loud voice came out of the speaker. "Franklin, I want you to meet someone, a government investigator, who is interested in Joe's death."

The library was closed on Sunday but she and the cop were at Sylvia's Slices, a little restaurant on the river. Julia suggested that I meet them for brunch. I agreed and Julia hung up without further explanation.

A few minutes later I approached the reception desk at Sylvia's searching for Julia and a stranger who looked like a policeman. I found Julia first.

"So where's this guy you want me to meet?" I asked.

Julia gave me an amused smile and flicked her eyes toward a spot behind me.

I turned. A woman about my age wearing a neatly tailored charcoal suit with a knee-length skirt approached. Gray eyes sparkled behind a splash of freckles across her nose. Layers of jet black curls surrounded a face more suited to a fashion model than a cop. She moved between the rows of tables with an easy, athletic grace. "Mr. Breault?" She pronounced Breault like it rhymed with salt. She waited for a reply.

A pleasant kind of warmth spread throughout my body, like a hot shower and a refreshing swim all rolled into one. Something about the shape of her, the sound of her voice, even the faint scent of her perfume settled in my brain like a long-lost road home. I stuffed my hands into my pockets to avoid reaching out and touching her to see if she was real. "It's Bro."

"Bro?" She repeated "Is that a nickname, short for brother?"

My tongue and brain seemed temporarily disconnected, but I certainly didn't want this woman to confuse me with her brother. With supreme effort I managed to utter a few syllables. "No, my family name is pronounced as if it was spelled 'B R O."

Her completion edged toward pink. "Oh."

"Hi, I'm Franklin Breault."

Her chest heaved as she fought the urge to giggle. "Yes, I know." She studied me for a second, probably attempting to assess my level of cognitive functioning. "I'm Virginia Maxwell from the Boston office of the IRS." She extended a hand. "We share an interest in Dr. Simpson's death."

It took me a couple of heartbeats to notice the business card she held. I pulled a hand out of my pocket, took the little cardboard rectangle, taking care not to touch her fingers. I held it at eye level. The message below the government seal identified Ms. Maxwell as a Criminal Investigator. She looked more like an IRS version of the popular dress-up doll that Amy and Eric's daughter coveted.

"Is there some place private that we can talk?" she asked Julia.

Julia nodded toward the table farthest from the river views. "Take a table back there. I have a board meeting of the Historical Society in a half an hour, so I'll leave you alone now that you've been introduced."

I couldn't interpret her expression as she exchanged hugs with Ms. Maxwell before hustling out the door. I reflected that Julia Judge was a person of secrets. Although a willing conduit of local gossip and the prodigious knowledge accessible through the library resources, I suspected she had secrets she wasn't sharing, like knowing this beautiful young woman. If I was right, Julia's expression reflected her delight in my surprise at the introduction and a hint that she had more surprises in store for me. I was glad Julia was an ally and not an enemy.

Agent Maxwell led the way across a room filled with scents of freshly baked rolls, hot metal pans, garlic, and tomato sauce. The view of her going was as impressive as that when coming. Like a moth to a flame, I drifted in her wake.

She selected a table in an alcove separated by a low wall from the clicking of flatware and conversation of the other diners. She slipped into the booth. I slid onto the opposite bench. "Julia tells me you're investigating a connection between Dr. Simpson's death and the Monument Condominiums project. Why are you interested?"

I reflected that the pleasant kind of hot and bothered I was feeling was similar to the way the sun feels before it burns you. With a supreme effort I remembered the importance of eye contact, looked directly into her penetrating eyes, took a ragged breath, and launched into the story. "Joe Simpson was my mentor until he died last week. His widow, Nora, thinks that his death was not an accident. Before he died he had visits from several people connected to the Monument Condominium development demanding that he sell them an old Queen Anne that he had already promised to me. I want to know if his offering me that house had anything to do with his death."

Criminal Investigator Virginia Maxwell sat stiffly in the chair and treated me to a tight smile and a serious expression. "Franklin, I hear that you're capable, but you could be getting into something really dangerous. If you have any information about Dr. Simpson or Monument Condominiums you should give it to me and back off."

Of all the things I wanted to hear from this goddess, being warned off wasn't one of them. I had already thrashed this out with the love of my life, and no stranger was going to order me off this case. "Can't do that. I promised Joe's widow I'd look into his death. In return she's helping me to go forward with plans to restore the old Victorian and get my career back on track."

The IRS agent studied me carefully. "So financial interest is the reason for your involvement."

Her distortion of my intentions caused me to snap out an angry reply. "Joe and I shared a passion for neglected historic buildings. Classic architecture is our link with the past. These buildings give our town its soul. The thought that someone might kill a fine old man and carelessly demolish pieces of history only to make a buck makes me sick."

I looked down, suddenly embarrassed at my outburst. The little speech sounded very corny coming out of my mouth.

Agent Maxwell didn't brush off my outburst as I thought she would. She relaxed a little, leaned back in her bench, and stretched her legs until they brushed mine. When my gaze reached her face again, a friendlier smile had replaced the earlier formality.

"I know exactly what you mean about lovely old homes. I grew up fifty miles from here in a Victorian on Smith Street in Providence." She flashed a heart-melting smile, reached out and placed her hand on mine. It felt soft and warm. "I'm here in a sort of unofficial capacity, and I need the help of someone local. If you're willing to work with me, maybe you can save some old Victorians and I can catch a few bad guys. Can I count on you to keep what I tell you now in confidence?"

I stared at Ms. Maxwell. What exactly did an unofficial capacity mean? Personal? A little voice reminded me that anything I said to an IRS agent was likely to become official whenever she wanted it to. Despite the alarms going off in my head, my attraction to Agent Maxwell eliminated the option of refusal. Being with her was thrilling, like unwrapping a new tool. "Okay, Agent Maxwell, count me in."

She relaxed and leaned slightly toward me. "Since we're working on this together you can call me Ginny."

I enjoyed the thaw in her voice. "Okay then, Ginny."

Ginny leaned forward as if to share a confidence. "I understand the widow's suspicions about Dr. Simpson's death. I talked to the state police by phone and Joe's death looked accidental, but a few questions remain."

"You mean the expired paint, the big footprints, and an eighty-year-old man on the roof painting the trim on a house that didn't need it?"

"Yes, and people the police interviewed mentioned Joe's knowledge of building materials and his record on safety issues, which are inconsistent with an accidental fall while painting. I'm not sure about the footprint—a local cop who stepped out on the roof could have made them."

"Where does that leave us? Did someone murder Joe or not?" I really hoped that Joe's death was the result of an accident, but something was wrong with that explanation. I could hear my pulse beating in my ears as I waited for her reply.

Ginny's eyes bored into mine. I could see that she was still trying to decide how much to tell me. Her cop sense probably told her not to share anything she didn't have to, but she needed me.

"We don't know that, but his opposition to large scale development in Groton Bank provides strong motives for someone to want him out of the way." She hesitated again, and then made a dismissive gesture as if the next question wasn't especially important. "I don't know if it means anything, but his widow told the police that Joe had been searching the storage room and some files may be missing. Do you know anything about missing files?"

A waitress stopped by and inquired about our meals, gaining me a few minutes to decide how much I wanted to tell her. We ordered a fried calamari appetizer, white wine for Ginny, and club soda for me.

"AA?" she asked.

"Concussion."

I wasn't ready to tell her about the break in at Joe's office, or that Nora had given me the missing box. "How does the IRS fit in? Did Joe cheat on his taxes?"

Ginny shrugged and shook her head, causing her dark curls to sway. "No more than anyone else." She stared hard at me, aware that I had ducked her question about the files. She must have decided to try to break me down by sharing more details, because her next revelation was explosive. "Dr. Simpson didn't seem to be directly involved but he had influence over some people who were. They may have embezzled millions of dollars from a real estate scam a decade ago, but the money has never surfaced. Their names kept coming up in relation to Joe's preservation efforts. We're hope that with Joe gone they'll get careless."

"And this is a case you're working on from Boston?"

"It isn't my case. I came down here to visit my family in Rhode Island on the south shore. My dad, a tax lawyer, heard about Joe's death and suggested I come down and try to break the old case. The Rhode Island south shore where I'm staying is only a short drive to Groton City so I came over to check with the local police about developments."

She lowered her chin, but looked up and flashed a devious smile. "It won't hurt my career if I help break this case."

"What about Julia Judge? Is she a suspect too?"

Ginny's face lifted as she tried to contain her amusement. Finally the mirth erupted in a smile. "Julia and my mother are sisters. While making a social call I found that Aunt Julia knows everyone and everything that goes on in Groton City."

She reached forward and put her hand on my arm. "Franklin, this case involves embezzling of very large sums of money, a disappearance, and possibly two deaths. Promise that if you know anything or learn anything you will let me know and not go off on your own."

So, she wanted to run the investigation. She had described her involvement as unofficial but hadn't adequately explained what was in it for her. I could understand her wanting a promotion, but there was more going on here than she was telling. "I promised Joe's widow to ask around and I can't quit— but we could work together. As a sign of good faith, how about you get me the police report of Joe's fall so I have something to talk over with Nora."

We shook on it. "I can help you with that. Let me have your cell phone." She accessed my phone directory and added an entry. "I've given you my personal cell number and the address of a motel where I'll stay tonight." She declined to hand me her phone, but asked for my contact information and entered it into her phone. "I'll ask for a copy of the report on Joe's death when I meet the locals tomorrow." She looked me over, as if she had a second thought. "If you're not busy maybe we can discuss strategy over dinner."

The prospect of an intimate dinner with Ginny kindled a pleasantly aroused feeling. Guilt that a date with Ginny was a betrayal of Linda, extinguished the mood. Besides, I still didn't know what Ginny's agenda was. "I've got a couple of projects to finish this afternoon. Why don't we talk later today and set something up?"

Ginny gave me the look that pretty girls use to seal a deal. "Sure. I'm looking forward to it." We finished and Ginny insisted on picking up the tab. She stepped out of the booth and stuck out her hand. Touching her was exciting—I didn't want to let go. She didn't pull back.

As I left her and returned to the truck, my giddiness gave way to confusion. Had I promised her a date? What was I thinking? Despite my quarrels with Linda, I'd never even considered seeing anyone else. I shook my head in denial. Ginny Maxwell was an IRS cop down here on a job. Whatever her personal interest was, I was merely a means to an end.

That thought eased my conscience a bit. Nothing personal was going to happen between us. But I still didn't know why she was interested in Joe. It might help my investigation to hang out with her and learn what she knows. That might be easier said than done. She clearly wanted me to stay away from the case. Maybe that was why she was here—to keep me from investigating Joe's death and the Monument Condominiums project. Too bad. If that was her goal, she was going to fail.

Chapter 10

I returned home, determined to be more careful around Ginny. I felt like a sap for being so attracted to her especially when I was technically still with Linda. Although I had no idea how, I was committed to working through the rough patch Linda and I had hit. If I was going to work things out, I needed a clear head. I put the box of Joe's files out of sight in my kitchen to save for later.

The best way to get a break from brooding about my love life, Joe, and everything that required any effort other than spacial intelligence and manual dexterity, was to pick up some tools. I left the apartment and headed for the barn.

The tranquilizing effects of the shop kicked in at the door. The smooth rotation of the lock released scents of wood dust and fresh paint that mixed with the sea breeze. Heavy machinery covered with petroleum lubricants gave off odors strong enough to register on the tongue. Yellow power cords dangled from the rafters like ribbons of fat spaghetti. My boots thumped on worn plank floors as I crossed the room. The familiar surface of the workbench was as grooved and gouged as an old man's face. I reached up and touched a row of antique chisels hanging on the wall. I could almost hear faint squeaks and feel the sensation as sharp blades sliced wood fibers.

I liked the way I felt in the shop, centered, creative, and powerful. There everything was orderly. Matter and force obeyed fixed rules. I could solve any problem by applying age-old principles and techniques.

Relationship problems should be that simple, but the obligatory behavioral science I took in school confirmed that people are unpredictable. Human behavior is so changeable that psychological laws are stated in probabilities rather than fixed rules. I couldn't imagine building a house where the laws of gravity applied only sometimes. But that's what relationships, especially with women, felt like to me. How could we build a relationship when the rules were in flux?

I flipped on a light switch and illuminated a worn dining room set in the center of the floor. I ran my hand over the nicked and scratched legs of one of the handmade wooden chairs built around the turn of the century. The set was beautifully formed of local hardwoods and joined with considerable skill. Until a week ago the one-of-a-kind set had rested in our furniture graveyard, along with a mountain of castoff chairs, sofas, loveseats, benches, and tables that reached the ceiling.

The furniture mountain was one place where my passion for restoration and Linda's enthusiasm for the new and bright worked harmoniously. Early in our business partnership we persuaded a customer to allow us to refinish her worn living room furniture to give the feeling of new on a small budget. I applied bold paint and bright fabric that Linda had chosen to compliment her design. The makeover was a hit and since then we've collected and restored worn castoffs to add low cost, custom furniture to Linda's concepts.

I collected the necessary tools and began filling and sanding scratches and dents. Soon the shop was filled with the sounds of buzzing tools, the air laden with dust, and the floor with wood chips. One circuit with a router returned the battered outer edge of the table top to a crisp bevel. After sanding I cleaned the pieces and created a dust-proof tent of polyethylene sheets. I painted all surfaces with a gray primer. The finish coat would be glossy black. While the paint dried I selected pre-cut plywood seat backs from a pile in one corner, pulled new padding from a bin, and fastened it to the plywood blanks with an electric stapler. I started to wrap the blanks with crimson upholstery material that Linda had dropped off earlier. The fabric glowed as I placed it across one of the seat backs.

A pattern in the fabric, rows of diamonds stamped into the nap, caught my eye. Linda hadn't mentioning how she wanted the design to lie. This was the opening I needed to call her and start the process of making up. I reached her in the studio. "Linda, I need to ask you a question."

"Frankie, I'm trying to work here."

"Me too."

"What do you want?"

"How do you want the upholstery to lie on those dining room chairs?"

"I don't understand."

"The material has a diamond pattern embossed on it. How do you want that to line up on the seat cushions?"

"Oh, I thought you called about something else." Linda paused as if unsure how to proceed. "I'll look up the fabric."

The clicking of the keyboard in the background signaled her efforts to find the fabric on the Internet. Sighs and tongue clicks said she didn't like what she found.

"Frankie, the fabric I ordered has no pattern. You're sure you have the material I dropped off?"

"Yes, and it's stamped with diamonds about an inch long and a half-inch wide."

"Don't do anything. I'll call the supplier and get the correct material sent out."

"That could take weeks. I want to get this done now. Besides, this could look good. You should come over and check it out."

"I have a design proposal to draft."

After my encounter with Bobby at the library and the subsequent argument with Linda, I had a pretty good idea why she was so focused and why she didn't want to talk to me about it.

"So you've started on the staging plan for the model homes in the Monument Condo complex."

Linda's voice had all the chill and none of the buzz of a frosty glass of beer. "Is that why you called, to talk me out of preparing a bid for Monument Condominiums?"

I'm not sure if it was the dust in the shop or my temper raising but suddenly it was getting hard to breathe. "That's not why I called. But since you raised the issue, I'm having a little trouble understanding how finding out about this bid from Bobby fits into your insistence that couples talk about important decisions first."

Linda ignored my complaint and returned to making excuses. "He told me he mentioned it to you. He was trying to jerk you around and it sounds like it worked. Frankie, I told you we need the work. This contract could keep us going for a long time. It's business."

Yeah, business. Linda didn't mind breaking her relationship rules as long as the violation advanced her business. I could feel us heading for another fight—not something consistent with my goal to make up for the last one. Too angry to continue I snapped out a reply. "Look, forget about it for now. I need to know how you want this fabric cut. You know how to find my shop, so come or don't come. It's your choice."

I snapped the cell phone shut and threw it in my tool box. I slammed the lid and started cleaning the shop.

By three o'clock the floors were clean and the equipment dusted. Under the plastic tent, the primer had dried so I put on the glossy black topcoat. By four o'clock Linda hadn't showed. I opened my tool box and picked up the cell phone. She hadn't called either. My finger hovered over Linda's speed dial number.

Before I could make up my mind to call, the phone rang. The screen identified the caller as Ginny Maxwell.

"Hi Ginny. What's up?"

"I'm following up on your suggestion that we discuss the case over dinner."

I thought that had been her idea. "Sure, how do you want to handle this?"

"I'll pick you up at your place in an hour."

I was waiting in front of the house when a Toyota FJ Cruiser in Sun Fusion yellow with a roof rack, rock rails, and sixteen-inch alloy wheels pulled up to the curb. Ginny's curly black hair bounced as she hopped down and headed my way. She had exchanged the gray skirt and white blouse for tan cargo pants and a gold knit top. A faint odor of expensive perfume drifted my way.

"Nice wheels. Nice outfit too."

"Thanks. I like a guy with good priorities." She looked over the raised ranch. "So you live with your parents."

"Worse. I live in my parents' basement. Want to have a look?"

I led her through the foyer and down the stairs. We stepped into the kitchen. Ginny crossed the red and white checkerboard tiles, ran her hand across the white-topped breakfast bar and looked out into the living room. "Wow Franklin, what a surprise. I love the retro look. The bar, the open floor plan and the mirrors are great."

Ginny's compliments stirred up mixed feelings. I was pleased at her approval, but these were Linda's designs and Ginny didn't belong here. "Linda intended a 50's look."

"Linda Kisslovich, your business partner, designed this?"

"You know Linda?" I asked.

"Aunt Julia mentioned her." Ginny crossed the room, put her hand on my arm and looked wistful. "She said that you and Linda are more than business partners. How come you aren't with her tonight?"

Caught off guard, I fumbled the reply. "Lately we're going through a rough patch. We fight a lot these days." As soon as I spoke I regretted the words.

Ginny glanced up at me as if she was evaluating my discontent with Linda. "I ended a relationship with a guy this summer and spent most of the season moping and feeling sorry for myself."

It registered that she had revealed her availability. I pictured myself as her new guy. It was an intoxicating image. "A guy would have to be crazy to let someone as gorgeous as you go."

She blushed slightly. "You could get in trouble saying things like that to a woman on the rebound."

I felt insane. I was flirting with Ginny hours after I had committed to being cautious around her. So what if I crashed and burned on the first attempt to make up with Linda? "I wasn't hitting on you, I meant, wow, you're so...."

She laughed at my discomfort. "Any chance I can get a tour of the rest of the place before you swallow that foot in your mouth?"

I took my eyes off her and shifted my attention to architecture. We crossed the kitchen and living room and toured the custom bathroom. Ginny ran her hand across the smooth, sparkling granite double sinks admiring the flecks of mica in the stone that picked up the light and scattered it like hundreds of tiny suns. She peeked into the stone alcove containing the shower. "Wow, a whirlpool and a sauna. This must have cost a fortune to build."

"Glad you like it. I used a lot of quality recycled materials to keep the cost down."

We peeked into my bedroom and Ginny made appreciative noises at the dark lacquered furniture, sunny drapes and soft lighting but didn't enter, a blessing in disguise considering the fantasies running in my head.

I led her back to the living room. "Sit down and I'll get us something to drink."

Ginny slid gracefully onto the couch. "Make mine ice water for now." Her eyes scanned the room and settled on the wood trim around the bookcases. "I like all this high quality finish. You did all this?"

"I like finish carpentry the best, although I do pretty much all the trades," I called from the kitchen. I scooped some ice cubes into glasses, filled them from the dispenser on the refrigerator, brought them to the living room, and handed one to Ginny. I sat across from her and redirected the conversation toward the investigation. "Did you talk to the police today? What did they make of Joe's death?"

"It's pretty much what you said Nora told you. Joe sustained multiple broken bones and bruises. He wasn't young and his heart gave out before the paramedics arrived on the scene." Ginny must have seen the painful expression on my face because she leaned into me, put her hand on my arm and spoke softly." I'm sorry if that sounds impersonal. I know he meant a lot to you."

"Yes he did." I realized that no stranger could feel about Joe as I did. "Nora thinks someone murdered him. Any sign of that in the report?"

"I don't have the written report, but the detective said a few things don't add up. Joe had a bump on the back of his head that didn't seem consistent with the fall."

"What could account for that?"

Ginny considered the question. "He might have hit something on the roof when he fell out of the window but they didn't find any blood or hair. Someone could have hit him on the head. A paint can the police found at the scene could have been used as a weapon."

"Could someone have hit him with the can and later opened it to create the appearance of a painting project in progress?"

Ginny looked at me as if reassessing my powers of deduction. "Possibly. The scene didn't make it clear what happened on the roof and in the attic."

This detective stuff was proving more difficult that I'd expected. "So the police have questions and I have questions but none of us have answers. Some investigation."

"Questions like this come up in most cases and often lead nowhere. It's possible that we'll never get conclusive answers."

I had promised Nora I would investigate but if the police or medical examiner didn't find any reason to continue their inquiries, I didn't know what I could do. "What would it take to persuade the police to take a second look?"

Ginny thought for a few seconds. "A suspect with motive and demonstrated opportunity would get their attention. Maybe something in Joe's personal records could help. Do you think that his widow would let us look at his files?"

"Someone already did that." I explained about Nora's discovery of the break in.

Ginny moved to the edge of her chair. "What did the police say? Do they think that the break-in is related to Joe's death?"

"I don't think Nora reported it. She believes the police have given up on the investigation, so she's given up on them."

Ginny looked relieved. "So the police don't know what the intruder removed."

I thought about the wall-to-wall clutter. Every drawer and box had been emptied on the floor. "I don't think they found what they were looking for."

"Why do you say that?"

"The room was completely trashed. They would have stopped searching and left something untouched if they had found whatever they wanted."

"So we may never know what the thieves wanted."

I had a pretty good idea what it was, but still wasn't sure about showing the picture to Ginny. I remembered the box Nora found in the trunk of Joe's car. It was sitting in my kitchen. I decided to see if Ginny could help figure out the significance of the contents. "Nora gave me a box of records that were removed hours before Joe died. I wonder if what the burglar was looking for is in that box."

Ginny's expression reminded me of Linda's cat as she stalked the birds on the window sill. "Do you have the box? Have you looked inside yet?"

"The contents appear to be mostly books and other documents to help with the restoration of the old Queen Anne. Do you want a look?"

Ginny leaned forward, as eager as a hunting dog on the trail. "Love to."

I retrieved the carton from the kitchen and put it on the coffee table.

Her hands shook as she began shuffling the contents. She cut her eyes in my direction. "I'd like to catalog this stuff before we go out, but I'm getting a little hungry. Could you fix a little something while I take a look?"

Banished to the kitchen I watched Ginny from the far side of the breakfast bar. She dove into the box with zeal worthy of an IRS agent. I put together a tray of crackers, cheese, fruit, and refills on the water. When I came around the corner of the bar, Ginny discreetly covered something she had been reading and reached for the water. She consumed a couple of mouthfuls of snacks and pushed a pile of colorful books at me. "Take a look at these and see if anything about them hits you as unusual while I sort the rest of the stuff."

"I don't know what to look for."

"Look for anything that seems out of place."

"But we still aren't sure that anyone murdered Joe."

Ginny looked up. "You're right. We don't know for sure that it was murder, but maybe something here will give us a direction to attack this from, like a motive."

"What does a motive look like?" I asked.

"People kill for lots of reasons. As an IRS agent I tend to look for the money."

I remembered all the battles with developers. "Joe's opposition to development has cost builders a bundle. That would make a pretty long list of people with motive."

We worked for nearly an hour. I started with the Victorian architecture books. I probably spent more time enjoying the contents than looking for clues.

Every now and then I sneaked a glance at Ginny. As she bent to the task I couldn't help but notice the contrast between her muscular, athletic build and Linda's slender body type. Ginny's raven hair and pale skin contrasted sharply from Linda's ash brown curls and golden tan. I wondered about other ways they might differ. I had experienced Linda's sharp tongue in response to frustration but I hadn't yet seen how Ginny responded when she didn't get her own way.

Ginny removed the last of the contents of the box, dropped the folder on a pile and looked up. "Here's what we have so far. This pile contains architecture books." She gestured toward a colorful stack. "The second pile has floor plans, plot plans, two-dimensional drawings, copies of assessor's property cards, and folded blueprints."

I looked at the drawings; the same or a similar house appeared in them all. "Probably the history of the Queen Anne." The remaining pile was the largest and contained smaller pieces, scraps of newspaper, photocopied pictures, little note books, and manila folders bulging with invoices and receipts. "What's in that third pile?"

"Those file folders contain records of a large construction project, material orders, invoices, and check registers. I haven't looked at that pile yet."

"What do we do now?"

"I want to inventory the last pile in more detail. Then I could run some analyses looking for less obvious patterns." Ginny removed a notebook computer from the bag she had carried in. She took a pair of glasses from the computer case, put them on, fired up the computer and started creating a data base of events, times and classifications. My stomach growled and I looked up at the clock. After seven—no wonder.

"Ginny, I'm getting hungry for something more substantial. Why don't we break and get something to eat?"

Ginny looked up. "I'd like to continue working on this but how about some pizza? You do have delivery in this town, don't you?"

Having issued her gentle order, Ginny turned her attention back to the computer. I grabbed a takeout menu from the kitchen and ordered an everything pizza and a garden salad for two.

The delivery guy arrived forty-five minutes later. I picked up the food at the door carried the box down to the kitchen. I retrieved a couple of salad bowls, plates, knives, and forks, and set them on the counter next to the box.

In the living room, the smell of the hot food roused Ginny from her labors. She saved the data base she created, shut down the computer, took off her glasses and executed a stretch that took my breath away. She gracefully lifted herself from the couch and made her way to the kitchen.

Ginny took a deep breath of the fragrant smells of our supper. "Wow that smells good. I'm starved." Still standing, She reached into the pizza box, slid out a greasy wedge covered with tomato and cheese. She devoured it with the intensity of a brush chipper on a soft log. On the chance that Ginny was ready for an adult beverage, I popped the top of a Sam Adams, retrieved a glass from the bar and handed both to her. She ignored the glass, took the beer with the hand not covered with pizza sauce, pressed the bottle against her lips, and tilted her chin toward the ceiling. The pale white skin on her throat throbbed as she gulped the fizzy liquid. I stood and watched her. She attacked the meal with a relaxed, strangely erotic gusto. I had the impression that she approached everything this way—with confidence and enthusiasm.

Ginny finally came up for air and gave me a smile. She still stood with her raven hair flowing around her as she licked the sauce from her fingers.

"Wow. I didn't realize I was so hungry."

I shoved a plate at her. "Have a seat and enjoy yourself."

Ginny slid onto a bar stool and stuck her hand back into the pizza box and pulled out another slice. She pushed the box my way as she stuffed a second wedge into her mouth. She watched as I retrieved a slice, placed it on my plate, cut off a piece with the knife and fork, and popped the morsel into my mouth. Ginny choked with laughter.

"What? No tape measure?"

I blushed like I'd been caught with my fly down. "I like to do things a certain way. I don't measure everything, but I like a neat workplace. Look at you, you've got crumbs everywhere.

Ginny's eyes held a wicked glint as she removed a crumb from her blouse. "You must like dainty girls—the ones who pretend that they don't like to eat."

I couldn't think of a thing to say. Ginny was hot, in my kitchen, drinking beer, eating pizza, and asking me what kind of girl I like. When did we transition from an investigation to a date? I attempted to stutter out a denial of the dainty girlfriend charge, which resulted in gales of laughter from her.

Ginny and I spent an hour talking, laughing and revealing bits of our lives, the kind of stuff that goes on during a good first date. "My physician mom and lawyer dad will celebrate their 26th anniversary in a few days." She described summers spent working at beach-front restaurants, four years of college at Brown and at twenty-one her move to Boston to take a job as a criminal investigator at the IRS. We discovered a shared love of historic architecture and the ocean. I asked about her unadorned ring finger and she said her career left little time for romantic entanglements. "Besides, I meet two kinds of guys in my job, cops and crooks. Neither matches my criteria for a good mate."

"I'm not a cop so that makes me a..."

Ginny treated me to a smile and placed her hand on mine. "A rarity, a nice guy."

I looked at her hand and felt heat surging through me. We sensed the change in our relationship and gently disengaged with awkward smiles. Ginny turned her attention back to the files while I cleaned up the mess from the meal. I watched her, curled up gracefully on my couch, and decided that the mess in my head was going to be much more difficult to straighten out.

When I returned to the living room Ginny scooped up a pile of papers and set them in front of me. She produced a handwritten list of names and pointed to the pile of miscellaneous papers.

"Make a separate pile of any documents that mention these names."

I recognized the names on the list right away: Steven Smith, Victor Bennett, Anthony Gorky, and Robert Caspar. "I know these guys. Why them?"

"The IRS is watching the first three for possible fraudulent activity. Caspar was on the watch list, but he disappeared and is presumed dead."

"The fraud concerns their involvement in Washington Way?" I asked.

"How do you know about that?"

I had become much more comfortable with Ginny after our evening together and decided to share what I found on Joe's roof. "I found a copy of a picture of the three of them at the groundbreaking. It shows Steve, Tony and Victor and a fourth guy no one is able to identify."

She blanched. "Do you still have the picture?"

"Sure, want to see it?"

Ginny nodded but looked sick, like the pizza and beer weren't settling well.

I dug out the faded clipping. Ginny practically snatched it from my hand. Her fingers twitched as she held the little square of paper under the light. "Do you recognize the fourth person?" I asked.

Her skin turned a pale gray. When she spoke her voice quivered with barely controlled emotion. "The face is pretty washed out, but I'd like to take this and show it around the office."

"I should show it around here. Maybe Steve, Victor, or Tony remembers who the guy in the back is."

Ginny looked horrified. She practically screamed. "No. One of them could have killed Joe to get the picture. You can't let anyone know you have this. Let me ask our lab to enhance the image." She folded the photo, put in her pocket, and scooped up a little pile of pages she had placed aside. "I've got to go, but I want to take these pages and study them some more." With that she packed her case and asked for her coat.

"If you find the original of that picture don't show it to anyone and let me know right away. It may have a better likeness." She took her coat, shook my hand, and left.

The change in Ginny from warm and relaxed to panicked and eager to get away had my head reeling. The shift reminded me of Linda's response when my objection to designing kitchens for life upset her plans. I wondered if the picture had upset Ginny's plan, and what that plan might be.

Why did a picture of four old guys in a public place upset her? As a government agent she probably had agendas and information she couldn't share with me, but her strong reaction suggested that the picture had personal significance. I realized that she probably already knew who the fourth person was. One thing was clear. She wouldn't have folded the picture if she was serious about having the lab enhance it.

I began shelving the picture books of Victorian houses in the book cases. As I moved the last pile, a volume titled *Field Guide to Victorian Styles* fell, tearing the colorful dust jacket. The tear revealed a thin sheet of paper taped to the inside. I gently removed the tape and reversed the page. The inner side of the sheet contained writing and explained a lot about why someone would want Joe dead.

Chapter 11

Dear colleague:

Although your coconspirator escaped with the funds skimmed from the investors of Washington Way, your signatures on certain documents in my possession show that you were not blameless. I suspect that a jury would find your billing practices meet the definition of fraud. However, prison would waste your talents, so I will contact you shortly with a proposal concerning how you can use your skills to benefit the community.

I stood with the paper in my hand, wanting to ignore the obvious implications. The letter wasn't addressed, but I could guess the intended recipients. Dad and Ginny had said that Steve, Victor, and Tony narrowly avoided prosecution for fraud when their partner skipped out with the money. They were probably the targets of this bit of blackmail. The letter wasn't signed, but the scrawl matched that which appeared on my correspondence from Joe. How was I going to spin this one to avoid ruining Joe's reputation?

I sat down on the couch with a thump. Joe had been

blackmailing the Washington Way partners. He had given the crooks who ripped off my dad and dozens of other investors a way to avoid prosecution. I felt like a builder who discovered that a formerly trusted contractor had used substandard concrete. How could I build a life as a restoration architect if the man who laid the foundation was corrupt? I had to get to the bottom of this and find out what Joe had been up to.

Maybe the letter wasn't the whole story. I flipped through the pages of the book but found no other surprises. Assuming that Joe had written the letter, what did he get from the deal? In a small town I would have known if he gambled, drank, or used drugs—which he didn't. Joe didn't need money, which he often described as merely the means to an end. He appeared to live what he preached. He furnished his old Greek Revival simply and he lived the lifestyle of a modestly successful small town architect. Joe did have a few vices, a passion for historic preservation that bordered on obsession, a demanding nature, and a tendency to get into other people's business. But Joe had used his influence for good, like preserving the region's history. Joe had always looked for ways to make things better. How could he have been involved in extortion?

If I thought of blackmail as using what you know to get your own way, I could almost believe it of Joe. Julia had confirmed that Joe bullied owners of Victorians to assure that they were preserved but she didn't say how. It wasn't much of a stretch to see him squeezing contractors with things he knew about them. I still didn't like thinking of my mentor as a blackmailer and I wasn't looking forward to telling Nora what I'd learned about the man that we loved. I would take my time and gather more facts before going down that path

That was why Steve and his cronies wanted to have a look at Joe's papers. They hoped to remove anything that incriminated them. I didn't know how I could continue to work with them. If they stole from investors, would one of them commit murder to hide their role? The blackmail involving them had been going on for nearly a decade and they hadn't done anything about it. Unless something had changed the status quo, they probably hadn't killed Joe. But they might know something that would help my investigation. As long as they thought I had the files they would probably cooperate.

Where could Joe have kept his files? The archive in his attic had nothing of interest, only pictures, newspapers, and magazines. He must have the blackmail files somewhere else, somewhere safe. I remembered a pile of papers with the name of one or more of the conspirators on them that had been in the box Nora gave me. I searched through the documents, but couldn't find the stack. Then I remembered that Ginny had taken some papers with her. Had she known about the blackmail? If so, why hadn't she told me? Was she attempting to protect me from the knowledge that my mentor had conspired to conceal evidence of a crime against my family?

There also was her flirting. Ginny was one of those beautiful girls who could get any guy she wanted. Why settle for an underemployed handyman? The painful answer was she was using me. Maybe her motive was to impress her boss and get a promotion, but she said her involvement was unofficial. Then there was her reaction to the picture. She wanted the original. Either something she was looking for wasn't clear on the copy, or she wanted to have all the copies for herself. I resolved to keep my libido to myself until I figured out her motives.

The night was warm and humid. Rotting leaves and other smells of nature cleaning house in preparation for winter floated in on the moist air and made it hard to breathe. The stuffiness and the discovery of the blackmail scheme led to a restless night and a series of dreams of which I could only remember the intense feelings of betrayal and anger. The Queen Anne hovered in the background of all my dreams. I woke up in a sweat with the strong impression that it was no coincidence that Joe died weeks after agreeing to sell the building to me. The basis for this insight drifted just out of consciousness as dream images tend to.

When Monday morning finally arrived I picked up the bedcovers from the floor, staggered into the bathroom and cleaned up. The soap didn't do much for the dirtiness I felt digging through Joe's life. If my investigation kept going in the present direction, I would demolish his reputation. As I struggled to find some benign explanation for the letter I found, my cell phone rang.

"Franklin, it's Nora. I checked Joe's phone. His last call was to Steve Smith."

I called Steve's service and found that he would make a rare appearance in his real estate office around noon today. I puttered around the apartment for most of the morning, catching up on chores and bills. As I prepared to leave I noticed Linda's ankle bracelet on the nightstand. I put it in an envelope and stuffed it into my pocket, intending to stop by the jewelers after I confronted Steve.

I drove across town to the realty office, and arrived a few minutes before noon. I didn't see Steve's 'SELL2U' vanity plates shimmering in the heat coming off of the pavement. I rolled down the truck window, breathed in the September air, and considered my complicated relationship with Steve. I often found jobs with builders who needed my specialized skills working on historic buildings, but most of my jobs came through Steve. I repaired deal-breaking flaws in houses he hoped to sell. Whenever business got really slow, Steve would come through with a project for Linda and me. Besides the business he had sent us, he taught me the practical side of real estate renovation—how to size up a house the way a buyer would, what to fix right away, and the kinds of finishes that would close a sale. But now that I had learned about Steve's participation in real estate fraud, he seemed a little too clever—the kind of guy who might know someone who hoped to get away with murder.

A victory red H3 Hummer pulled into the parking lot and crunched to a stop under the shade of a tree. Steve slid out of the driver's seat. He looked like Humpty Dumpty dressed in gray slacks, Italian loafers, and a tightly stretched polo shirt. He leaned against the truck and studied some papers on a clipboard. His thick glasses sat on the end of his nose.

I had intended merely to get his attention, but I couldn't keep the anger from my voice when I called him. "Steve."

He jumped nearly a foot. His eyeglasses slipped off and rattled onto the clip board. He scrambled for his glasses. "What the...," He finally got them back on his broad nose, squinted, and recognized me. He leaned against the van and placed a hand over his heart. "Geez, Franklin, you scared the crap out of me!"

"You're pretty jumpy. Are we still on to inspect the Queen Anne some time?"

Sweat glistened on Steve's face. He really did look shaken up by my sudden appearance. At the mention of the Queen Anne he began to scowl, but raised his hands in a gesture of futility. "Sure but why bother? You've seen the disclosure report. This place is a mess. Walk away from this one and start looking for a place worth restoring."

"I want to preserve that building."

"The chance to do that passed years ago."

Steve's casual dismissal of a building that had survived for a hundred and twenty-five years made me angry enough to start my confrontation sooner than planned. "Steve, does that judgment have anything to do with your involvement with the Monument Condominium development?"

Steve stared at me with an unreadable expression. He took a deep breath and extended his hands palm up and shrugged. "Sure, I'll make money selling units if the developers build the condos, but my profits and the developer's need for a road don't change the facts. That old house is ready to collapse."

"I can fix it."

Steve glanced at my beat-up old truck. "I know you can fix it, but should you? I've always treated you right, haven't I? Trust me, here's a better deal. I'll bet that Nora Simpson will sell the place cheap. Buy it and then let me sell it to the Monument

Condominium people for you—they'll give you full price. You'll make enough money to buy yourself a decent truck and still have money left over for a down payment on a house worth having."

Steve didn't know me very well if he thought that I'd betray Joe's widow for a truck and a down payment. Sure I needed the money and wanted to find a house to restore but I believed in loyalty and honesty too much to betray my mentor's widow. It made me angry to think that those values weren't shared by Steve, or apparently by Joe. Both men had cut deals with the people who swindled my dad. "You want me to cheat Nora?" I asked, not concealing my anger.

Steve knew he had pushed me too far. He smiled and tried again. "Think of this as business. Joe was only interested in preserving the place. He didn't care if you got stuck pouring hundreds of thousands of dollars and years of work into the Queen Anne. He was using you. You don't owe him or his widow anything."

Steve didn't understand the first thing about integrity. That made me think he probably had another angle too. "What else do you get out of it if I let you sell it?"

"My usual six percent commission and maybe a bonus for solving a sticky problem for the developers. Trust me. This could be a good deal for us."

When I didn't reply he straightened and pushed off from the truck. "It is a sad thing to love old houses too much, Franklin. They only want you for your money."

I wondered if Steve had slammed the hatch cover on my head. If I could get him over there maybe he would give himself away. "Maybe you're right. I tell you what, let's look over the Queen Anne one last time and see if it is worth saving."

At first Steve refused to go, but when I said I'd go alone, he agreed to accompany me. "Only to knock a little sense into that head of yours." Interesting choice of words.

We made the ten minute drive to Groton Bank in separate vehicles. The Queen Anne sat on a small rectangular city lot about seventy-five feet wide and a hundred feet deep. The land sloped up sharply from the street to the house fifty feet in. The postage stamp front yard provided a view of the river at the end of the street. A shallow back yard extended to the tangled slopes of the Monument Parcel. I checked my pocket for something to write on. The envelope with Linda's bracelet inside and a short stub of a carpenter's pencil would have to do the job.

Steve read the property card from his net book. "Number thirty-three Arnold Street. Located on the corner of Arnold and Smith Streets, a Queen Anne built in 1886. Two stories, three bedrooms, one bath, finished attic, stone foundation, and a dirt basement."

I turned away from the structure and faced the street. Between the trees I could see the Thames River roiled up by the incoming tide. "What a view."

Steve looked at the house, the river, and then me. "It's not the view that has me concerned."

Despite his personal agenda, Steve's extensive experience selling real estate made him a competent house inspector. House lust tended to make me blind to the faults of old buildings and Steve usually provided a much-needed reality check. My goal in this visit was to pump Steve for information about Joe's death, but I found myself focusing more and more on the old house.

We started our inspection around the exterior. Steve tilted his head up and squinted. "The roof seems sound, but the asphalt shingles are nearing the end of their lives. The ridge lines are straight so the supporting walls and sills are probably okay. The siding is weathered but most of it looks solid. The windows are intact but they need glazing. Everything on the shell needs paint and caulk."

I said made a note on the envelope. "That means the interior should be free of water penetration across the shell. I could have the whole exterior painted in a couple of weeks if the weather cooperates."

Steve held up his arms and gestured for me to slow down.

"Don't get ahead of yourself." He gestured toward a gap in the row of foundation stones. Someone had cut an opening into the foundation stones to ventilate the basement and stuck in a small wood-framed window. A shallow lake had formed next to the wall and rotted the widow frame. Steve strained the seams of his polo shirt to peer into a void near the foundation. "This doesn't look good. The gutters above this spot have failed and the water excavated the soil near the wall. Those foundation blocks are about to fall into the basement."

"Yes, but look at that square cut stone. Most of the houses in this era have foundations made of round field stones. These quarried stones are real quality."

Steve rolled his eyes at my efforts to find something to like. I felt the same way about his efforts to find things that would condemn the place. Neither of us tried to hide our disgust at the other's transparency.

We continued around the outside Steve took an old-fashioned ice pick from his pocket and poked at the sill boards that lay on the foundation. The wood resisted the hard jabs. "That's an encouraging sign. The sills are sound."

I looked for more good news. "The doors and windows are square, so the foundation isn't settling either."

We continued our inspection around the back. Steve examined the bulkhead that provided access to the basement from the back of the house. My head throbbed as we neared the spot where someone had slammed the hatch cover on my skull. I watched Steve for signs that he knew what had happened to me here, but detected no reaction.

He gestured toward the back yard. "Here is another potential source of water penetration,"

I wasn't impressed. So what if the poorly sloped yard had allowed water to undermine the concrete walls surrounding the stairs, and a steady stream trickled in from the rear of the yard, down the steps and into the basement. "All it will take is a little concrete and gravel to fix this up."

Steve gestured toward the back yard. "You need an engineer to tell if you need a curtain drain back here to catch the runoff from that hill."

We finished our circuit around the house and ended up back at the front porch. By then the barbs we were exchanging had become increasingly more unfriendly. Steve gave me a quizzical look as he probed the sills of the porch. The ice pick sunk in up to the hilt on the rotted outer sills of the porch. The base of the columns that supported the second floor balcony crumbled under Steve's probing. "You still think this house is sound? The whole porch is about to fall into the street."

I pictured what the porch had looked like a hundred years ago. "OK, but think about how great it will look with the original wrap-around veranda going up two stories."

Steve shook his head in disgust. "Franklin, stay focused. Your checklist should say remove and rebuild the entire front porch, not fantasies about what it once looked like."

I was plenty irritated by his negativity. "Let's go inside."

We climbed the steps to the first floor. The main entrance opened into the living room which included nine-foot-high ceilings capped with intricate crown molding and an octagon-shaped space inside of the turret tower. I stopped for a few seconds in front of three tall windows framed with fluted Victorian trim. Despite the dirt, I could see the river clearly. I thought about what a great place this once was, before the owner, Robert Caspar, had disappeared and let the home fall into neglect.

Steve was right about my problem keeping the potential of the place separate from the reality. My mind's eye transformed the dusty, run-down interior to a modern version of its former elegance. I imagined refinishing the rough, scratched hardwood floors into gleaming rich wood. I could see crews replace the old windows with energy-efficient replicas of the original double-hung, twelve-pane uppers, and single-pane bottoms. Imaginary paint coated the walls with a soft, lustrous color. Linda, dancing in a flowing gown, completed my fantasy.

Steve barked out a cynical laugh. "I haven't seen that expression on anyone's face since Danny Springer asked the head cheerleader for a date back in high school. I can see that this place has really gotten to you, but try to be objective. This is a dump masquerading as a Queen Anne."

We picked our way across the debris toward the back of the house. The dining room was beyond the living room in the left rear, and the kitchen covered the right rear of the first floor.

We had only been in the house for a few minutes but the smells were already bothering us. The stale air reeked of mold, mildew, and dust. Each breath burned my throat like pepper.

Steve sniffed. "Smell that? There's black mold in here. That stuff needs moisture, so water is getting in somewhere. You're going to need professional help to remove it."

I started for the basement to look at the furnace and chimney. "It smells like dust and soot to me."

Instead, Steve took my arm and guided me toward the stairs that led to the upper floor. "Let's start here and leave the basement for last. I don't know how much of this crap I can breathe in and I want to see the bedrooms and bath."

The small rooms on the second floor were covered with cracked plaster and peeling paint. In a closet we found an artifact of early electric supply wiring: a row of ceramic guides with bare copper wires running between them called knob and tube wiring. In the bathroom, several generations of plumbers had contributed to a cobbled-together mess of pipes made of lead, cast iron, copper, three kinds of plastic, and even a stretch of rubber hose held in place with stainless steel clamps. None of this was complicated to replace, but time-consuming and expensive.

We climbed the final staircase to an attic room occupied by nesting pigeons and, from the quantity of droppings, quite a few mice.

Steve took exaggerated steps up the stairs. "These stairs are major code violations. The irregular height of the risers and the missing handrails are dangerous."

"Yes, but how can you discount the value of the bonus room because the stairway needs repair?"

We made our way back to the kitchen on the first floor. The mineral-rich Connecticut water had turned the original white cast iron sink into a filthy, rusty mess well before the arrival of a municipal water system. The rest of the room wasn't any better. Steve shook his head in disgust. I agreed. The kitchen required complete demolition and replacement.

"Franklin, let's skip the basement. I've seen the report on the mechanicals. The furnace, water heater, and fuel tanks require replacement. The dirt floor really should be covered with concrete and the whole basement waterproofed. There's a spring running through there. You can record the basement as another total replacement." Steve coughed heavily and sagged against the blistered kitchen counter.

"I'd like to see how much damage the water around that window has done to the foundation stones and the footings."

"If you insist," he sighed and started down the stairs.

As Steve predicted, the foundation blocks bulged in where the window had been. The furnace and water heater sat on cement blocks and were covered in rust. I moved in for a closer look.

Steve grabbed my arm and turned me toward the muddy floor near where he stood. "Look at this. It's a hundred bucks. I guess this is my lucky day." He bent to the floor with effort, grasped the paper, wiped it off, and put it in his pocket.

This little bit of petty larceny was the last straw. I had heard of agents taking trinkets from vacant homes, but his stealing reminded me of my intention to confront Steve about some more serious ethical lapses.

"Don't you mean Nora Simpson's lucky day?" I asked. I held out my hand. "Give it to me and I'll return it to her."

"Sure, that'll save me a trip." He fished out the bill and handed it to me with enough bad grace to make me doubt his intentions. He gestured toward the stairs. "Come on, let's get out of here."

I finished filling up the back of the envelope with my notes on the condition of the basement mechanical systems as I stumbled back up the narrow stairs. By the time we reached the foyer we were coughing steadily. The pepper taste made it nearly impossible to breathe. Steve motioned toward the front door. "Let's talk outside."

Back on the street we leaned against Steve's Hummer and filled our lungs with the smells of low tide. I had to admit that the putrid fishy odors were an improvement over the smell in the house.

Steve gazed at the Queen Anne with obvious distaste. "You have no way to bail out if you start this. No one is going to buy a dump if you can't afford to finish it. A demolition machine now would save you a lot of cost and aggravation." He saw my shocked expression and lifted his arms in defeat. "I know. It's like telling a guy he is dating a girl who is bad for him. You really aren't listening to anything I say. Speaking of dates, have you ever given any thought to what your stubbornness might do to Linda?"

"What has she got to do with this?" I asked knowing full well the answer.

"Linda is an up-and-coming designer and Bobby Lester is courting her for more than those model units. That job is a chance in a lifetime for her. And you are ruining it because of your love affair with this dump. It's none of my business that you're driving her into Bobby's arms, but your real estate decisions are my business, so quit acting like an ass and dump this house."

I put the notes in my jacket. "I'll think about it."

"Damn it, Franklin, you need to decide if you're a businessman or another house nut having a romantic moment with a building. Let this one go before you lose everything," Steve warned.

"You aren't objective enough about this deal for me to trust your judgment."

Steve shrugged his shoulders. "Have I ever steered you wrong?"

That was a good question. Joe had linked me up with Steve, and I had trusted the real estate broker the same way I'd trusted Joe. I wondered what I had missed by not being a little more cynical. His question signaled that it was a good time to press Steve for answers about Joe's death.

"There's something I want to tell you. I know about your arrangement with Joe."

Steve blanched. "Arrangement?"

"Joe knew about your role in Washington Way. Now I know about it too."

I expected remorse or confusion. Instead Steve's face tightened with anger and he spat out a hate-filled reply.

"You little shit. After everything I have done for you. This is the thanks I get?"

"How could you? You ruined my Dad."

Some of the color returned to Steve's face. "Franklin, it wasn't like that. It was only a few kickbacks, normal stuff, until Robert Caspar got greedy and stole everything."

"Steve, I have seen Joe's notes," I bluffed, surprised how easy the lie came.

Steve's shoulders slumped in defeat. "Okay, well I guess you know the whole thing then. What do you want—the same as Joe or something else?"

"I want to renovate the old Queen Anne without interference. Someone hit me over the head with the hatch last time I was here. I want you to find out who is trying to keep me out of the house. And I want to know what happened to Joe. Did someone push him off that roof or did he fall?"

"If you are determined to renovate, I'll keep everyone off your back. About Joe, I'm not sure what I could tell you that the police can't."

"You talked to Joe before he died. I want to know what you talked about and if it was important enough to kill him over."

"Franklin, you have to believe me, I don't know anything about a killing. No one does. It makes no sense for someone to want him dead. The blackmail was a pain, but nothing worth killing over. He asked for a favor every now and then to save some ruin. It can't have been anyone in my circle. Joe agreed to leave us alone if we did our little things for him. We made money anyway."

"He argued with you and said you wouldn't get away with it again."

Steve's beady eyes opened wide with surprise. "Did that old buzzard record everything? Franklin, it wasn't like that. He found out I was working on the new condominium development. I told him it was an honest deal, but he had this thing about Washington Way and the money never turning up. And there was something else—he wanted to know who taught project management to Robert Caspar."

"Why did he want to know that?"

"He said our setup looked like a copycat of Caspar's handiwork. But I had no idea who, if anyone, advised Caspar."

I thought about this for a moment. Had Caspar returned? Joe's question to Steve made me think he suspected that someone had been behind Caspar. "Okay, I'm asking you the same question. Who could have given Robert Caspar the idea for the fraud? Check for any former associates who may still be around."

Steve gave me a shrewd look. "Franklin, trust me, I want to know too. Look, if you'll keep the whole Washington Way thing between us, I'll help you find out what happened to Joe. Give me a week."

"One week, and then you and I'll have another talk. And keep away from the Queen Anne."

Steve gave me a hard look. "I've got some advice for you. Blackmail is a tough game. When the word gets out that you have the files, not everyone is going to take this as good as me."

Before I could protest that I wasn't taking over the blackmail, Steve jumped into his hummer and roared off.

As he drove away I remembered something Dad told me. He said that any salesman who has to ask you to trust him is probably someone you shouldn't. Steve had asked me to trust him. Twice.

Chapter 12

I sat for a few minutes after Steve left. I had a sense that a moral milestone had passed and I hadn't ended up on the side of the angels. Using secrets I didn't have to shake down people wasn't only immoral, it was a bad idea, like showing up to a gunfight armed with blanks.

It was probably too late to recant my claim that I had the files. No one would believe me if I changed my story now. The victims would conclude that I was holding out for more. It would be much better if I found Joe's records and used the knowledge to keep my enemies at bay.

I wondered if those files were what Victor was looking for up on the Monument Parcel. I took out my cell phone and speed dialed Albert. "Hey man, how'd you like to go on a treasure hunt up on the Monument Parcel later today?"

"Sure, Monday's a slow day here. What's up?"

I described my earlier altercation with Bennett, and my plan to visit the Monument Parcel. I didn't want to alarm Victor or Steve by poking around too obviously so we planned to go in through the park when few visitors would be around later in the day. In early September the sun didn't set until after seven, so we would have plenty of daylight even late afternoon when park visitors had gone home to their suppers.

I had some time to kill so I went home. In the back of my

mind I still felt the pleasant twinge of desire for Ginny. So as a kind of penance I busied myself by cleaning, starting with the apartment. I saved the truck for last but as usual I ran out of time before emptying it out. The junk in the bed would have to wait a bit longer.

By the time I pulled up at Albert's mother's house, the sun had crossed the river and started to descend toward the lighthouse in New London Harbor. Linda would have noticed the mess in the truck bed, but Albert slid in without comment and buckled up. His big feet encased in red high top sneakers reminded me to tell him about the footprints on Joe's roof and next to Bennett's truck.

When I gave Albert a summary of my last couple of days he lapsed into an uncharacteristic quiet. "You think Victor or Steve killed Joe?"

"I don't like Victor, but I think he gets his kicks from crunching buildings, not killing people. Steve is more devious than I thought, but he is all about the money and had nothing to gain by killing Joe."

"You hope. But with enough at stake people will do almost anything."

Albert had a good point. The Washington Way partners might be counting on the Monument Condominiums to recover their losses from Caspar's double-cross. That might make any one of them desperate enough to throw an old guy out a window and do the same to a nosey handyman like me if I got in the way.

The drive from Albert's house to the park wound through streets crammed with little two-story bungalows and Cape Cod Style homes built around the turn of the twentieth century. Originally these were built to support the families of workers in the manufacturing plants that dotted the seaside. By the twenty-first century, scientists and engineers who worked at the shipyard and pharmacy research centers were the only ones who could afford these little houses by the water. Rows of black shutters and the occasional red door provided the only relief from the ubiquitous white clapboards. The austere color preferences of the original puritan settlers still dominated in the land of steady habits.

I drove past the service road and continued on Smith Street to the entrance of Fort Griswold State Park at the top of the hill. "We'll leave the truck in the library parking lot and approach through the Park. If we hike south we'll pick up the service road somewhere near the middle of the Monument Parcel. That way if Bennett is still hanging around Arnold Street he won't see us."

By the time we arrived at the park most of the history buffs, joggers, and pet walkers had left. The entrance to the battlefield was on a hill that overlooked the Thames River.

We stopped next to two large cannons on the spot from which colonial volunteers had rained cannon balls on British ships led by the traitor Benedict Arnold., Their attempt to defend New London harbor failed and the defenders all died.

The Revolutionary War was awash with moral dilemmas. The conflict pitted neighbor against neighbor, set personal financial interests against loyalty to the king, and raised thorny moral questions. Today most people would call the revolutionaries terrorists and a person like Benedict Arnold would be a patriot. People's relationship with the law was more complicated than was taught in school. Maybe Joe's choice to handle Steve, Victor, and Tony without consulting the authorities had a clear precedent in Yankee culture.

We crossed the mowed lawns of the park for a quarter mile or so to the south border and the beginning of the Monument Parcel. I pointed toward a barbed wire fence overgrown by a dense tangle of scrub oak, kudzu, wild raspberries, and wood vines. I found a break in the brush, and gently nudged aside the remains of the fence. The fragile, rusty wire tacked to shriveled husks of cedar posts yielded easily. "This is where we go in."

We proceeded straight south intending to meet up with the old service road in the middle of the parcel. The sun cast slanting shadows over the rough ground. We struggled through the brush for nearly a half hour. The boulders, fallen trees, and dense undergrowth forced us to take a winding path. Twigs and thorns snagged our clothes.

I wiped a smear of blood from a long scratch. "These thorns are making me regret leaving my jacket in the truck."

Albert pointed to a ribbon of light in the trees ahead. "It's pretty rough going here, but there's the service road." We stepped through the vines and bush onto what looked more like twin bicycle paths than a road. Grass grew between two narrow tracks, brush crowded the sides, and large limbs crossed overhead. Despite its neglected appearance, the road had been used recently. Pale cracks in twigs which had fallen across the track revealed that they were newly crushed and the moss had been scraped off stones that lay in the ruts.

We stepped into the filtered sunlight. I gestured toward the sun. "Let's follow this track west toward the river. If we don't find anything on that segment, we can follow the road back to Smith Street."

We started down the trail and scanned the sides of the road for signs of human activity. The thinning leaves shimmied on spindly branches and filtered the sun. The shifting, dappled, effect made searching difficult.

Albert stumbled on a branch. "At least walking is easier than it was on our shortcut through the brush."

A half an hour later the trail ended on a cliff overlooking the back yards of the houses on Thames Street. Over the rooftops we could see the New London Light House on the far side of the river. The setting sun sketched a golden path across the blue-black river. Below us on the Groton City side of the water, little boats sparkled in the glare.

I was disappointed that we hadn't found anything yet. "Whatever Bennett is up to it must be at the other end of the road." We followed our lengthening shadows back toward the point where we picked up the service road and continued our exploration on the eastern half of the parcel.

We hadn't gone far when something deep in the trees flashed. "Albert, do you see that?" He peered intently into the tangled growth on the south side of the trail, took a step back, moved forward and repeated the move.

"Yeah, but it's pretty far away." We trekked on, keeping watch on the flash. Albert pointed toward an opening between the trees. "Look."

A narrow corridor, little more than a crease in the dense vegetation, appeared. We slipped between the trees and temporarily lost sight of the flash. The path continued for about a hundred feet, to the edge of a deep ravine.

Albert stepped out on a natural stone bridge formed by enormous boulders. "Come on."

At the far end, the bridge ended against a nearly vertical rock face. I guessed that the crest was twenty feet above our heads and the bottom of the gorge was fifty feet below. A narrow shelf was etched across the rock face and stretched to both the left and right until it disappeared around a bend. I pointed. "That is some rock. It's hundreds of feet wide."

Albert pointed toward a stack of flat stones on the ledge. "What do you make of that? It looks like a foundation."

I pointed to a shiny object sitting on top of the stone stack. The screen on the face of an open cell phone reflected the light of the setting sun. "Here is where the light came from."

Albert picked up the shiny device. "This is a pretty advanced phone. We sell this model at the store."

"This can't be what Bennett was looking for. It's a phone."

Albert was incredulous. "You're kidding, right? People keep their whole lives on these things." He looked at me with a silly grin on his face. "Do you know why some guys would rather give up their girl friends than their smart phones?"

"I know I'm going to be sorry for asking, but why?"

"Phones are less demanding and easier to turn on."

I groaned, but couldn't suppress a grin. "You're a regular comedian. But is there anything interesting on this one?"

Albert pressed a few buttons and then closed the cover. "The battery is dead and it may have been out in the rain. Even if it is okay, it's probably password protected."

Another dead end. "I guess we'll never know what's on it."

Albert gave me his superior geek grin. "Wait until I get it back to the store. I may not be much with a hammer, but I have never found an electronic device that can keep secrets from me for long."

A gust of wind caused something to rustle behind the stack of stones. I wasn't expecting to find anything but to my surprise two packages each about the size of a saw case were hidden behind the stones. The parcels were wrapped in green tarps that looked new. We removed a bungee cord holding the top package together and peeled back one corner. Below the wrapping was an old fashioned hard-sided briefcase.

Albert pointed to the exposed edge of the case. "It has a combination lock. What are these doing here?"

I looked around for anything that might explain our find. "This is a good place to hide something. Except for the light reflecting off that phone we wouldn't have found this spot. Let's see what's inside."

Before we could open the package the sound of a truck motor growled across the ravine. We stopped and strained to determine the direction of the sound. A pickup truck was bouncing along the service road, its white paint pulsing beyond the slender tree trunks. It stopped at the head of the path that led to the cliff. Two doors slammed.

Albert looked puzzled. "What are they doing out here?"

"Same as us, something they don't want to be seen doing."

The snapping of twigs became louder. I couldn't see the walkers but Bennett had a white truck and this was not a place where I wanted to meet him. "Albert, quick, let's split up. You follow the ledge to the left. See if you can get around the bend behind the cliff before they get here. I'll go right. Let's wait until they leave before we head back."

Albert moved down the path. I refastened the tarp and then worked my way around the cliff in the opposite direction. The ledge narrowed to less than boot width, and I stopped and glanced back. I could still see the stone bridge, so I faced the wall, and resumed sliding to my right. By the time I was hidden fully, the ledge had narrowed so much that my heels were suspended over the edge. I stood facing the ledge wall, balancing on the balls of my feet, arms spread, and cheek pressed against the cool stone. The setting sun on my back did nothing to warm the chills I felt.

Feet scraped and stamped. "I don't see the damn phone, do you?" growled Victor Bennett.

The second man had a familiar voice. "I can't believe that he wants us to leave the cases out here."

"With all the people who were nosing around it was too risky to leave them in the basement any longer, Tony," Bennett said to his companion.

Tony Gorky! He was the third Washington Way partner.

"That may be true, but I'd like to get the cases out of here as soon as the money man says it's okay."

"I know. This is a dumb place to leave them, but it's temporary," Bennett agreed.

Tony sounded eager to leave the gorge. "Let's take a quick look around for the phone and get out of here. It's going to be dark soon and I don't want to attract attention by running lights out here at night."

As they came my way I inched a little further along the ledge. I stopped, thinking I'd gone far enough. Then the ground beneath my right foot crumbled.

Chapter 13

My foot propelled a cascade of pebbles down toward the forest floor and my stomach lurched. I shifted my weight back toward what had been firm ground below my left foot, but the added pressure crumbled the rock there too. My goal to wait quietly until Victor and Tony left disintegrated with a roar as I slid down the slope in a shower of dirt and stones.

I dragged my hands and arms against the rock wall in a futile attempt to slow my decent. The burn of the scrapes and the ache of multiple collisions with small outcroppings of ledge barely registered until my feet slammed into another narrow ledge. The avalanche continued around me. For a few minutes my heart thundered too loudly for any other sound to penetrate. Finally I caught my breath. The noises in my head diminished, and my internal organs returned to their normal resting places. The rocks under my hands were streaked with blood. I pressed against the stone and dug my fingers into small cracks. Securely anchored, I molded myself against the wall and tried to be invisible.

A voice snapped from above. "What the hell was that?"

I clung to the cliff face in the middle of dark shadows cast by a stand of oak trees between me and the sun. Bennett probably couldn't see me, but I froze. I would hold still and be quiet until he left and then climb back up and see what was in those cases.

As I waited something fuzzy crawled out of the crack in which

114

my fingers were jammed. A large spider tentatively touched my finger with a furry leg. When I didn't move, it strolled, out tickling my naked hand. Beads of nervous sweat burst out on my skin. I considered pushing off the rock face and flicking the gruesome pest into oblivion below but stopped when Victor's voice came from somewhere overhead.

"It came from over here."

I forced myself to relax. The arachnid strolled up my forearm. I blew gently, trying to dislodge the furry trespasser. The spider reared up and pawed at the air with several legs but held its ground.

"Probably a limb off a dead tree," said Tony.

The fuzzy legs lowered and moved a couple of inches closer to my elbow. It tickled, not in a pleasant way. A nervous rash broke out on my arm. All I could think of was how much I hated spiders. My whole body was a wound-up spring.

"It didn't sound like a limb to me," said Bennett.

"There is no way I'm going back there to look. The ledge is too narrow past this point," said Tony.

The determined arachnid continued its slow progress up my arm and stopped below the cuff of my short-sleeved tee shirt. I wriggled my shoulder to close the gap between the shirt and my arm. More than anything in the world I did not want that critter to go inside my sleeve.

"All right, let's get out of here before dark," said Bennett.

I heard the sounds of footfalls becoming increasingly faint as the pair moved back down the ledge. The spider placed two legs on my shirt sleeve, and scooted to the top of my shoulder, inches from my neck and face. It wasn't inside the shirt, but close enough to my collar to make me burst into a cold sweat. Sounds of crackling brush faded, doors slammed, and the truck started up.

Unwilling to hold still a moment longer, I gently released my left hand from the rock and made a circle with my thumb and middle finger. I leaned back slightly and reached in front of my chest. Gently I moved my hand across my body, toward my right shoulder. I rested my thumb in front of the spider, my middle finger braced like a kicker taking aim on the ball.

With a quick snap my finger lashed out and I flicked the fuzzy pest on its way toward the forest below. A quick shiver flowed through me like a wave, and I felt a sudden need to pee. It took a few minutes for my heart rate to slow and the sweating to subside. As my innards returned to normal I shook my head and marveled at the irrationality of my reaction. There I was, stuck on a steep rock face without any climbing gear at least sixty feet above the forest floor. Two guys, at least one of whom was very large and had threatened me earlier, had been only a few feet away. With all that going on the thing had frightened me the most was a bug.

"Damn! I hate spiders." I shivered to throw off the feeling.

I renewed my grip in the crack, leaned back and studied the slope above. My slide had loosened too much gravel for me to climb back up without a climbing harness. I looked over my shoulder toward the forest floor below. If I could get the rest of the way down I could probably hike out around the base of the cliff. The problem was how to get down without falling. I looked longingly at the fluffy tops of large oaks below me but resisted the urge to jump into their leafy green arms.

The cliff face had a feature that left me some hope for a successful traverse. Below me several cracks cut diagonally across the rock, like shallow ramps. The nearest crack would allow me to anchor my feet if I could reach it without slipping. I jammed the fingers of my left hand in a small fissure at about waist height, and locked my knuckles in the little crack. Anchored, and with my heart beating fast I stepped down until I found a toehold. I moved my hand down on the top of an outcropping next to my knee, stepped down with my other foot, and stuck my toes into the diagonal crack. Once on the crack I shuffled across the cliff face and slightly downward. When I reached the end of the fissure I was still high above the forest but I found another crack that moved down and back to the left. I carefully slid along the face until I ran out of foot holds.

"Damn it!" I had run out of cracks about twenty feet from the bottom. My only hope was to lever off the trunk of an enormous oak that had grown only a couple of feet from the cliff face. With my back wedged firmly against the rough bark and my feet flat against the cliff, I inched down.

I nearly made it, but eight feet from safety the rough bark caught on my shirt. When I tried to squirm free, my feet lost their grip on the mossy rock face. I slid the rest of the way to the packed earth at the base of the tree. My feet hit first, but I slammed down on my back, knocking the wind out of me.

I lay on the ground for a few seconds, feeling knobby roots pushing on my back. Finally my wind came back. "Crap, that's going to leave some bruises."

I must have spoken that thought, because Albert called down from above. "Hey, Franklin, is that you?" In the rapidly diminishing sunlight I couldn't see the source, but recognized his voice.

"I'm okay, but be careful. That ledge ends abruptly."

"Can you climb back up?"

"No. I'm going to hike around the base of this cliff and meet you at the road."

Albert sounded concerned. "Okay, if that's what you want to do, but be careful. It's too dark to go back the way we came through the park. Follow the service road back to Smith Street. If you don't make it in an hour I'm coming to get you."

It took me nearly the whole hour to climb around the boulders and deadfall trees that littered the base of the cliff. Several times I was so close to the back yards of the houses on Arnold Street that I could see the lights in their windows. The moon was coming up over Groton City as I limped out of the brush and onto the service road.

We turned east, toward Smith Street. When we arrived, Albert looked at my scratches under the street light. "You don't look so good,"

"I have been banged up worse than this shingling a roof."

Albert peered at the back of my shirt. "Turn around." He picked up a stick from the gutter and flicked something off. A large spider lay in the dirt. "Come on. Let's get going before someone asks what we're doing here."

It was nearly a half mile back to my truck. When we got there I stopped for a few moments to catch my breath. I ached all over and was covered with scratches. "Damn, we never got to see what was in those cases."

"Speak for yourself." Albert powered up his cell phone and turned the screen toward me. "Someone had already pried the locks open."

I took the phone from Albert. The image was an open case with dozens of pictures of Ben Franklin. "Are both cases filled with these? That has to be several million dollars."

Albert flashed a hundred dollar bill. It was old and smelled of mildew. "Well, they're no longer completely filled. I didn't take enough to buy you that Victorian, but this one did find its way in my pocket. He studied the bill. "This has to be dirty money. Why else would it be hidden in the woods?"

I thought of my new investigative partner from the IRS. "I know someone who will be very interested to see this."

Chapter 14

I pointed a scratched finger at the hundred-dollar bill in Ginny's hand. The pictures Albert had taken of the open cases displayed on a nearby monitor. "Why would someone be hiding thousands of these in the woods?"

It was Tuesday morning and we were in the reading room at the back of the library. I still didn't know if the money had anything to do with Joe's death, but that much money could create plenty of trouble. I hoped that Ginny would help me put the pieces together.

She turned the bill up to the light and then studied the images on the computer. She zoomed in on the pictures of the cases of money that Albert had taken with his phone. "You're right. This is a lot of money. Big hoards of cash always signal illegal activity."

I had always thought about the money swindled from my dad as sitting in an offshore bank account somewhere but maybe I was wrong. "Could this be the missing Washington Way money?"

Ginny thought in silence. "I need to talk to someone from Treasury, but these bills look old enough to be from that era. The only problem with your theory is that this isn't enough money. Washington Way involved hundreds of millions."

"What if this is only part of the take? You said that the IRS has been monitoring these guys. Has any of the money showed up?"

"I can't discuss an ongoing investigation, but let's say that for several years the volume of money passing though Steve, Victor, and Tony's businesses was out of proportion with the depressed building climate."

"Like maybe they have been laundering money?"

"It's not impossible but we haven't had enough evidence to catch them yet."

"Was Joe's income in the same shape?" I asked dreading the answer.

Ginny clicked into her e-mail and attached the image files to a message. "No. Either he was better at hiding it or not involved directly in the money. I'm sending the pictures to my office so the technicians can get the serial numbers and check them against lists of bills taken in robberies."

"If this is the missing Washington Way money, why is it still in cash?" I asked.

Ginny held the bill up to the light. "Washington Way imploded a few months before 9/11. Changes in bank reporting since then made it difficult to launder large sums of cash. And maybe they lost their money laundering expert."

That made sense to me. "So the crooks got caught with piles of cash they couldn't spend or deposit."

Ginny nodded. "If the economy had been better and building activity higher it would have been easier to move large sums by feeding it into business accounts. The economic slowdown meant they had to launder it in small batches over a longer time," She explained that cash deposits over ten thousand dollars were likely to be investigated, but most people didn't know that deposits over five thousand were reported too.

It had been a decade ago that the money was stolen. Even broken down into small batches, the cash should have been deposited long ago. What had delayed the process? I had overheard Bennett say something about moving the cases from a house that was no longer safe. I wondered if Joe had them in his attic and the person who killed him was looking for them. Bennett hadn't said anything about the money when I ran into him, but now I knew what questions to ask when our paths crossed again.

Ginny closed her computer and put it and the bill in her case. "The first thing we need to do is go back to the Monument Parcel and retrieve those cases and the money."

"Can we do that?"

"Since Congress passed the Patriot Act, the government can do pretty much whatever we want to. But to avoid weakening our case in court I'd like to get permission from the owners to examine the property. I don't want to give some defense lawyer a chance to throw out the evidence because I was trespassing or didn't have probable cause."

"You'll need to talk to the executor. The property is in probate."

Ginny packed away the rest of her papers and headed for the door. "I'll contact the court and local law enforcement. We'll retrieve the packages later this morning. I need to go back to my motel for some gear and to change. Meet me back here at 11:00 a.m. if you want to come along."

I drove to Silicon Shack and picked up Albert. He would want to be in on the action. "Have you found anything on the cell phone yet?" I asked as he climbed in. Albert and I had decided not to tell Ginny about the smart phone. I was still uneasy about her personal agenda and I wanted to know the contents of the files before she took them away like the files from Joe's record box. Albert and I also thought that Ginny might be unwilling to let Albert hack into it without a warrant. Since standard procedure at Silicon Shack required the store to try to locate owners of phones that were turned in, Albert felt justified searching the memory for identification. If the passwords were broken and files revealed in the process, so much the better.

At 10:50 Ginny's Toyota pulled back into the library parking lot. She was wearing no-nonsense hiking boots, camouflage pants and shirt, topped with a baseball cap. I introduced her to Albert.

"Wow. You look like Combat Barbie."

Ginny did a little pirouette and ended up in a fighting stance like a female action hero. "Don't forget, I'm armed and dangerous." She was practically glowing with excitement. "This will be my first big seizure of cash in the field."

"What, you haven't done this before?"

"Look, Franklin, my job usually involves getting court orders to release records and studying the books of companies. I wasn't even on this case until my dad passed along a tip suggesting a possible connection between Joe's death and the missing Washington Way money."

That still didn't tell me what her interest was. "Your Dad's an IRS agent too?"

Ginny's face lit up and she laughed. "He's the opposition, a lawyer specializing in tax law and corporate finance."

An IRS agent with a personal agenda acting on a tip from her dad who was in the business of helping corporations avoid paying taxes—what was going on here? "So, what's the connection between Joe and the money?"

"We haven't found a direct connection yet but there are too many coincidences. In the span of a few weeks Joe, a powerful man who controlled our prime suspects, dies suddenly, Steve, Victor, and Tony are up to their eyeballs in a suspicious-looking condominium development, and now a hoard of cash turns up."

"What happens if this is stolen money?"

"If we can prove it and identify the perpetrators, I arrest them. I get a promotion, you get a reward, we return what we can to the victims, and the bad guys get some jail time. Everyone except the bad guys is happy."

"Does it usually work that way?"

"When nothing goes wrong. Don't worry. I'll take good care of you."

A few minutes later we arrived at the intersection of Smith and Arnold streets. Through the trees I could see the back of the Victorian.

The local police had assigned Officer Daryl Williams to

accompany us. The giant of a man, easily topping six feet five inches from the top of his curly black hair to the soles of his highly polished boots, led the way with Albert at his side. Ginny and I followed a few steps behind as we started down the trail.

Trees grew right up to the track and their branches formed a natural canopy of green and gold that was much more inviting in the daylight. Ginny's hand brushed mine and our fingers momentarily become entwined. I was a little shocked. Ginny gave me a quizzical look and made no effort to pull away. "Don't you need to keep your hand free to draw your weapon?" I asked.

She glanced ahead at Officer Williams and Albert who were discussing electronic surveillance. She leaned near me and whispered. "Don't worry, that's not my gun hand." I looked for where she might be keeping a weapon but after a pleasant but fruitless inspection I was convinced that her artillery was symbolic.

Our tender moment was broken by a roar from up ahead. I recognized the sound of an eight-cylinder Ford engine laboring at high revolutions. The sound was coming from the far side of the hill we were climbing. Seconds later a bouncing white pickup came over the crest and filled the narrow path. The truck was above us so the driver probably couldn't see us. I realized that the narrow track couldn't hold the truck and pedestrians.

"Look out," shouted Officer Williams as he and Albert leapt for the side of the path. They crashed into a stand of young pines, cracking limbs as they fell.

Like one of those dreams where we move in maddeningly slow steps, Ginny and I leapt for the other side of the road. Our hands were still linked as we dove into the brush seconds before the truck filled the space behind us.

The brush yielded to our battering and we plummeted down a steep slope. Branches and thorns tore at our clothes. Small trees bent and broke under our assault. We ended our tumble in a heap at the bottom of the ravine. I was on my side completely enveloped by a wild rose bush that had wrapped tightly around my limbs. My jacket had a new tear and I'd added to the previous day's scratches.

Ginny was on her back in the leaves. She had missed the thorn bush but the force of landing had knocked the breath out of her. She had lost her hat and her raven hair was loose and filled with leaves. I couldn't help noticing that the primary casualty of the fall was Ginny's shirt. Several buttons, which had been doing a valiant job earlier, were ripped out during the wild fall, revealing lace and freckled white skin. Ginny coughed and groaned. Her eyes focused and she turned her head and glanced my way.

I remembered the eye contact rule in time to see her catch me checking out the show. Without doing much to cover up she rolled on her side and faced me.

"Can I assume from that leer that you are okay?"

"Yeah, except that I'm spending too much time tumbling down ravines lately." I risked another glance. "The view is improving, though."

Ginny rolled her eyes. "Men." She swiveled around to a sitting position with her back toward me, removed a couple of clips from her hair, and used them to close her shirt. She retrieved her hat from a wild rose bush. She approached me and used a branch to push aside the thorns that had me locked in.

Officer Williams and Albert appeared above us.

"Are you hurt?" Albert called.

"We're only a little scuffed," Ginny replied.

We arrived at the top of the slope in time to see Officer Williams on his cell phone. "I alerted the department to keep an eye out for the pickup." The truck had been moving too fast for identification, but to me it looked a lot like Victor Bennett's.

Ginny gestured down the service road. "We may as well continue to the site." None of us were optimistic that we were going to find the crates where they had been yesterday, but we had to check.

Minutes later we arrived at the site of the cache. There were no signs of the money-filled cases. Ginny produced a small camera and took several photographs of impressions in the path left by numerous boot prints.

We returned to Smith Street and our awaiting vehicles. I thought that Ginny would be a little down due to missing her first big cash capture, but I was wrong. There was mischief in her eyes as she took my arm. "Franklin, I'm heading back to the Days Inn for a shower, first aid, and a late lunch. Want to join me?"

Chapter 15

I was about to ask Ginny which of those three activities her invitation covered when my cell phone rang. The interruption was about as welcome as the sound of a stalled chainsaw half-way through a tree trunk. I read the caller I.D. "It's Linda. I need to take this." I moved back toward the truck. "What's up?"

Linda's voice was much more pleasant than I expected. "Frankie, I'm so glad I reached you. If the dinette set you've been working is ready, can you get it to my studio today? The Petersons want to see the kind of work we do."

I recognized her professional voice, the always pleasant, cheerful one she used with clients. I hoped she was through ripping me up but probably she was in character and forgot for a moment that she was angry with me. I decided to take the chance that she was beyond her irritation. "Sure. If you need them right away I can bring them over in an hour."

"That would be great." There was a pause as if she wasn't sure what to say next. "It'll be good to see you. I really want to talk." I may have imagined the longing in her voice, but her anger seemed to have burned out. It would be good if we could finally work out some of what had been bothering us.

"Okay, I'll be there soon." While I talked to Linda, Ginny had climbed into her Toyota and started the engine. She lowered the window and waited. I closed the phone. "I need to deliver some furniture to Linda's studio, and we have a couple of things to talk out. I don't know when I'll be done."

Ginny's smile reminded me of Linda's cheery voice, professional but not entirely genuine. "Sure, if you finish up early, give me a call. I'd like to talk to you." I was a little surprised and disappointed that she let me go so easily.

Back at home I pulled a soft canvas drop cloth off the finished pieces. It was like undressing a lover. I ran my fingers across the smooth lacquer on the frames. The crimson fabric against the glossy black wood frames gave the old set a timeless and elegant look. Linda's great eye and my restoration skills had triumphed again.

I wrapped the top of the table and each of the legs with cardboard and taped them securely. Canvas drop cloths or carpet scraps would have worked as well, but Linda liked to deliver furniture with the stress points wrapped with clean new cardboard sleeves and bright colored packing tape. That left lots of finished wood and new upholstery showing. Crisp packaging helped the clients forget that the pieces were refinished. Buyers liked to experience the pleasure of purchasing pieces that looked new and expensive, while congratulating themselves on being frugal.

Linda's attention to the emotional needs of her clients was another of the reasons why she had a lot of repeat business. I admired her skills with customers, but my recently acquired cynicism made me suspect she used the same talent to manipulate me.

It took a while to wrap and secure the furniture, but only a few minutes to reach Linda's storefront studio in the plaza behind Poquonnock Road. I parked my old truck in front of the store and began to untie the load. Linda stepped through the front door of the studio. A band that coordinated perfectly with her sunny yellow dress held her hair back. The prettiness of her took my breath away.

"Thanks for coming over so quickly, Frankie. I appreciate

this." She ran up and gave me a hug. I scanned the storefront to see who the show was for but we were alone. She relaxed her arms but only enough so I could look into her eyes. Linda parted her lips and tilted her head, granting permission for a kiss on the lips.

We pulled back to take a breath. "Linda, I missed you."

"Me too Frankie. It hurts so much when we fight."

My heart skipped a beat as I felt the heat building between us. She held the door open and gave me a look that said this visit was about much more than furniture.

"Will you put the set in the storeroom out back? I want to show it to the Petersons. I'll keep it wrapped so you can deliver it to the clients who bought it."

It felt good that my efforts were helpful at bringing in new business. It made me feel like a real partner. "Let me know when you are ready for the delivery. Do they need anything else? We have a barn full of furniture in need of a new home."

Linda smiled at what she must have seen as my newfound ambition. "Come in after you put this stuff away and I'll show you a new project that is going to need some of that furniture and custom built-ins too."

It took only a few minutes to unload and tuck the furniture away in the store room. I carried the last chair in and realized that when I was away from the loveliness of Linda, doubts about her began to surface. Our cycles of fighting and making up were familiar, but this one had been different. The anger had been much greater and the barbs stuck much deeper. A few days ago she called me a loser and said that we were over as a couple. Then I got my face slapped for questioning Bobby Lester's intentions. She might be over it, but I wasn't. I noticed that when I delivered her furniture, she was warm and friendly again. A question popped unwelcome in my head. Did she want me as a mate, or was she playing me for what I could do for her career?

I pushed my doubts aside and resolved to not be so petty. I met Linda in the front of the studio. We sat at her work table reviewing the designs she had been working on during our phone call. She didn't say so, but I could tell that they were for the Monument Condo project.

"I've created four basic layouts. If we get the job each model unit will need to be completely furnished. We can offer more elegant designs and still underbid the completion if we refurbish some of the pieces in your shop."

Linda's ideas were fresh and appealing and I saw the skeletons in the shed being put to good use. "Great concepts. I wish I didn't have such a bad feeling about that condo project."

Linda hardly paused a second to register that she heard me. Only a slight bunching of the muscles at the jaw line signaled her displeasure. She forged on, describing what we needed to do. It was all I could do to concentrate on her words. She smelled like a spring day. Everything about her was exciting: her passion for decorating, the smiles that stretched all the way to her eyes, the soft curves under the sunny fabric. I finally pushed my doubts aside and gave in to the feeling.

"Linda, can you close up early? We have a lot to talk about and I haven't eaten yet. Why don't we go to that little place overlooking the river and finish this discussion over lunch?" What I really wanted was to get her back home for a roll between the sheets, but my experience told me that I would need to do some more courting first.

"Sure, these designs are done and Tuesdays and are pretty slow this time of year. Go ahead and put a sign on the door. I'll clean up and then we can go."

While I waited I looked around the studio. It was filled with evidence of Linda's rising success as a designer. Fabric books, floor plans, and pictures of homes that Linda had decorated covered the shelves and walls. This studio belonged to a competent and determined businesswoman. There were no signs of the insecure teenager I had fallen in love with. Was that the root of our problems? She had been growing and I hadn't noticed?

The bell on the front door jingled before I put up the closed sign. The visitor was as unhappy to see me as I was to see him.

Bobby Lester frowned. "Oh, it's you. I expected Linda."

"It's amazing what will sneak in if you forget to lock the door. We're closed."

"Last time I checked Linda's name was on the lease. So if you would call your employer, I have business with her."

Physically throwing him out on the sidewalk was looking like a good option until Linda emerged. The effect of her efforts with her hair and makeup was stunning. She greeted Bobby with a level of enthusiasm that left me wondering about their relationship, but then Linda always had the ability to turn on the charm when she needed it.

As she addressed Bobby, she glanced nervously in my direction. "Did you come about the sketches? I didn't expect you today but they're done." She stepped toward some large prints on a display table.

Bobby picked up one of the sketches and turned back to Linda. "The timetable for the project has been moved up. The investors want to choose a decorator for the new condos right away. I want to go over your ideas today and I haven't eaten yet. How about if we discuss them over lunch," he asked.

Linda's eyes cut toward me but she wouldn't make eye contact." I don't know. Franklin and I were going to ...."

The panic in Linda's expression told me that she wanted to go with Bobby. I needed to make a decision: go cave man and punch the creep in his protruding nose, grab the girl and drag her off, or act like a business partner and a gentleman and, graciously, let Bobby take her. I leaned toward the former but then she lifted her eyes and I caught her pleading look. Surrounded by everything that Linda had built, I couldn't see myself jeopardizing her business by punching a client, even Bobby.

"Linda, we can get together another time. This is business," I hoped that it was true. I longed for her to turn him down but knew that she wouldn't.

Bobby's eyes did a slow sweep across Linda. "Business and pleasure. Don't wait up for us."

Linda blushed and said nothing.

"Well I'll be going then. I'll call you later."

"Tonight?" asked Linda.

"I don't know. Maybe. I have something to do."

As I backed the truck out of the parking space I saw the two of them huddled over the drafting table. Bobby had a proprietary hand on her arm. His eyes were focused not on the drawings but on her. He glanced at me through the window and smirked. I put the truck in gear and drove out of the parking lot. I may have managed to behave like an adult, but my inner adolescent longed to see how well the tread pattern of all-season tires would look over a pinstripe suit.

Chapter 16

Since I missed my chance to spend the afternoon with Ginny or Linda, I decided to go for the next best thing and wrap my hands around something electronic. Silicon Shack of Groton City was a few streets down from Linda's studio. The little store was a hole-in-the-wall establishment tucked in one end of yet another strip mall. I pulled in at the back of a large parking lot that looked almost as bleak as my life. The dark windows of a couple of vacant stores gave the mall the appearance of a smile with teeth missing. For Rent signs taped behind dirty glass storefronts announced the obvious in shades of gray. Discarded fast food wrappers peppered the parking lot and sidewalks.

The businesses that were still open would have been bankrupted by the big box mall stores down the road except that each survivor possessed a unique attribute that the large stores couldn't or wouldn't duplicate. In the Silicon Shack the secret weapon was Albert Henley. To me Albert was a best friend and wise cracking, know-it-all-pain-in-the-ass. But to customers who wandered into the shop, he was a genius who could exorcise electronic demons and soothe silicon chips into serenity. What customers didn't know was that Albert was also a master salesman who could sense the needs, hopes, and fears of his customers better than their mothers. He never sold anything right out of the box. He always enhanced, tweaked, and customized his products to fit needs the customers didn't even know they had. Silicon Shack patrons always left a little poorer, but feeling richer, smarter, and more fulfilled.

I found Albert in the back room at a long work bench, specially raised to accommodate his gangly frame. He wore his work uniform, red sneakers, dark jeans, blue dress shirt with an open collar, and a white name tag. He looked like a skinny black version of a TV appliance repair man.

"Hi, Albert, has the phone given up its secrets yet?"

Albert peered into a monitor connected by a USB cable to the smart phone. A printer buzzed in the background. He looked surprised that I had to ask. "Do you mean this little pile of chips? You don't honestly think that a dead battery, some water damage, and a little security software could keep me out?"

"Albert, it's as hard to get an answer from you as it is to get a date lately. What do you have?"

Albert turned toward me with a sly smile. "Do I detect a little unrelieved sexual tension? I take it that you and Linda are still feuding. You must have come to watch the master at work to distract you from your sorrows." Albert never let modesty get in the way of a grand unveiling.

"Please, let's not get into my messy love life. Give, what did you find?"

Albert clicked a few keys. The image on the screen changed and began to scroll. "See these? They're text messages, dozens of them. Now look at this." He poked the keyboard again and the screen filled with more characters. "These are scans of documents, megabytes of them. There are also lots of regular word processor documents. The owner was using this phone for general purpose information storage."

"Any idea what it's all about?" I asked.

"I read a couple of the text files. Some were invoices. The others were receipts for down payments on something very expensive."

"You mean like down payments on a condo? Could this have

anything to do with the Monument Condominium Project?" I asked.

"Don't know. I only looked at a few files to make sure they displayed properly."

Albert's fingers darted toward the keypad of the phone faster than a herring gull on a bag of discarded French fries. "What are you doing now?" I asked.

"I'm trying to access the voice mail files. I can produce transcripts using speech recognition software."

Albert's skills were amazing. I still hadn't figured out how to make the GPS application work on my phone. "Did you find out who owns it?"

Albert didn't reply but pressed a few keys. A row of numbers and letters appeared on the monitor. "I'll need to check this serial number and track down where it was sold. If the owner sent in a warranty card we could get lucky and the info will still be around."

"Great, so do it."

Albert shook his head. "Not so fast. Once I know who owns it, I have an obligation to return it. We should concentrate on getting copies of these files first."

I approved of Albert's priorities. It also occurred to me that the growing stack of printouts might contain the solution to my lack of companionship for the evening. "Can you give me those prints?"

"Sure, what for?"

"I think that Ginny might be able to make some sense of the document files."

"And does the urgency of this have anything to do with your frustrated libido?"

I was getting a little irritated with his barbs about my love life. "Man, you really are a pain. Ginny is an IRS criminal investigator. Her only interest in me is if I can help close her cold case." It felt good for me to say those words out loud, even if I didn't want to believe them.

"If you say so, Bro."

Albert selected a box from a stack on the back wall and filled it with the prints. He plugged the phone into a docking station and copied the contents to a USB drive. "Hold onto this drive. It may be enough to get you a second date if your charm fails."

"Let it go, Albert."

He had on a smile that said that he was a genius, knew all, and could see right through me. "You may be a one-woman-at-a-time man, but which woman will it be this time?"

A strangely knotted tongue prevented me from making a retort. I took my phone out and dialed Ginny. What was Albert thinking? Of course it was Linda. I tried to reject the idea that I wanted to be with Ginny and almost succeeded until her voice in my ear snapped my thoughts like a fresh ocean breeze on a loose sail. Despite my irritation with Albert, I felt the corners of my mouth pull up. "Ginny, it's Franklin."

"Hi, Franklin, what a nice surprise. I didn't expect to hear from you before morning. I thought you were spending the rest of the day with Linda."

"That was business. She called to ask me to deliver some furniture before she left for a meeting with a client."

"Oh, so it really is only business between you two?"

That was the very question I had been asking myself. Not sure of the answer I tried to deflect with a little humor. "I'm not sure I should be discussing business with an IRS Criminal Investigator without a lawyer present."

Ginny laughed. "Fair enough. Why did you call?"

I hesitated, unsure how Ginny would react when she realized that I hadn't been completely candid with her about what I had found along with the cases of money. "It's about our investigation into real estate fraud and Joe's death. I have been meaning to tell you that Albert and I found something else up on the Monument Parcel."

The line was silent for a few seconds. When Ginny spoke her voice was still friendly but the breezy quality had been replaced by a firmness that communicated her displeasure. "Franklin, if we're going to work together you can't hold out on me. I'm sure you had a reason for not telling me but withholding information is a bad idea."

Ginny's gentle rebuke stung. Her opinion of me mattered more than I expected. "Sorry I didn't tell you before. When Albert and I were up checking out the Monument Parcel we found a smart phone sitting on a rock. The battery was dead, it had been outside for a while, and I didn't even know if it worked. We picked it up and I asked Albert to see if he could revive it and find out who owned it."

"I assume you didn't tell me this before because you knew we would probably need a warrant to look at the contents."

"That did occur to me. I thought that if Albert came across some interesting files while looking for identification it wouldn't be an illegal search and mess up your case."

Ginny laughed. "That is pretty complicated thinking for a handyman. I bet your genius friend came up with that one."

"Don't you want to know if we were successful?"

"Of course, and I want to see what you found."

"Albert was able to access the files. There are a hundreds of documents, phone calls and text messages. We don't know what to make of them but that's the kind of thing you do. I have some paper copies. Do you want to get together and look them over?" I decided not to tell her about the flash drive.

"You bet. When and where?" Her voice had the eagerness of a gambler waiting for the dice to stop rolling.

"How about tonight? While we're at it, you could clarify the invitation you made in the library parking lot."

"Got you curious with that one, didn't I?" Ginny's voice had regained its playful, flirtatious feel. "The offer to join me for dinner is still on. We'll need some time and a quiet place to spread out the files so a restaurant is out. My motel isn't suitable. Can we work uninterrupted at your place?"

This was exactly what I wanted to hear. I felt a warm glow racing around my veins. "Great, when?"

"I'll bring the food and arrive around five?"

"That's early, but I had forgotten about that appetite of yours. Sure, that's fine. I'm in town so I'll pick up some wine and meet you at my place. I'll leave the door unlocked so ring the bell and come on in when you get there."

* * *

The door bell rang much earlier than expected. I stepped out of the shower, toweled off, jumped into a pair of jeans, and ran barefoot toward the kitchen pulling up the zipper. "Come in," I called. Ginny let herself in and met me halfway down the stairs carrying two large deli bags. She handed me one and followed me toward the kitchen. We placed the bags on the counter and faced each other.

Ginny was dressed more for a date than a business meeting in a short skirt over sheer stockings and a cross-over blouse. Like everything she wore, the fit was perfect, accentuating her athletic form without appearing to be intentionally provocative.

I was considerably more casually dressed. Ginny studied my tight jeans, damp, shirtless torso and bare feet. When she saw me watching her check me out she blushed. "I should apologize for arriving early but you look pretty good in that outfit."

We turned toward the living room at the same time, nearly colliding, "Sorry," we said in unison. Ginny's hands had landed on my shoulders. She slid them down my chest. The sensation was a cross between a caress and an electric shock. Ginny's eyes opened wide and her lips parted. She had felt it too. I grinned, enjoying the panicked look on her face. She glanced from my eyes to her hands and back again, pushed me away gently, and stepped back. Her face was a collage of emotions with surprise, longing, and good old-fashioned lust.

Her eyes dropped and then shifted behind me toward the piles of paper on the counter. "Wow, are those the files? Let me have a look." She rushed to the pile and picked up a page. Her hands quivered slightly with anticipation. "Why don't you finish getting dressed while I look at these?"

I retrieved a shirt and sneakers from the bedroom. I was disappointed that Ginny had pulled back but there was no mistaking the hunger in her expression. I had thought her touch-me-not flirtation of the past several days was merely manipulation. I had no idea that the thunderbolt that had struck me at our first meeting had hit her too.

She was studying the paper files at the far end of the breakfast bar when I returned. I removed steaming plates of steak, mushrooms and onions and French fries from the bags she had brought. I transferred the food to dishes and opened the wine.

The smell of the food broke Ginny's concentration and she looked up. She pushed the papers aside and came to my end of the bar. Her eyes met mine; her expression was vulnerable and tentative. "Franklin, I'm sorry about the way I reacted the last time we were together. The IRS has been working on this case for a long time and seeing those faces in the picture threw me. They look like ordinary guys but a lot of people were hurt by that theft, and it's possible that Caspar and Joe were killed over the money. I kind of freaked out at being on the ground with a real investigation."

I looked at her, acutely aware that she was holding something back and that she knew that I knew. "I understand about professional responsibilities. You can't discuss ongoing investigations, but you have never explained exactly what your personal interest is."

Ginny looked around the apartment as if unsure where how much to say. "My interest is a lot like yours. I want to rule out someone as being part of the conspiracy."

"OK, so I have Joe and you have Mister X. I don't mind helping you but..."

Ginny stepped up to me, pulled my head down and planted a serious kiss on my lips. She didn't pull back for a long time. She looked thoughtful, like she was analyzing the kiss. "Damn it. This isn't supposed to happen. You're supposed to be a local contact. I'm usually better at managing my priorities."

We looked at each other like a couple of puppies in front of an empty food dish. Food. "I tell you what, let's have some supper, do something about getting to know each other better, and put the rest on hold for now," I suggested.

Ginny's rueful smile matched my own. "You're right. I guess there is no putting this attraction back in the bottle." She shook her head, as if to erase the impulsive gesture. She plucked a French fry from my plate and popped it in her mouth. She shivered with a mini food orgasm.

I reached for a morsel on her plate. "Do you want to put it back?"

She intercepted my hand before I reached her plate, pushed it away, and picked up the piece herself. She placed it in my mouth. "No."

I don't remember how the morsel tasted, but I burned where her fingers touched my lips.

Ginny attacked the meal with her usual gusto. Between bites and sips of wine we filled in more of the gaps in our knowledge of each other. A picture of Ginny emerged as a talented, privileged woman who had excelled at nearly everything she tried. Her parents were encouraging and wealthy enough to support her interests. An only child, she had a powerful work ethic, liked things neat and orderly, usually played within the rules, and had the expectation of a fairytale princess that everything would work out right. Other than being gorgeous, talented, and rich, the only vice I could find was an excessive need for achievement. She was officially on vacation in nearby Charlestown, Rhode Island, but eager to crack a cold case concerning a real estate fraud that had baffled the IRS since Ginny had been in high school.

We laughed, touched, fed each other, and drank both bottles of wine. We were flushed and aroused by the time the plates were empty.

"Why don't we relax in the living room for a while," I suggested, hoping to keep her mind on me and off the files for a while longer.

We started for the narrow doorway and once again ended up chest to chest. Ginny played with my buttons and giggled. "This was more fun without your shirt." Before our lips could touch she turned me around, propelled me into the living room, and pushed me down onto one end of the couch. She stood over me for a second, undressing me with her eyes while I did the same to her.

"Wait here. I have something for you." She turned and returned to the kitchen.

Ginny stepped back in the living room cradling a large bunch of grapes in her hand. She saw my perplexed expression, executed a quick twist and collapsed, laughing, on the opposite end of the couch. The move was a little short of her usual grace, and I suspected that the wine had taken its toll. Her legs were angled toward me, and her torso was propped up by scatter pillows. Apparently unconcerned that her skirt had slid deliciously far up her thighs she plucked a grape and placed it between her lips.

I hadn't been on a date with anyone except Linda for years and I was not sure if Ginny's posture was more flirtation but it was the right position for some serious romance. A grape fell out of the bunch, rolled down her chest, and slipped between the folds of the crossover blouse. My innards lurched as I tracked its course.

Ginny giggled. "Wow, that's cold. Well if you want some, come and get them." She lifted the bunch with one hand and groped for the errant grape with the other.

"I know which one I want." I slid across the couch and kneeled on the floor between her legs. I cupped my hands around the bunch of fruit. Ginny took a deep breath as my knuckles grazed the lightly freckled skin on her chest. She removed the hand that had been groping for the runaway fruit and with a teasing smile placed the grape she had retrieved between my lips. Her blouse slipped down over one shoulder and revealed a delicious patch of creamy skin.

Before I could take my first taste of an IRS Criminal Investigator the door at the back of the kitchen rattled. In a panic

I hoped that Mom wasn't violating her rule about uninvited appearances in the apartment of her bachelor son. The voice that came from the kitchen signaled that the interruption was much worse than a maternal visit.

It took a few seconds for my new guest to realize that I was not in the kitchen.

"Frankie, where are you? I have something for you."

In the mirror's reflection I saw a coat come off. All that was left were a few specks of red lace, matching fiery red high heeled shoes, and long cylinders of tanned skin.

"Frankie," called a seductive voice, "I think it's time we made up."

Linda appeared in the doorway looking like a lingerie model. She stopped and stared.

I was kneeling in front of Ginny so only her legs and bare shoulder could be seen from the doorway. From Linda's vantage point it probably looked like Ginny was wearing less than her. My face, which was already flushed with desire and too much wine, glowed even hotter. I straightened up which did nothing to improve the situation. Linda looked from Ginny's reclined form to me. Tears of shock and anger filled her eyes. She mumbled something about what I could do with myself and bolted for the kitchen. Ginny raised an eyebrow and waited for me to say something.

I had a brain freeze.

Buttons clacked as Linda scraped her coat off the counter, threw it around her shoulders, and stomped up the stair. I struggled to my feet. With her clothes in mild disarray, and an amused expression on her face, Ginny was as sexy and desirable a woman as I have ever known. But any guy older than ten knows that two hot women in the same place and time were likely to result in no hot women before long. I cursed inwardly at the timing of it all.

"I've got to talk to her," I said.

I rushed after Linda, and caught her at the top of the stair.

She turned an acid stare on me. "You creep! How long have you been cheating on me with that slut?"

There are very few constructive things that a man can say in a situation like that. Nothing was going to save me, not the newness of my relationship with Ginny or that I hadn't done anything yet. "Linda, I'm as surprised about all this as you are," was the best I could do.

The hands that gripped her coat were balled into fists. Linda looked like she was going to punch me and this time I deserved it. Instead she let go of the coat and put her arms in the sleeves. The sides slipped open revealing her flawless, nearly naked body. I ached for her and involuntarily reached out toward her golden skin. "I thought you and Bobby..."

Linda breathed in sharply when I reached for her. The fire in her eyes was all anger and no passion. Instead of covering herself she took the lapels and spread the coat wide. "Take a good look, Frankie. This is the last time you'll ever see this," she snapped. With that she closed the coat, turned, and left without another word.

When I returned to the dining room Ginny had her cell phone out and a wry expression on her face. She stood up, pulled her skirt down and lifted the blouse back up over her shoulder. "Franklin, I see that you need some time to figure out what is going on with you and Linda." She waved off my attempts to explain. "I've had too much wine to drive so I'm taking a cab back to the motel. I'll talk to you when I pick up the car tomorrow."

Chapter 17

"Franklin, are you up?"

It took a few minutes for me to realize that it was Wednesday morning and that the women who had been chasing me with sharp knives all night had faded with my dreams. A real woman addressed me through the speaker phone. I recognized the voice and punched the talk button.

"Ginny," I managed to croak in my scratchy, hung-over voice.

"Men! You break two hearts in one evening and sleep through the night like a baby." I hoped that was mock disgust.

Had she said two hearts? I felt a cautious optimism, the way it feels when a bolt I have been trying to break free gives a little. It could either be about to come free gently or snap off.

"I didn't sleep well, Ginny, and I'm too groggy to have a relationship discussion right now. I have enough trouble keeping my foot out of my mouth when I'm awake."

"Your foot isn't the appendage that's getting you in trouble."

"Very funny. I was shocked to see Linda. Earlier this week she told me it was over and when I asked to talk things out yesterday she had been on a date with an old boyfriend. Does that sound like someone who wants to make up?"

"So you want me to believe that you are not a manipulative two-timing louse, but a guy unable to figure out a woman you have been with since high school?"

143

"That sums it up pretty well. It's not flattering, but fairly accurate."

"Well, your gender makes stupidity at least a good first guess. And besides, I had a clear look at Linda. She is hot. You'd have to be a major moron to cheat on someone that beautiful."

"Listen, Ginny. When it comes to being hot, you aren't second place to anyone. But that is not the point. Linda doesn't want me. For a long time she has been trying to remake me into her ideal boyfriend, and has finally figured out it isn't working. When she does stunts like last night I think she's trying to go back to what we had."

"You expect me to believe that Linda is clinging to you until someone better come along? Why would you let yourself be used like that?"

"Ginny, I'll be straight with you. I have a lot of history with Linda. We've been together since high school and it has been difficult for either of us to admit that it is over. We still love each other, but I don't know if we're in love anymore." That was the first time I admitted that to myself.

"So where does that leave you and me? You can't have us both, it doesn't work that way. And I'm not willing to be your consolation prize either."

Along with her statement there was a soft vulnerability that I hadn't heard in her voice before. I began to suspect that it might be easier to hurt Ginny than I thought. "Ginny, I have been with only one woman my whole adult life, and that is coming apart. I'm doing my best to do the right thing, but I'm not always sure what that is. One thing that I'm not confused about is that you're smart, funny, pretty, and great to be around. Let's continue to work together, go slow and I promise no pressure for sex until I end it with Linda."

The laughter at the end of the phone told me that Ginny had maintained her sense of humor. "That's not a particularly flattering proposal, but okay, friends for now and later we'll see. In the meantime we have a case to solve. I want to see those files."

"When and where?"

"Well, your place is out. Let's meet at the library. See if Albert has been able to get anything else off the chip and we'll look over the files there. How does ten o'clock sound?"

"You've got it. I'll call Julia and ask her to reserve the quiet reading room."

"No need Franklin, I've already talked to her. Don't worry about my car, I took a cab and picked it up earlier. I'll meet you at ten."

True to her word, Ginny's Toyota was gone when I stepped into the Wednesday morning sunshine. Before meeting Ginny at the library, I made a side trip to drop off Linda's ankle bracelet. I owed her that.

Over the years the little family jewelry shop had morphed into a superstore, but they kept the same Fort Street location across from the fire station. The repair window is at the back of the room, past rows of glass cases filled with flashing gems set in gold, silver, and platinum. At a plain black counter I pulled out the white envelope containing Linda's bracelet. I opened the flap intending to pour the chain into my hand. It was empty. I stammered my apology to the clerk. I looked at the construction notes on the envelope and realized that I must have dropped it somewhere in the Queen Anne.

With no time to look for it, I made a quick drive past Washington Park, through the homes on the east side of Groton Bank, and a left at the Congregational Church to reach the library parking lot. I arrived a little before ten and stepped inside looking for Ginny. A few of the library regulars were already there. A row of gray heads bobbed behind a line of computers. A woman who appeared to be taking a break from her life in the tattoo parlor held a copy of the *Wall Street Journal* between highly decorated arms. A red-faced young woman was attempting with little success to quiet two preschoolers.

I opened the glass door to the quiet reading room where Ginny and Julia were sorting a large stack of papers into piles on a long table. The two women moved from the stack to the table in graceful steps. They reached around each other and smiled whenever they brushed elbows or hands. Their graceful harmony was broken when they grasped a document together and engaged in a brief tug of war.

Julia noticed me in the doorway, smiled, and put her arm around Ginny's waist. The pair turned in my direction. Julia inspected me with one upraised eyebrow that made me think that either I was late or Ginny had filled her in on the fiasco last night in my apartment. Ginny's crooked smile didn't give me a clue which it was.

For the first time I noticed the family resemblance between the two. They were around five four with athletic builds. Both had fair skin and jet black hair. Julia's was well cut and pleasantly short whereas Ginny's fell across her shoulders in long, curly tresses. I could see Ginny's pert nose evolving into the sort that supported Julia's glasses. Even their choice of clothing had a symmetry I hadn't noticed earlier. Julia wore an attractive knee-length dress in tan and gold that fit well enough to have the senior men out front lining up with reference questions for her. Ginny was wearing tan slacks with a cream shirt that made the most of her figure. The most striking similarity was the bright intelligence shining out from two pairs of gray eyes. I realized that in different ways and for different reasons I was inordinately fond of both. "Good morning ladies, you're looking fine today."

"Good morning, Franklin." Julia's expression changed to a wry smile. "Well, you've got yourself in quite a mess this time." She swept her arm in a direction that could have signified either the pile of papers or her niece. Ginny's eyes flicked uneasily toward Julia, aware of the ambiguity of her aunt's comment and gesture.

I looked into Ginny's eyes, and promptly lost my ability to speak. I stood there for a minute or so, like a goofy slobbering puppy, with neither of us saying anything.

Julia rescued us from our romantic trance. "Look you two,

146

you have some chemistry to work out, but we have crimes to solve. Where did these files come from?"

Ginny touched the older woman's arm. "Aunt Julia, these are prints of files that Albert extracted from a smart phone he and Franklin found on the Monument Parcel. It was near a lot of money that we're trying to trace. I called Albert this morning and asked him to send copies of the remaining files to my computer as attachments. Franklin and I are looking for clues concerning the source of the money and how it fits into Joe's death and the new condominium development."

"Well, I'm always game for an interesting puzzle," offered Julia.

Ginny looked pleased. "Thanks. We can use your help."

Julia plugged the drive directly into a printer and soon pages were spitting out like cards from the fingertips of a professional gambler. The sheets filled the out basket and spilled onto the floor.

I returned the pages to the out basket "How are we ever going to make sense out of all this mess?"

The two women stopped sorting and looked at each other with amused expressions. They turned to me with pleasant but condescending looks, like Sherlock Holmes might have given Dr. Watson. Julia waved her arm toward the stacks of books outside of the room. "I'm a librarian trained to bring order to the chaos of the literary world. Ginny works for the agency which is home to about a million pages of tax codes. Do you really think we can't handle this?"

Ginny laughed and gave a high five to Julia. "Piece of cake."

"It is nice you two are having so much fun together. What do I do?"

Ginny smiled. "After you have picked up those papers spilling on the floor, you can go out for coffee. Aunt Julia and I both like it light and sweet."

"That figures."

"And, Franklin," said Julia. "When you return be discreet. I don't want the other patrons getting the idea that food and drink are allowed in the Library."

I had noticed a Dreamy Donuts coffee cup in Ginny's Toyota, so I headed across town to their nearest store on Shore Route 1. Reasoning that drive-up windows are intended to assure that the staff will screw up my order, I grabbed a parking space and headed inside.

A few minutes later I exited the store juggling three large coffees, and ran right into trouble. Two men wearing worn jackets, faded jeans and heavy boots leaned against my truck. Their clothes and boots didn't have a trace of mud. These guys hadn't been doing any construction recently. They pushed off from the truck and started my way with sharp eyes and heavy steps.

"Hey, is this piece of crap your truck?" asked the big guy in a Boston Red Sox baseball cap.

"That isn't a truck," said the hatless second man. "It's scrap metal on wheels."

The men looked like a couple of tag team wrestlers. I suspected that the message they wanted to deliver had nothing to do with my choice of transportation. My chest hammered and my tendons and muscles tightened. From long experience I had learned that the best approach to bullies was to show no fear so I stepped forward and got in the face of the nearest one.

"Very funny, guys, but I really don't give a damn what you think about my truck. I'm not dating it. I drive it to work. Insult it if you want, but get out of my way."

The pair seemed surprised at my aggressive response. I was betting that they wanted to intimidate, but not to make too much of a scene. It only took a second for the pair to recover from their surprise. "We drive our truck to work too, but thanks to some stubborn jerk we don't have any work to drive to," said the Red Sox fan.

The hatless man stepped forward. "We heard that some moron who drives a truck like this one is blocking the condo development we're supposed to be building. We think you're that guy." He grabbed my arm and pushed.

The guy was pretty strong. My arm whipped back and the three coffees tumbled to the ground. About the time I was thinking that I was going to be late returning to the library, I spotted a familiar face. Approaching me was Officer Daryl Williams looking like a two hundred and sixty pound black avenging angel. He approached with long measured strides, his highly polished black steel-toed size twelve boots making a sound like a Clydesdale on patrol.

The two thugs saw him too. They exchanged startled looks. As they moved off, the one with the hat lowered his head and hissed at me. "Maybe you don't care what happens to your truck, but I would keep close watch on your family if I were you. If you keep getting in the way of progress they could get hurt." He followed his partner who had jumped into a red pickup. The truck accelerated out of the parking lot.

Officer Williams watched. "What was that all about?"

"A couple of guys didn't like my truck." I picked up the now empty cups and stuffed them in a nearby trash receptacle.

The policeman glanced from the receding red pickup to my truck and back to me. "I can't blame them. This is a crummy looking excuse for a vehicle." He watched as the red truck turned on Fort Hill Road. "That's all they wanted—to talk about your truck?"

"I don't think they like historic buildings either." Officer Williams waited for me to continue. "Can you tell me if there are any new developments concerning Joe Simpson's Death?"

The policeman looked down the street again and then back toward me. "Is there some connection between those two and Dr. Simpson's death that I should know about?"

"I've never seen them before. Someone told them that my plan to renovate the Queen Anne up on Arnold Street is blocking the condo development on the Monument parcel. I don't see what that had to Joe's death. Besides, he fell, right?"

Officer Williams' eyes turned down at the corners and he shuffled his feet. "I probably shouldn't tell you this, but since you're working with the IRS on this I'm going to let you in on something. It's looking less and less like a fall and more like a murder. The coroner identified a blow to the head that doesn't seem to be related to the fall, like someone hit him and then dumped him off the roof."

Officer Williams' revelation made the day seem colder. Nora Simpson was right after all.

I bought replacement coffees, and returned to the library. A smooth faced student intern was staffing the front desk. The girl pushed straight black hair away from the olive skin of her cheek and greeted me with soft dark eyes filled with youth. She peered skeptically at the tray of plastic cups with bright purple and orange logos. Her dainty mouth straightened with disapproval. "Sir, food and drink are not allowed in the library."

I practically groaned. There is nothing as deflating as being called sir by an attractive young woman. I gestured toward the quiet reading room where Julia and Ginny were working behind the glass. "These are for the boss and the Fed." The smile returned to the intern's face and with a graceful gesture she waved me in.

Julia and Ginny had sorted the papers into neat piles. Ginny typed into her computer as Julia dictated descriptions of the files.

Julia accepted a coffee. "I see you got by Kristi. Her dad is a naval officer at the base and she's a stickler for rules."

Ginny took the other cup and lifted the plastic cap to her mouth. She closed her eyes and pressed her parted lips against the rim in a coffee lover's kiss. Her throat pulsed several times before she lowered the cup. Her eyes were bright and playful. "Thanks, Franklin. I love coffee, but it wasn't necessary to go to South America to get it."

I could see that she was trying to find out why it took so long, and I played along with the banter. "Yeah, sorry about the delay. I ran into some people along the way who thought they knew me. We got to talking about trucks."

"You men are such gossips," said Julia. "So you were hanging out with the boys while we were doing all the work?"

"It was something like that. What have you found?"

The women exchanged conspiratorial expressions. They communicated something with their eyes that signaled Julia should begin. "These files appear to be records pertaining to the Monument Condominiums Project. There is everything from correspondence about permits and supply orders to purchase and sales agreements, and bank deposits."

"Sales agreements?" I asked.

"Yes." Ginny picked up a stack of receipt forms and handed them to me. "The developers are already taking down payments on units. A lot of money has already flowed in."

Julia looked up from a spreadsheet on the computer. "Yes, too much money."

"What do you mean?" I asked.

Ginny took the stack of receipts back from me and brought up a balance sheet on the computer. "I analyzed the receipts, and compared them to what is ordinary for this phase in a development. They have sold a lot of units already, but even with that there is too much money in their accounts for the number of deposits taken. Quite a few of the deposits were reported to have been in cash and below the federal reporting limits. "

I thought about what I had heard, large cash deposits and too much money in the accounts. Even a finance dummy like me could figure this one out.

Julia voiced what we all were thinking. "It's a money laundering operation. They are inflating the cash deposits given as down payments on condominiums to get the money into legitimate accounts."

Ginny nodded in agreement. "Look at this receipt. It says that Eric and Amy made a down payment of $9,000."

"They told me they didn't put any money down."

Ginny gestured to a pile of similar receipts. "All these are probably inflated or made up."

Julia rested her hands on the table and leaned forward. There was triumph in her eyes like the first time I mastered the math for figuring out the load requirements for a roof. "I know where the money being laundered came from."

Ginny leaned forward, her eyes sharp and focused. "We think that this is the cash from Washington Way. The hundred-dollar bill Albert found is the right age. I can't figure out why it was left out on that cliff. Washington Way was ten years ago and that bill hasn't been outside that long."

Something I had overheard when I was balancing on the cliff face came back to me. Victor said something about moving the money out there because people were hanging around the location where it had been hidden. "What old building do we know about that hasn't been disturbed for eight years and suddenly has become subject to scrutiny?"

Julia appeared to have already worked this out too. "The old Queen Anne. Robert Caspar owned that house. He must have hidden the money there before he disappeared."

"Could Joe have found the money when he bought the house?" asked Ginny.

We all thought about this for a minute. I guessed that Julia didn't know about the blackmail, and would be certain that Joe wasn't involved with the money. Julia had her own theory. "It's more likely that someone who knew about the money panicked when they heard Joe bought the house."

While we talked, Ginny had been typing on the computer. "Look at this." On the screen was a spreadsheet displaying the kind of management chart that might be used to keep track of a construction project. She pointed to a string of events arrayed along a time line. "Here is when the Queen Anne came up for auction, here is when Joe bought it, when the Monument Condominium project application was filed, and when Joe died. The only date I'm missing is when you and Joe filed for a building permit to start the restoration."

I gave her the date and she entered it. It fit in a day before the

Monument Condominium project permit application and a week before Joe's death.

Julia gestured toward the screen. "It's too bad we don't know when the money was moved, we could add that."

"I may be able to find out." I dialed Albert's phone and asked him if there was any way to determine the last time the cell phone we found was used to send an outgoing call. He consulted his copies of the files, found the call log, and gave me the date and time. I wrote it down. "Thanks, man, you are great."

I gave Ginny the paper with the date. "Assuming that the phone was left up there the day the money was moved, this is the date." Ginny made the entry and the time line revised. It showed that the money was already hidden on the Monument Parcel two days after the restoration application was submitted. "It could be that whoever dropped off the Monument Condominiums building permit learned about the permit on the Queen Anne, and raised the alarm to whoever is laundering the money. They moved the money the next day. It also makes it unlikely that someone's fear Joe would discover the money in the Queen Anne was the reason for his death. He died well after the money was already moved," Ginny reasoned.

Julia looked thoughtful. "Of course there are lots of alternative explanations, but that does fit the timeline very well. It's interesting that the Monument Condominiums project was set up a month after Joe bought the house from the City. Someone felt the need to launder the money quickly."

All this reasoning was giving me a headache. There were still too many unanswered questions. First, if the Monument Condominiums were a money laundering scheme that would never be built, why was I still getting threats from the developers for blocking the construction? Second, none of this got us closer to understanding the circumstances surrounding Joe's death. "So who killed Joe and why?"

"Aunt Julia thinks that we can use all the e-mails and text messages to look for some suspects. Besides the calls made to and from this phone, many of the text and e-mail files have the history attached including calls made to and from other phones that were forwarded here. We may be able to identify who is behind Monument Condominiums and narrow down the list before we start looking for motive and opportunity."

Julia pointed toward a chart in an open book on the table. "This is called a sociogram. People tend to organize themselves into hierarchies and networks that can be identified by looking at patterns of communication. See the name in the middle of this diagram with a cluster of names connected to it with arrows? The person in the center is probably in a position of authority since most communications flow through him."

"Can we apply this technique to the files in the computer to figure out who is behind the Monument Condominium development?" I asked.

Julia smiled at me. "There is a little complicated math involved, but the computer will do that. Albert was able to recover the logs on most of the e-mails, so we have the URLs for the senders and receivers of a whole string of conversations. Ginny and I have entered the data for most of the e-mails and texts while you were gossiping about trucks. We need to link to a program and do the analysis."

I watched as she brought up a data base listing hundreds of e-mails and texts. Dozens of different names appeared on the lines. "There are a lot of names here. Will this work?"

"It is worth a try," said Ginny.

"I vote for Bobby as the organizer," I said.

Julia accessed a program on the Internet and linked to the data base. She set some parameters and seconds later the computer emitted a chirp. "Let's see what we have."

The report on the computer contained several diagrams that resembled the one in the book Julia had showed us. In all there were five diagrams, each looking like a wagon wheel. Ginny looked at the report on the screen and gasped.

"Franklin, look at that cluster of five people at the top."

The names Victor Bennett, Tony Gorky, Steve Smith, and Bobby Lester were clustered around a sender labeled as mm4000. Each of the four named men was also at the center of a cluster further down the page.

"This confirms it; these guys are at the top of the networks and most likely are the partners," I said.

"Right," Ginny said. "Bennett, Gorky, Smith, and Lester all talk to each other and this person labeled mm4000@gmail.net. In turn each of these communicates with a circle of contacts that reflect their area of responsibility. This is a typical hierarchical structure. But who is mm4000?"

"I don't know. The position of the node suggests this is the mastermind behind the whole thing," Julia said.

I looked at the clusters lower down on the page. I recognized groups of building material suppliers, equipment rental companies, and government officials. When I got to Bobby Lester's network I stared with surprise at a name in his circle. "What is Linda's name doing there?"

Ginny and Julia engaged in some more non verbal communication. They squirmed and made eye contact with each other, but not me.

Ginny spoke. "These lists are based on the volume of back and forth e-mail, text messages, phone calls, and correspondence. There was only a little from Linda. It's recent and mostly between her and Bobby Lester."

"I would guess that it is about the design contract for the condo interiors but she could be part of this. There's no way to know, is there?" I asked.

"We don't have the contents of the messages, only the senders, receivers, and dates," Julia said. She gestured toward the screen. "Look at this cluster. Joe Simpson exchanged a little flurry of e-mails with the Washington Way trio days before he died. Our four suspects also sent a lot of e-mail to each other after he died."

"Doesn't it stand to reason that the person who owns the smart phone is the mastermind behind all this?" I asked.

"Not necessarily, but it seems highly likely," said Ginny.

"Let's call Albert and see if he's identified the owner," I said. "If he doesn't have a name yet, I know another way to find out."

Chapter 18

Julia stepped out to answer a question for a patron. I called Albert and asked if he had learned who owned the phone.

"Does the name Miranda Murphy mean anything to you?"

"No. Who is she?"

"That's the name on the warranty card for the smart phone but the contact information is out-of-date. I can't find an address or phone listing for her anywhere."

"I'm still at the library with Ginny. Let me ask if she knows that name." I put the cell phone down and repeated the question. Ginny shook her head. She typed the name into her data IRS base. She shook her head again, no matches.

"Nope, we haven't any idea who she is," I told Albert. "It's probably an alias. Will you hang on to the phone at the store? I'm going to try to get the owner to come to you."

I explained my plan to Albert with Ginny listening in. "In addition to his skills as a realtor, Steve Smith is a prolific gossip. If I tell him that we have the phone, and are looking for the owner, the word will get around quickly."

"But what if he is the owner and Miranda Murphy is his alias?" objected Albert.

"No problem, I'll tell him it's broken and we couldn't get anything off it except the serial number. If he shows up to claim it, we'll know." Ginny approved of the plan.

On the way out of the library I noticed the intern, Kristi,

scowling at the contents of a folder. When our eyes met she smiled sadly. "I'll never understand why people feel it is okay to steal library property. Look at this." She held up an old town economic development brochure. Someone had used a razor blade to cut a big square out of the center. The headline over the missing portion read "New Condominium Complex Breaks Ground." I had a good idea what the picture had shown. "Kristi, does the library have a backup copy of this?"

"There's probably one in our old microfiche system, but all that antique stuff is in storage." Kristi tossed her long straight locks behind her shoulder and gave me a shy smile. "I'd be glad to track this down for you, but it's going to cost you a coffee."

I sealed the bargain with a handshake and a smile. I held her hand a bit too long which caused the intern to blush.

Before I left library parking lot I called Steve to set my plan in motion.

"Smith Realty, Mandy speaking."

"Hi, Mandy, this is Franklin Breault."

"Hi, Franklin. How have you been? I haven't seen you around here for a while."

I pictured Mandy, a curvy brunette who spent the time between calls doing her nails and studying fashion magazines. All dreamy ambition, she was waiting for her prince to come in, buy a castle, and decide she was one accessory he had to have.

"Blame Steve, he hasn't sent me any work lately."

"I always thought you came in to see me."

"Is he around? I want to talk to him."

"He is in the conference room. I'll ask if he can talk to you." She put the phone on hold and was gone only a few seconds. "Dad said how about meeting him here at 1:00?"

"Good. Tell him I'll see him then."

Mandy hesitated. "I heard that you and Linda had a fight and you're with someone new. You know that I'm here if you need some local company."

How did she know about Linda and me? Life in a small town

was like living in a glass house, no privacy and fragile walls. I tried with my usual lack of verbal skills to reply. "Mandy, I …"

My stammered reply raised a laugh from Mandy. What is it that makes women first proposition me and then laugh?

It was only a ten-minute drive from the library to the real estate office on Fort Street, and I had an hour to kill. I took the long way around and drove by Groton Bank. That neighborhood is a half a square mile packed with historic structures dating from colonial times to the turn of the twentieth century. Several hundred years ago this was the home of wealthy seafaring families who demonstrated their status by living in homes designed by leading architects of the period and built by local craftsman.

I cruised by the stately Greek Revival home built in 1842 by Deacon William P. Harris and saw a familiar form on the sidewalk. The thinning hair, open-neck dress shirt, and shiny shoes were pointed toward the classic home. I pulled the truck over to the curb, got out, and strolled over. "Dad, what are you doing here?"

For a couple of seconds Dad appeared confused. He looked from me to the house and then back again. "Frank, I didn't expect to see you here. What are you doing in the Historic Village?"

"I was at the library. I'm taking a drive through the old neighborhood before meeting Steve."

"These buildings are beautiful," he said. "Look down there. See that Federal Style home? It was once owned by Captain Ebenezer 'Rattler' Morgan."

"Do you want to walk a bit, Dad?" I suggested. All around us were Victorian era homes. We wandered around the narrow streets. Dad pointed out structures built in Italianate, Carpenter Gothic, French Mansard, Cottage Style, Stick Style, and Queen Anne Style scattered below the dark green canopy of mature hardwoods.

"There is so much history tied to these homes," he said savoring the moment.

We ended up in Fort Griswold Park near where Albert and I

had started our trip to the Monument Parcel. "Want to sit?" I pointed toward a bench facing the river. We looked out over the homes below, across the wide mouth of the river to where it met the sound. The sky was so clear we could see the gray shadowy cliffs of Montauk Point Long Island in the distance. "You're a long way from home. Did you walk all the way from home?"

"Heavens no. I left the car somewhere, but for the life of me I can't remember where." He released a guilty laugh and pulled a crumpled brochure from his pocket. "I found this old walking tour guide prepared by the Groton Bank Historical Society and thought it would be nice to locate all the registered buildings. Do you know that there are twenty-seven of them within a half mile?" He studied the brochure for a few seconds. "The car must be next to one of these houses."

"Does Mom know where you are?"

"She is out with the ladies. They have this afternoon thing. Harry was coming over and we were going to play some cards but he cancelled on me."

My cell phone played the ring tone assigned to Mom. She sounded upset.

"Franklin, Dad is missing. I called the house to check on him and he didn't answer. I called a neighbor and she said that the car is gone. Where could he be?"

"Relax, he's with me. We're doing the historic home tour up in Groton Bank."

"Thank goodness! I was so worried."

I promised to follow him home after the tour.

Dad and I spent the next half hour in friendly companionship. He retold the story of the captain who found the HMS Resolute floating abandoned out in the North Atlantic, the legend of the ghost who haunts the Ledge Lighthouse, and tales of the rich families who settled this area in the past three hundred years.

"Are you getting cold?" I asked. The sun was bright, but the sea breeze was cool.

"Yes. I probably should get going."

"Okay, let's take my truck and look for your car."

"Come to think of it, I bet I left the car out in front of the church on Meridian Street next to the pretty Queen Anne on the corner."

The Grand Marquis was parked safely at the curb.

"Dad, what is all this forgetting about? Are you okay?"

"The doctor called it a mild case of cognitive impairment. It sounds more serious than it is. When I stopped working, I kind of lost my bearings, like someone pulled up the survey stakes."

"Is there anything he can do for you?"

"I have some medicine, but mostly it is stuff I need to do for myself. Find a hobby, exercise, keep connected with people."

Dad pulled away from the curb ahead of me. He made only one wrong turn, corrected at the next block, and ended up in the driveway at home a few minutes later.

"This has been great," Dad said. "I feel sharper already."

All the reminiscing triggered a thought. "Dad, do you know someone named Miranda Murphy?"

Dad was silent for a moment. "I know that name but I can't place it."

Great. My big lead was in the hands of my dad, who had managed to misplace his very large car not an hour ago.

Chapter 19

"See you later, Dad. After I visit Steve's office I'm going to stop at the Queen Anne to get some info off the furnace. I'll be home later."

I met Steve in the parking lot. He had a tight expression that said he remembered our last conversation. "I don't have anything to report about Joe's death yet," he said.

"That's not why I'm here. Did you hear about the raid up on the Monument Parcel?"

"Yeah, I heard the cops didn't find anything."

"The cops didn't, but Albert did. He found a busted cell phone."

Steve blanched, like the phone had meaning to him. "Who has it now, the cops?"

"Nah, it's at Silicon Shack. The store manager wants Albert to try to return it. The problem is he can't find the person who signed the warranty card, someone named Miranda Murphy."

Steve flinched again but quickly recovered his composure. "So why tell me?"

"I thought that maybe you could get the word out that the store has the phone and is looking for the owner."

"Why all the fuss over a busted cell phone?"

"Business at Silicon Shack has been bad lately. I think Albert wants a chance to sell a replacement to the owner."

Steve looked thoughtful as he twirled the pencil attached to his clipboard. "Okay, I'll ask around. If I find the owner I'll send them to the store."

I made a quick drive over to the Queen Anne. I wanted to get started on costing out the restoration, and needed to check the capacity of the old furnace. I left the truck on the street in front of a neighboring house and walked back to the Queen Anne. If the person who had hit me on the head was still around I didn't want to advertise my presence by parking in the driveway. I went to the back of the house and used the hatchway to enter. I lifted the hatch carefully and made sure the stops were firmly engaged. Once in the basement I found the label on the furnace and cleaned off the plate containing the serial numbers and output rating. Those numbers would make locating a proper replacement easier.

I had started searching for the missing ankle bracelet when a black Cadillac Escalade pulled into the drive. It was Tony Gorky, Steve and Victor's partner. I guess he hadn't got the message yet about the Queen Anne being hands off.

Before I had the chance to put the fear of prosecution on him, he pulled out a laser tape measure and began shooting the dimensions of the building. I was still behind the building, partially concealed from the front by brush. When he had calculated the dimensions of the foundation, he pulled a slim computer from his jacket and began clicking keys, probably entering the measurements. Next he removed a device that looked like a little telescope and squinted in one end, calculating the height of the building.

Tony's cell phone rang. He reached in another pocket and lifted it to his ear. "Yup, I'm right in front of it. I'm updating the dimensions, but I figure a 20-ton demolition machine and a couple of dump trucks could take care of it in an afternoon."

He stopped and listened to whoever was on the other end of the call. I realized he had been estimating the volume of debris that would be left to haul away after the Queen Anne was demolished. He held the phone at arm's length and looked at it like it was defective, shook his head, and placed the phone back against his ear. "What do you mean leave the house alone, Steve? We agreed that this place has to go."

Steve must have given him an earful, because Tony listened for a whole minute.

I didn't wait for the rest of the conversation. I stepped around the corner. Tony seemed surprised to see me, said a hasty goodbye to Steve, and hung up.

Tony wore a shiny gray suit, creased from too much sitting. In physical size he resembled Victor Bennett, except that more of Tony's bulk was wrapped around his middle. Tony's cool, intelligent stare reminded me of Steve but Tony wasn't even trying to fake friendliness. He looked more like a feral cat defending a dumpster.

"Well, Steve tells me you're Groton City's newest extortionist. When that stubborn old curmudgeon died, I expected an end to being shaken down."

I hadn't planned to use my knowledge of the extortion to pressure anyone. Victor and Steve had jumped to conclusions. Faced with the malice in Tony's eyes I couldn't resist doing it again. "The demands will stop when the money you stole is all back where it belongs. Until then I own you, like Joe did."

If my aim was to piss Tony off, I succeeded. He strode up to me, looked down and hissed. "Be careful, Franklin, blackmail is a game for grownups, and kids can get hurt." With that he returned to the Escalade and drove off.

I thought about extortion all the way home. I didn't notice the familiar red Miata parked on the street until I stepped out of the truck. I entered the house with more than a little dread.

I heard voices coming from the kitchen. I followed the sounds and encountered a familiar scene. Mom was preparing supper and dad was sitting at the table entertaining a young woman with a real estate story. It was easy to see that he was fond of her and she was enjoying the attention.

"Hi, Franklin," called Dad, catching my eye in the doorway. "Look who's here. She was waiting for you in her car so I invited her in for a cup of tea. She wasn't sure she would be welcome. She is welcome, isn't she?"

I approached Linda. The blue eyes that I had loved for so long were opened wide. I leaned in to kiss her cheek, but to my surprise she turned her head and our lips brushed lightly. She spoke softly. "Hi, Frankie."

Linda smiled at my parent with fondness. "Your Dad has been explaining his theories of remodeling stress."

"Will you and Linda be staying for supper?" Mom asked.

"No, Mom. Linda and I have some things to talk about. I think we'll go out."

A few minutes later Linda and I were on our way to a local eatery that offered more privacy than the family dining room. Consistent with our relationship problems, we took separate vehicles.

The South End Deli didn't have to fake the old warehouse décor. From the exposed pipes in the ceiling to the flagstone floors it was the real deal. We passed a sea of wood-framed, glass-topped tables, a worn lunch counter, and the stainless steel appliances in the full view kitchen.

"Is this okay?" I asked pointing to a booth tucked on the back wall. A young girl with more hardware on her face than in the bins at Johnson's Hardware had been stalking us since we entered. She handed us a couple of menus, brushed back a wisp of hair from an ear outlined in spikes, and inquired about our drink orders. "A couple of Sam Adams Winter Lagers?" I asked. Linda nodded. The waitress made a note on a pad and disappeared.

Linda stared at her menu. We were reluctant to start the conversation so we spent more time than usual studying the worn, plastic folders. As the silence ticked on between us, the poison ivy rash I picked up on the Monument Parcel began to itch. I scratched it.

"Frankie, you're hurt!" Linda exclaimed noticing for the first time the scrapes and red rash on my arms. She took my wrist in her hand, turned it over and cradled it between her soft hands. "Does it hurt? What happened?"

I told her about the field trip that Albert and I took to the Monument Parcel. I described the smart phone and the cases of money but not the files that we downloaded.

"Sam Adams Winter Lager isn't available yet," interrupted the waitress who reappeared at my side.

"Oktoberfest?" I asked.

Without a word the waitress turned and departed.

"What were a smart phone and a pile of money doing out there and where are they now?" Linda asked when we were alone again.

"Albert has the phone. He is going to try to find the owner. We returned to pick up the money but it was gone. The four of us nearly got run over on the service road by someone making a quick getaway."

"Four? I thought it was you and Albert."

"We took a local cop and a lady IRS agent with us."

Linda gave me a sour look. "I assume the IRS agent was that woman who was sprawled over the couch in your apartment."

"Her name is Ginny and that wasn't what it looked like. We were..."

"Frankie, it's pretty clear what would have happened if I hadn't interrupted. At least you're a louse with taste. She is pretty, even if she is a little too muscular."

"She was impressed at how pretty you are. She said you were hot."

The waitress showed up with our drinks and asked us for our food order. Fish and chips times two got her on her way quickly.

"She did? She thought I was hot?" Linda looked eager and interested. Why she would care what her rival thought is one of those many things about women I don't understand.

"Yes. She said she got a good look at you and said you were smoking."

166

"How did she say it, like she meant it?"

"She meant it. She said that I would be a nut to cheat on someone like you."

"Then why did you?"

"Why did I what?"

Linda looked down at the table. She was trying without success to keep her face composed. The corners of her mouth twitched, her eyes dropped and her brow furrowed. "Why were you going to cheat on me with the tax tramp?"

I could see that it had hurt her plenty to see me with Ginny. Once again I was confused and angry at the mixed signals from Linda. "We were working and then drank too much. It wasn't planned. Besides, two days ago you told me I was a loser, that we weren't a couple. You said that it was over between us. What do you want from me?"

Linda lowered her eyes and swirled the straw in her soft drink. She sighed deeply. "You're right. I did say those things, but I didn't expect you to run off and find someone else so soon. Frankie, I'm so confused. One minute we're in bed and everything is great and the next I'm so angry with you that I can't stand to be in the same room. I've loved you for a long time but we've lost something and we can't get it back."

I was not sure what to say to that.

Obviously looking for some way to keep the conversation going, Linda asked if the ankle bracelet was back from the jeweler yet.

"I've misplaced it. I must have dropped it."

"Frankie, I loved that bracelet, how could you?"

I thought back to the places I had been since I picked it up. "Don't worry. It must be at the old Queen Anne. I pulled the envelope out to take notes and it must have fallen. I'll go back and find it."

"That's so like you," she complained. "You are obsessed with old buildings and nothing else matters. You can't even make a decent living repairing them. Frankie, I don't want to work for rich people–I want to be one. I want to be able to afford a nice home and car. I want a husband who talks to me and a baby."

So that was it. This is about finding her ideal husband and starting a family. Linda had had a baby once, our baby, until she miscarried. We were pretty young and I thought she had been relieved. I guess there are some things a woman never gets over. "Linda, I know what it is like to have dreams. I'm not going to be a handyman forever. Renovating the old Queen Anne is my ticket to becoming an architect. That's not only for me, it's for us."

Linda looked at me with the kind of angry determination I had been seeing a lot lately. "You made it clear that you are going to pursue the restoration of the Queen Anne even if it ruins our business. Well that kind of decision works both ways. I'm taking the design contract for the Monument Condominium development. Bobby says it will take my career to the next level. He has lots of money and likes my work. He says that we can get rich on this project."

The thought of her with that weasel infuriated me. "So how long have you and Bobby been sneaking around? Is that what this is all about, you want someone richer, someone who will tell you what you want to hear to get you in the sack?"

"It's not like that. Bobby and I have been friends as long as you and I. You're the one who decided he wasn't friends with Bobby anymore, not me. But you're right. This is more than business. He really likes me."

With great effort I resisted the urge to curse. If we weren't going to be together what did I care who she ended up in bed with? In a rare flash of self-awareness I realized that while Linda wasn't in love with me anymore, I still cared about her. "Linda, there's something you should know about that condo development."

I stopped. I had promised Ginny I would not share the details of the investigation with anyone. "Linda, there are things I can't tell you, but those are not people you want to peg your dreams on."

Linda's eyes narrowed and her hands clenched the table hard enough to make her knuckles turn white. "There you go with your secrets again. I don't believe you. You want to get back at Bobby by stopping the condos from being built."

I reached out and took her hands across the table. "My feelings about Bobby aren't the point. All I'm saying is please be careful with the Monument Condominium people. I'm not sure they really want to build anything at all."

"That makes no sense," she snapped. "If they don't plan to build the condo complex why are they making such a fuss about demolishing the Queen Anne?"

Our porcupine look-alike waitress arrived, her attitude as prickly as her jewelry. She placed a large tray containing steaming plates on the vacant table next to us, reached over our hands and dropped the dishes on the table with a careless grace. "You two love birds want anything else?" she asked, misinterpreting our linked hands.

Hot fried potatoes and steaming, crusty fish provided a welcome excuse to stop talking, but it tasted like ashes. We had reached an impasse. In order to achieve my dreams I needed to stop the Monument Condominium development but Linda's dreams required it to go forward. Linda expected me to give in as usual, but I was through with that. We chewed in gloomy silence.

Linda made a good point about the developers' intentions. If the conspirators were planning to take deposits and run with the money before anything was built, why would they need a road? Why were they so intent on the destruction of the Queen Anne? Something Bennett said gave me a chill. Maybe Joe wasn't killed for what he knew, but for something he didn't know about the house. Joe had controlled the conspirators for a decade. Something about that house had changed the status quo and raised the stakes high enough for someone to commit murder. The race was on to find out what it was before I became a victim too.

We gave up on the food by consensus. Linda insisted that we

split the check. On the sidewalk we said our goodbyes and parted without touching. The impasse didn't mean that our passion for each other was gone. We were like matches and gasoline, and neither of us wanted to take the risk of igniting another fire that we couldn't put out.

Chapter 20

After spending the night alone, I awoke on Saturday morning determined to separate my love of the Queen Anne from the practical matter of calculating what it would cost to restore it. The notes on the back of the jewelry envelope told a grim story. Even deducting the cost of my labor and professional discounts, the numbers were not good. It was going to take a sympathetic banker, strong earnings on my part, and maybe years, to make this work. I had to admit that Linda's pessimism had not been entirely unfounded.

When I tired of staring at the bottom line, I headed upstairs to enlist Dad's help to drum up some new business. He was at the kitchen table reading the paper when I found him. I helped myself to a cup of coffee. "Dad, I need to start prospecting for some more work. Want to help?"

"Sure. Mom is out and I'm bored. What are we looking for today?"

"Recent and pending sales involving old classical homes."

If there is a constant with old buildings, it is their need for maintenance. My ultimate business plan was to be the first person owners of classic buildings thought of when they decided to renovate. Until my name became better known, finding work meant scanning the papers and making lots of cold calls.

Dad fired up his laptop and connected to the Online Listing

Service. "I'll start looking for purchases in older neighborhoods during the last year. Some of those owners will have exhausted their do-it-yourself skills by now and be ready for your help."

Dad had a good feel for the real estate market. Those instincts saved his retirement after Washington Way went bust a decade ago taking his savings with it. "Will you look at that," Dad exclaimed as he pointed to a listing. "I never thought I would see homes in Noank dip below $500,000 again." Dad kept up a running commentary as we worked. He knew all the districts, the neighborhoods that were up and coming, and the ones that were deteriorating. He also knew which ones had an abundance of aging Victorian homes.

By mid morning we had twenty prospects. All had been sold in the prior six months. The property cards, which were conveniently on line, told us that nine were early twentieth century buildings now about a hundred years old. One was a classical Victorian built in 1870. Between the print newspaper and online files we soon had the names, numbers, and addresses of the selling agents and new owners. Dad picked up the phone and called a couple of the agents he knew to inquire if the owners had expressed their intention to renovate or upgrade. He managed to extract agreements that we could use the agents' names when we called the owners.

I made cold calls to the ones we couldn't find a connection to and asked the owners if they would like estimates on any immediate maintenance or renovation plans. For a while I felt like a writer peddling his debut novel. Ten owners hung up without a word, five muttered a curt "not interested," and three were more polite but still rejected me. I was finally rewarded by two owners who were looking for a contractor and willing to set up appointments for me to come and look at the properties.

By noon I had my fill of paperwork and phone calls. In addition to the two appointments I had set up, Dad had secured four promises of introductions from real estate brokers that we would pursue later.

Mom returned from her errands with three, foot-long submarine sandwiches and sides. "Are you staying for lunch, Frank?" she asked. "There is plenty." Mom divided the sandwiches into thirds and set out three plates while Dad and I cleared the papers off the kitchen table. We spent a pleasant hour eating and talking about life in town.

Mom stood up and started toward the living room. "Oh, Franklin, I saw Nora Simpson at the grocery store. She wants you to call her when you have a chance. She needs your help with something."

I called right away.

"Hi, Franklin. I need your help, but this has nothing to do with our other business. I'm giving an antique dresser to my sister in Ledyard and I don't have any way to get it to her. Can you deliver it for me some time?"

"Sure, when do you want it picked up?"

"Tomorrow would be nice, but you'll need some help. It is pretty awkward, and I'm not much help with heavy lifting."

"No problem, I'll bring someone. Oh, that reminds me I have something for you. Steve Smith found a hundred-dollar bill in the basement of the Queen Anne. I'll drop it off."

"That's extraordinary. I guess it's lucky that you were with him when he found it. It's hard to imagine Steve ever parting with a dollar once it is in his hand, no matter who it belongs to."

It was interesting that others had picked up on Steve's avarice, whereas I had missed or ignored it all those years I had worked with him. I agreed to call Nora back once I had a helper and a schedule worked out. Fortunately I knew a strong friend. I hoped she would be willing to lend a hand.

Ginny picked up on the second ring. "Hi, Franklin. What's up?"

"I have a favor to ask and something to show you."

"If you are asking me out on a date, that's a line I haven't heard before."

"Now that you mention it, a date is a good idea."

"Franklin, isn't there a matter you promised to attend to before we go out again?"

"I didn't really call for a date, but since you brought it up I had the talk with Linda yesterday. Nothing is ever simple with Linda, but we reached an understanding."

The silence on the line told me Ginny was processing the new information. "If you're not asking for a date, why did you call?"

"Nora Simpson asked me to move an antique dresser for her and I could use an extra pair of hands. We could turn it into a date if you let me buy you breakfast, but it might be fun either way. What I want to show you is a hundred-dollar bill I found in the basement of the old Queen Anne. I didn't make the connection then but..."

"But you think that it could be related to the missing boxes of money you and Albert found. When do you want to get together?"

"I was hoping to see you later today."

"No way. I'm in Rhode Island at my parents' house today. How about tomorrow?"

"OK. Do you know how to find the Simpson house on Arnold? Meet me there at 10:00 tomorrow morning."

"Make it 8:30 at The Breakfast Spot on Buddington Road and you have a date."

I was disappointed that she wasn't available today, but I had a date tomorrow. I called Nora back and made the arrangements for mid morning the next day, Sunday. Since Ginny was meeting me early, I loaded the truck with some items I would need. I collected protective mats and a two-wheeled dolly from the shed and lugged them out to the driveway. My cell phone rang again before I finished loading.

"Are you coming to the pot luck tonight?" asked Albert.

With everything that was going on I had forgotten. "Oh, Mexican night. Sure, I'll be there but it's a little awkward. Linda and I are not together right now." This was probably only the first of what was bound to be a string of embarrassing explanations about Linda and me.

174

"I'm sorry man, not surprised, but sorry. Come anyway. You and Linda are still our friends and we'd like you to come even if you aren't together."

"Okay, I'll be there and will bring my two favorite Mexican foods."

Albert laughed. "Corona and black bean soup. Good. I'll have Marti remind Linda she is still invited."

I resumed unloading the junk that had accumulated in the bed of the truck. The debris were only partially unloaded when I was interrupted again, this time by Linda's ring tones coming from my cell phone. I was beginning to feel like those pigeons trained to peck whenever a bell sounded and had a momentary image of a cell phone crushed in the jaws of a vise. The nature of the call didn't make the interruption any more welcome.

"I called to remind you about my bracelet. I know I'm not your priority right now, but it means a lot to me."

"I'm sure it's in the old Victorian. I told you I'll get it. I'm a little busy."

"Maybe you could go this afternoon and bring it to Marti's tonight?"

"What's the rush? The Queen Anne is going to be there for a long time, despite what your friends think."

"You're a jerk, Frankie." She hung up.

That hadn't gone well, but I had a feeling she was going to like me a lot less when I took down the persons behind the Monument Condominiums.

Chapter 21

It would take a few hours to prepare my special dish, so I stopped cleaning the truck and made a quick run to the big supermarket on Poquonnock Road to buy the ingredients. I gathered my purchases quickly and moved to a short checkout line. I was studying the back of a shapely brunette in front of me when she turned.

"Hi Franklin, what a nice surprise."

"Hi Mandy; did your dad give you a day off today?"

"You're joking. He asked me to pick up some coffee and creamer for the office. I'm taking my time." Mandy peered into my cart and stirred the items. "What have you got there?" She recited the list: pumpernickel rolls, four cans of black beans, chicken broth, lemon, yellow onions, green onions, garlic, sour cream, blue corn tortilla chips, and a case of Corona. "I didn't know you can cook."

"Hey, I have skills. It's all those hours of watching the food network, that and being single."

Mandy looked me up and down, bit her lip, and placed her hand on my arm. "Cooking is more fun together. I could come to your place later and help."

"Sorry, this is for a party with Albert and Marti tonight."

"Too bad I have to work," she pouted. "I'd rather cook something up with you."

Mandy had been a 24/7 flirt as long as I had known her. It was hard to tell if any of it was serious. When I didn't respond to her come-on Mandy shifted her attention to the checkout guy.

Mandy and checkout guy flirted in high gear. He obviously didn't have the kind of job prospects that attracted her, but she strung him along anyway and glanced back every couple of seconds to make sure I noticed. She slinked to the door and made the "call me" sign. The clerk waved, but Mandy held eye contact with me the whole time.

I paid for my purchases and headed for the exit in time to see Mandy shut the door on her Honda and burn a little rubber as she exited the parking lot.

As I loaded the groceries in the truck I noticed a plastic grocery bag flopping in the breeze. There appeared to be some mail inside, and from the pristine look of the bag it must have been dropped recently. That kind of thing happened all the time, someone put a bag on the roof while groping for their keys and then drove off in a big rush with the bag sliding to the ground. No one was around and I was in a hurry so I chucked the bag on the seat intending to track down the owner later.

I rushed back home, dumped the groceries on the bar, pulled out my crock pot, and set it on the stove. My plan was to cook the black bean soup in the slow cooker while I got a little work done outside. I sautéed the onion and a few garlic cloves in olive oil in a frying pan. While that was cooking I drained the beans and dumped them into the slow cooker along with most of the broth, the juice of the lemon and cumin, oregano, parsley, and black pepper. When the onions and garlic looked right, I added a little chicken broth to deglaze the pan, dumped the contents of the pan, the rest of the broth, and beans and spices into the slow cooker, covered it and set the temperature dial to high.

I left the slow cooker simmering and headed back outside. I had enough time before the party to pay a visit to one of the prospects on my list. Like many of the homes in the area the little bungalow was a merger of many architectural styles and turn-of-the-century mechanical and plumbing systems. The owner wanted to update the paint and replace several sections of damaged Victorian trim in the public areas. All the trim was custom-made in the years before standard shapes, and other contractors had proposed replacing it all with newer, uniform styles.

I secured the contract when I explained that I could duplicate custom molding. I would remove a small section of molding and use the cross-section the way a locksmith used a key as a pattern to shape a blank. In my case it wasn't a key I would make, but a blade for a shaper machine I'd inherited from Grandpa. That would allow me to reproduce the original molding. It was expensive, but much less than replacing all the trim. The owner was impressed and hired me on the spot.

I made a hasty run back to my place to check on the soup. Slow cookers are handy and probably safe, but I didn't like leaving any appliance unattended for long.

"Frank, is that you? You have a visitor," called Mom from the kitchen.

For the second time that day, a woman I didn't expect was chatting up my folks.

Dad and Mom were seated at the table. Steaming cups were in front of them as well as the visitor.

"Ginny, wow. It's great to see you. I see you have met my Mom and Dad," I stammered.

I was surprised and a little apprehensive but glad to see her. That was the first time she had met my folks and I hadn't figured out what to say about her to Mom and Dad. I stepped over to her and gave her a hug.

My fears of any awkwardness were unfounded.

"We were getting to know Miss Maxwell. Did you know that her mom and Julia Judge are sisters?" asked Mom. "The Maxwells live in Rhode Island. That practically makes them neighbors."

Dad jumped into the conversation. "We have been hearing

about the exciting life of an IRS Criminal Investigator. The broker I'd been suspicious of all those years is in prison for a too-creative interpretation of the tax code."

Mom looked at Ginny, suddenly apprehensive. "Frank is not in trouble, is he?"

Ginny gave me a mischievous look. "Not with the IRS. I'm working on a case that involves builders and housing development. Aunt Julia introduced Franklin as someone who could help me understand the local scene, but my visit today is social."

Dad gave me a stern look, the way he used to at parent teacher conferences. "I hope he is being helpful."

"He is." Ginny turned and addressed me. "My mom and dad aren't back from Europe yet, so I decided to come after all. I hope it is okay."

Her presence had already improved my day. "I'm glad you did."

Ginny placed her hand on mine. Her smile sent heat coursing through me. Mom and Dad exchanged a discreet, puzzled glance, suggesting that they had picked up on the chemistry between us, but they didn't comment.

We spent the next ten minutes with Mom and Dad discussing families and the community. "That reminds me, I have a quick delivery to make. Ginny, if you would like to help, you can make this your audition for the moving job tomorrow."

"So I need an audition to see if I'm good enough to help you move a bureau? What do you have in mind?"

I brought her out to the barn where an old-style gooseneck rocker I had restored was awaiting final inspection and delivery. The chair was sitting on a work table, gleaming with new finish. The materials and details of its construction had told me it was not a genuine antique, but it was handcrafted by someone who knew what they were doing. The arms and legs had nice curves that were attractive to look at and also very comfortable.

Ginny couldn't resist running her hands over the satin finish.

"It's beautiful, Franklin. Where did it come from and what are you going to do with it?"

I lifted it off the table and placed it on the floor. "Sit in it and see how comfortable it is. It is the right size for a woman. I found it at a yard sale for $5. It was a little beat up, but not difficult to restore."

Ginny sat in the chair, closed her eyes and rocked gently. "This really is heavenly. Whoever this is for, she is a lucky woman."

"I wouldn't exactly say that, but let's get it loaded. It is only a short trip."

I brought the chair outside and noticed that I hadn't finished cleaning the debris out of the truck. The bucket of junk I scraped off drain in front of the old Queen Anne a couple of days ago was still there. I was in a hurry so I pushed it aside, placed the rocker in the bed and wrapped it in the blankets I planned to use to wrap Nora's dresser.

The drive to the thrift store on Fort Street took only a couple of minutes.

Katy, the manager of the day, greeted us. "Hi, Franklin." She extended her hand to Ginny and the pair exchanged introductions. The women studied each other. Their smiles said they liked what they saw.

Katy gestured toward the package in the truck bed. "Is this the chair for the shelter?"

I slipped off the wrappings so she could see my handiwork. "It came out pretty nice, if I do say so."

Katy reached up and ran her hands over the smooth arms of the chair. "The mothers there are going to really appreciate this. I'll call the staff to pick it up. Can you bring it inside?"

I would have been glad to drop the chair off myself, but most shelters don't welcome random visitors, particularly men. Groton City is a pretty nice place to live, but the region has an unfortunately high rate of domestic violence. Instead of pretending the problem didn't exist, civic-minded residents established a place across the river in New London where women and their children could be safe.

Ginny and Katy moved off a short way while I untied the chair and lifted it down. Katy was obviously singing my praises because Ginny was smiling at me with an expression that communicated approval and maybe a bit of surprise.

When we climbed back in for the drive home Ginny linked her arm in mine, and gave it a squeeze with a dreamy look in her eyes. "I'm impressed that you donate furniture to women who could really use something nice. Katy tells me that you have practically furnished the shelter."

"You are going to embarrass me if you keep this up. It was really Marti's idea. She volunteers at the shelter and noticed the shortage of furniture. I always have more restored stuff around than we can sell so I send some of it over. Marti mentioned that the young mothers with infants would enjoy the ability to rock them to sleep, so I kept my eyes open for a nice chair."

We returned home and headed down to the stairs. Ginny followed me without hesitation. At the bottom she took my arm again and turned me to her. We were standing close and she looked so delicious that I couldn't resist her. I took her in my arms and placed a light kiss on her lips that quickly progressed to a full contact exploration of her mouth. She reciprocated enthusiastically. We pulled back a minute later, flushed, and a little dizzy.

"What's that wonderful smell?" Ginny kept hold of my hand and led me to the kitchen. The slow cooker was on the stove, nestled between the burners. The black bean soup bubbled slowly. Ginny lifted the glass top releasing fragrant steam. She noticed the rolls and chips on the counter. She blanched.

"Oh, Franklin. Did I do it to you again? Were you expecting someone for supper?" Her voice cracked with disappointment.

I laughed, pleased at what her distress implied, although I was sorry for upsetting her. "This is for Mexican night at Albert and Marti's house. I was planning to invite you before you told me you were at your folks for the night. I was planning to go alone. But now that you are here, you should come. You know Albert, and I'd like you to meet some of my other friends."

"Will Linda be there?"

"Ginny, my friends know that it is over with Linda and me. You will be welcome. Come on, you can help me finish preparing the bread bowls."

We used sharp knives to scoop out hollows in the bread rolls and broke up the remains into bite sized pieces. We sealed the rolls and fragments in plastic bags. When the preparations were done Ginny helped me clean up. She was about to toss the plastic grocery store bags when I remembered that one bag wasn't mine.

"Don't toss that one out. I intend to return it tomorrow."

Ginny looked in the bag, removed the package of coffee and a newspaper and placed them on the counter. She removed the single envelope from the bag, studied the address and gave me a quizzical look. "Where did you get this bag?"

"I found it in the Big Supermarket parking lot. Why?"

"The letter is addressed to Miranda Murphy. You've found the person who registered the smart phone!"

Chapter 22

Shouts of "Uncle Frankie, Uncle Frankie," rang out as Ginny and I stepped into the foyer of the Henley home.

Eric and Amy's daughter, Megan, was only the first trial in the gauntlet that Ginny would run tonight. I felt a little lurch in my gut and realized that having my friends accept Ginny was very important to me. I wanted this party to go well. The beaming three-year-old in a princess costume ran to me waving a bandaged finger.

"How's my big girl?"

"I hurted myself."

Megan's mother smiled at Ginny. "Hi, I'm Amy. I'd better take those. Megan isn't going to give up until you do your magic." She took the beer and bag of blue corn chips from me.

Free of my burdens, I bent down and lifted Megan. She held her tiny index finger in front of her like a sword. A colorful bandage circled the finger tip. Megan pressed the wounded appendage to my lips.

I did my best tiger growl and chased the finger with my mouth, snapping my teeth. "Mm, I'm hungry. That's just the thing, a tasty finger."

Megan giggled, not at all frightened by my antics. "No Uncle Frankie. Don't bite, kiss."

I did and the petite face burst into smiles and little arms locked around my neck.

Ginny stepped forward and looked at me with raised eyebrows.

Megan lifted her head from my shoulder and focused huge hazel eyes on Ginny. She jabbed the colorfully bandaged digit in Ginny's direction. "Who's that?"

"This is my friend, Ginny."

Megan curled her lower lip, buried her face in my shoulder and whispered, "I don't like her."

I lifted Megan off my shoulder and looked at her in surprise. Ginny, who hadn't heard Megan's comment, stepped forward and touched the sleeve of the frilly costume. "You look like a princess. I'm very pleased to meet you."

Much to my surprise Megan pulled her arm away and began to cry. "I want my mommy."

Embarrassed, Ginny stepped back with a pained look on her face. Amy reached for her daughter and cuddled her on her shoulder. "Megan, don't be silly. That is no way to act toward Uncle Frankie's new friend." Amy smiled at Ginny. "Hi, I'm really sorry. She is overtired. Despite appearances, it's nice to meet you."

While Ginny attempted to recover her dignity Megan let out a scream. Linda emerged from the kitchen, put her arm around mother and child, and brushed a tear from the crying child's cheek. "Megan Freelove, why are you screaming?"

The toddler sniffed and wiped her nose with her sleeve. Megan pointed the bandaged finger at Ginny. "It's her."

Linda appraised my date like a vice cop observing a pedophile suspect. "Well, Ms. Maxwell, I didn't expect to see you again so soon. What did you do to Megan?"

Ginny gave a crooked smile and shrugged. "I don't think she was expecting me."

Linda studied Ginny with an unfriendly smile. Her gaze flicked over the short black skirt and open necked white shirt. "I bet you get that reaction a lot. At least your clothes are a little better put together now than when we first met."

Amy still had the bag of groceries in her arms. She smiled awkwardly. "I didn't know that you two had already met."

There was frost in Ginny's eyes and voice when she replied. "Linda and I haven't been introduced, but we have seen each other around." Ginny cut her eyes back to Linda. "In fact, I saw quite a bit of you in that pathetic display in the stairway."

Linda's mouth sagged open. She sucked in her breath as if she had taken a punch to the gut and was struggling for breath.

I felt the heat rising in my face. This wasn't going the way I had planned. Before I could figure out how to salvage the situation, the last person I wanted to see entered from the living room.

Bobby Lester had obviously heard the interchange and also knew the story of Ginny and Linda's first meeting. "Hold on, you two. This may be Mexican night but I'm pretty sure the reenactment of the Alamo isn't scheduled until later."

He placed a proprietary arm around Linda's waist and gave Ginny an approving once-over. He leaned forward and stuck out his other hand. "You must be Ginny Maxwell, the IRS investigator. I'm Linda's date, Bobby Lester."

Ginny's expression gave away her mild surprise at the confirmation of my suspicions that Linda and Bobby were now involved. She took in the blue suit and shiny shoes and hair. "Yes, I'm Ginny, Franklin's date. Attorney Lester, I've heard so much about you, it is nice to meet you in person."

It was Bobby's turn to look at a loss, probably wondering what Ginny knew about him and if the information had come from an IRS file.

Despite being an oily snake, Bobby was defusing the tense confrontation between Linda and Ginny. Amy kept the recovery going when her husband wheeled his titanium sport wheelchair into the entry way. "Eric, will you take Megan to the den and see if she will lie down while I take this food into the kitchen?"

He rolled up to my date. "Sure. Hi, I'm Eric and you must be Ginny." He held his arms out for Megan. "Come on, princess, hop on your chariot for a ride." The little instigator climbed into her father's lap and he rolled his wheelchair toward the back room making horse noises to the little girl's delight.

Bobby pulled Linda into the living room and I led Ginny straight ahead to the kitchen.

Albert and his partner Marti were helping Mom Henley prepare refreshments. "Welcome Señor Breault," called Mom Henley as we entered her domain. She always dressed in costume for our Saturday night gatherings. Today she was decked out in a beaded, brightly colored vest and a broad-brimmed sombrero. "Welcome to Mexican Night. Who is your pretty new friend, Franklin?"

Albert did the introductions. "Mom, this is Ginny Maxwell. Ginny, this is my Mom, Ruth, and this is my girlfriend Marti."

Ginny glanced around as if looking for a friendly face. "It is nice to see you again, Albert. And it's so nice to meet you, Mrs. Henley. Marti, I have heard so many good things about you from the guys."

Marti looked over Ginny carefully. Marti's smile couldn't quite conceal the conflict between her loyalty to her best friend Linda and her natural tendency toward friendliness. "Albert says you are an IRS Criminal Investigator. How did you meet Franklin? I hope it wasn't on the job."

Ginny laughed and lifted the insulated bottle of soup in her hands. "I did, but I'm not investigating him officially. At least not yet. Tonight I'm a friend and the bearer of the black bean soup Franklin made."

Mom Henley collected the food, asked Albert to stay, but ordered Ginny, Marti and me out of the kitchen. We settled into the living room. I ended up opposite Bobby and Linda who were sitting together on a loveseat. Bobby was being overly affectionate, marking his territory. It made me sick to see them sitting hip to hip.

"So, Linda, you've brought your benefactor."

Marti glared at me. "Franklin, don't start up on those old

grudges of yours. Linda asked Bobby here to talk to you about the old Queen Anne."

"What could Linda's date have to say that would be of interest to me?"

Bobby looked at the faces around him. "See what I mean? Franklin is such a hardhead. There is no getting through to him. I don't know how you put up with him."

I jumped out of my chair and took a step in his direction. "It's not being hardheaded. It's a low tolerance for bull, and that is usually all you have to offer,"

Ginny reached for my hand which I shook off angrily. Linda stepped between Bobby and me and put a hand on my chest. Her touch felt so natural and familiar, and with our new status it tangled my gut in as many knots as my tongue. Linda looked up into my eyes. "Will you please stop it? Bobby said he would be willing to talk to you about saving the Old Victorian. I asked him to come and talk to you."

"The last time my family needed help from Bobby Lester's family, things didn't turn out so well for us."

Bobby stood, his eyes narrowed to slits. "Damn you, Franklin, Robert Caspar cheated your dad, I didn't. When he skipped out he left Mom and me high and dry too."

The two of us stood there breathing hard and glaring, years of festering resentment finally in the open. An unsettling thought slipped in and I felt my anger cool a notch. Bobby was probably telling the truth about his stepdad. I remembered Bobby and his mother moving out of their beautiful house on Groton Bank into some dump up by the Poquonnock River following Caspar's disappearance. They had suffered too.

At Linda's urging, Bobby sat down and she slid in beside him. Bobby sighed and took her hand.

Mom Henley came in from the kitchen decked out like an angry General Santa Anna, and with about as much authority. "Ok you two, that's enough. All this shouting woke up Megan. Amy, will you try to get her back to sleep? And, Franklin, if you don't want to talk about the house with Bobby, that's OK. Find something else to talk about. You both have beautiful dates and it's a party. So relax and visit." With that she turned on her heel and returned to the kitchen.

Bobby and I had already cooled down, but Linda was getting warmed up. "How does she expect me to relax when Frankie is being so beastly? Nothing I say matters to him. We've been broken up less than a week and he shows up with a new girl."

I thought about the fact that it was exactly the same interval before Linda showed up with Bobby, but the looks I was getting from around the room said that I had talked too much already.

Bobby flinched at Linda's complaint about my date. He rolled his eyes, stood and tugged Linda toward the deck at the back of the house. "Come on, we need to talk." He led Linda through the door to the deck and closed it behind him.

Ginny's grim expression said that she had noticed Linda's proprietary attitude toward me, and she did not like it any more than Bobby. She turned to Marti. "This is too awkward. I know that Linda and Franklin are your friends, and their breakup has been uncomfortable for everyone. Maybe I should go."

Albert came into the living room in time to hear Ginny's offer to leave.

"Don't do that. We're used to listening to their arguments without taking sides. You are Franklin's new friend and we would really like to get to know you."

Amy returned and agreed. "Yes, Ginny, please stay. Franklin, you and Albert go help Mom Henley in the kitchen and Marti and I'll show Ginny the rest of house."

With the combatants sufficiently scattered around the house, we resumed preparations for the party. As parties go, this one was pretty much a disaster already, so I concentrated on preparing the buffet and setting plates out in the dining room adjacent to the kitchen and living room. I brought a dish to the table and noticed that the women had returned from the house tour. Marti still looked a little stiff, but Ginny and Amy sat together, and from the looks of things a friendship might be beginning. Albert and Eric returned and took the seats across from Ginny, no doubt to better appreciate her short skirt. Marti, who was seated next to Albert, was well aware of her boyfriend's frequent glances at Ginny's legs and rolled her eyes when she caught my expression. Albert was telling a funny story about some of our exploits and the other three were correcting exaggerations and contributing their own.

As I finished setting out the last of the food, Linda and Bobby returned from the deck. Bobby's eyes were sharp and hard as he brushed by me and spoke with Mom Henley and then headed for the front door. Linda's eyes were red and swollen.

"Mrs. Henley, Bobby and I are going. I had hoped to work something out with Frankie, but I think we need some time and I don't want to ruin your evening."

Mom Henley put down the mixing spoon, dried her hands on a towel, and hugged Linda. "I know honey, these things can be difficult. But don't stay away too long. You're always welcome here."

Fresh tears flowed from Linda's eyes she kissed Mom's cheek and followed Bobby out the front door.

The shotgun design of the old bungalow let me see all the way from the kitchen to the curb. If there was ever a doubt in my mind about her relationship with Bobby it was dispelled when they embraced before climbing into his shiny Beemer. Score one for Bobby, he got the girl. But he and his clients were not going to get the old Victorian if I could stop them.

Eric rolled into the kitchen. His wheelchair barely fit through the doorway, but he popped a wheelie, executed a three hundred sixty degree turn on the back wheels, and ended up facing the refrigerator door. He opened it and pulled out a Corona.

"What is with the fancy moves, Wheels?" I asked.

He laughed. "Sobriety test."

"What do you think of Ginny?"

"She's gorgeous, smart, and funny. What's not to like?"

"Yeah, she is something else."

Eric grinned at me. "She does have one flaw, though."

"I suppose you mean her taste in men."

"You nailed that." Eric was quiet for a few seconds. "Are you serious about Ginny?"

"We have only known each other for less than a week."

"Did you see Linda's face when you showed up with Ginny? Are you sure it's over between you two?"

That was the question I'd been asking myself. "I don't know, but I don't think Ginny is into anything serious."

Eric snorted. "Did you see Ginny's eyes when you picked up Megan? She was seeing you with her child."

The rest of the evening was a blur. My friends apparently forgave my earlier bad temper, but my grouchiness became the joke of the evening. I didn't rise to the friendly insults. During the games, food, and banter, I kept looking at Ginny for signs of what Eric saw. Whenever I looked into her eyes, she got a silly smile and her face became soft and warm. I had given a lot of thought to what it might be like to get her into my bed, but what else was I getting into?

Chapter 23

Sunday morning announced its arrival with bright rays creating a light show on the mirrored surfaces around the apartment. I kicked off the sheets, groped for my phone, and speed dialed Ginny.

After the Mexican night disaster I had driven Ginny back to my place hoping she would spend the night. Instead she kissed me, climbed into her Toyota and drove to the motel she used the last time she was in town.

"Need more sleep," she moaned through the phone.

"Not an option. It's a beautiful morning and we need to deliver that dresser for Nora Simpson. Besides, we need to get back to work on our investigation."

I could hear mattress springs creak. "Are you angry about last night? I'm sorry I couldn't stay, but all the bickering at the party wasn't a fitting prelude to our first night in bed together."

"So there *is* going to be a night in bed together?"

Ginny was silent for a few seconds. "Maybe. I have to tell you, I didn't intend to fall for you. This is all so unexpected and complicated."

I had sensed the change in her yesterday. The banter and flirting that came before was fun, but I always felt that she was manipulating me. But she had become quiet and shy at the party, signaling vulnerability I hadn't expected. Maybe Eric was right. Seeing me with Megan had made her all dewy-eyed for a child of her own, and she saw me as a likely candidate for a dad. "I'll pick you up for breakfast in an hour."

I arrived a few minutes early and Ginny was waiting. She glanced into the back of the truck. "What's all that junk?"

"A hand truck for moving the bureau and the blankets are to protect it." She pointed at the bucket I still hadn't cleaned out. "That mud is stuff I shoveled off a drain in front of the Queen Anne last week and forgot to take out."

Ginny rolled her eyes. "You have carried a bucket of mud around all week?"

We were still getting to know each other but I hadn't noticed that Ginny was a neat freak. I guessed that a bucket of garbage spending the week in my truck was probably over-the-top for almost anyone.

Ten minutes later we were at The Breakfast Spot ordering outsized meals of ham, eggs, home fries, and toast. The coffee arrived first in thick white mugs. Ginny reached for a mug, and sucked down the fragrant brew like a wet/dry vacuum. "After a night like the last one I needed this."

"Last night wasn't a total disaster. You got to meet Amy and Wheels and they were impressed with you."

"Why do you call Eric 'Wheels'? Isn't it cruel to remind him that he is disabled?"

I laughed. "Wheels is short for 'hell on wheels'. It's what we've called Eric since he was a kid and in love with anything that rolled. The name stuck, and we saw no reason to change it after the accident. He said something about you last night."

Ginny hung her head and glanced up with hooded eyes. "Your friends blame me for breaking up you and Linda, don't they?"

"No way. The guys and Amy are cool with you. Marti's coming around. It's hard for her. Linda is her best friend."

Ginny took a sip. "I was pretty unkind to Linda."

"I thought she was kind of nasty to you."

"She was claiming her territory. She really isn't over you. Are you sure you are through with her?"

"We're not a couple, but I still care what happens to her."

"I'm not so sure that's all it is. You're jealous of Bobby—that's why you confronted her about bringing him.

I found myself getting angry at the accusation, even as I recognized the truth of it. "What are you talking about?"

"That display with Bobby was all about asserting your ownership of Linda. It was like two mountain rams butting heads."

"That wasn't about Linda. Bobby and his family were up to their ears in the Washington Way scam that swindled my dad. Bobby represents the same partners in the Monument Condominium development, probably another scam that threatens to gobble up more classic architecture. That makes this personal but not about Linda."

"Look, I don't want to fight but you're still possessive of Linda and it sometimes makes you miss things. I think that Linda manipulated Bobby into trying to help you with the Queen Anne or he wouldn't have come to the party."

"So I'm a jerk for jumping down his throat and ruining the evening?"

Ginny swallowed another load of eggs. "Pretty much, but let's talk about something else. How busy are you after this delivery? I have an idea how we might get a break in this case, and have some fun too."

"All we need to do is lug the dresser down, drive it five miles to Ledyard, and then we're free. Oh yeah, I also want to return that hundred-dollar bill that Steve found."

"You were going to show me that bill."

I pulled it out of my wallet and handed it over to Ginny.

She held it up to the light. "It's less worn than I expected." She studied the bill from end to end and then shook her head. "This isn't from the same series as the other money. All the bills that Albert photographed were more than fifteen years old. This one was printed much more recently."

"It looks pretty old, how can you tell?"

"This currency design was introduced in 1996, beginning with the $100 denomination. It has the new counterfeit-resistant features that make it easier to authenticate the notes without specialized equipment. I would need to look up the serial numbers to be sure, but this probably didn't go into circulation until two or three years after the Washington Way fraud."

"Then how did it end up in the Queen Anne? None of the people I know who have been in that building have hundred-dollar bills to spread around."

"Did you see where Steve found it?"

"No, I opened the basement door and he had already picked it up by the time I turned to him."

"Think about it. What were you doing when he found it?"

"We were finishing the inspection. Steve didn't want to go into the basement, the smell was getting to him, he said."

"And what happened after he showed it to you?"

"We left shortly after. He was acting kind of weird the whole time. I know he doesn't think the house is worth restoring, but there was something else."

"Is it possible that he faked finding this bill there?"

"Why would he do that?"

Ginny's eyes focused on the ceiling as she tried to make sense of Steve's action. "Could he have been trying to distract you from going into the basement?"

"If he was, it worked. Maybe we should go back and check out the old Victorian without him along."

Ginny nodded her agreement. "I'm game. It'll give me a chance to see your true love up close."

I took the shore route to Nora's house. We passed salt marshes with tall grasses and ponds reflecting blue sky. Beyond the dunes tall masts of sail boats in the marina stuck up like distant trees. We turned on Thames Street below the shipyard and drove north beside the river, pacing the Block Island Ferry on its way to its terminal in New London. It was Sunday, so the parking lots around the shipyard were nearly empty. At Arnold

Street we turned right and parked at the curb in front of Nora's.

Ginny gazed up at the windows. "Is this where Joe died?"

"Yeah, he fell from that attic window in the cross gable, over the portico."

Nora greeted us at the door. I introduced Ginny and mentioned that she worked for the IRS and was helping me with my inquiries as well as moving the bureau. Nora studied Ginny. "Are you making any progress on your investigation?"

Ginny looked at me and then answered. "We have some leads, but some of them are connected to an official investigation that the IRS was conducting so we can't talk about them yet."

"Joe wasn't in any trouble with the IRS, was he?"

"I can tell you definitely no on that, but several of his business associates are on an IRS watch list of probable tax cheats."

"Well, I'll trust you to keep me informed when you can. Thank you for helping Franklin with this," Nora said.

Inside, the home was littered with boxes. "So you're really moving?" I asked.

"Joe and I had started to clean out and pare down and I decided to continue." Nora dropped her eyes and voice. "There's nothing to keep me here now."

The Victorian dresser was in a second-floor bedroom and as heavy as a mechanic's tool box. It was built from dark stained hardwood with hand-carved ornaments and three full-sized drawers capped by a slim jewelry drawer. It looked to be mid-nineteenth century and was in great shape. We removed an ornate mirror that capped the piece, wrapped it in a blanket and brought it down first. I took the downhill side and backed down the twisting stairs while Ginny followed steadying the top. Next we wrapped the bureau in protective blankets and strapped it to the two-wheeled dolly. This time Ginny backed down the stairs steadying the piece while I gently lowered it one stair at a time. After much effort we got the old chest of drawers down onto the sidewalk.

By the time we reached the curb we were breathing hard from

the exertion. Ginny checked the bureau for dents or scratches and glanced at the truck. "This isn't going to fit with that bucket of junk in the way."

"Nora probably has a dumpster where we can dispose of that stuff. Will you get it out while I set up the ramps?"

Ginny climbed into the truck and gave a wry smile. "So that's how you operate. When your truck gets too full of junk you get a girlfriend to clean it out while she is still infatuated with you." She reached into the truck and tugged at the five-gallon bucket. Ginny was pretty strong but it was too heavy for her to lift over the side of the truck so she slid it along the truck bed. She almost made it to the tailgate, but the bucket hung up on the lip of the bed and tipped over. A cylinder of debris glued together with dried mud popped out, slammed down on the sidewalk, and shattered.

I finished placing the ramps. "Leave that for now and help me roll the dresser onto the truck."

We tugged and pushed and eventually secured the pieces for the ride. Before I had time to store the ramps and shovel up the spilled mess, Nora came across the lawn.

"Oh good, you are loaded. My sister's expecting you."

I pulled the Ben Franklin from my pocket. "Here is the hundred dollars Steve found up at the old Victorian."

"Franklin, why don't you keep that for all the help you have given me?"

"A hundred dollars is a lot of money for delivering one dresser, Nora."

"Consider it a retainer. I have lots of boxes to move and I would appreciate having someone I trust to help."

I could see that it was important to her to pay me so I put the bill back. "Thanks, be sure to call anytime you need me."

Ginny stepped up to Nora. "Mrs. Simpson, would it be all right if I go with Franklin to the old Victorian and look around? I'd like to see the place."

"Sure, Franklin has a key. Don't let anything fall down on you. Despite what he thinks, that place is dangerous."

Ginny looked pleased. "We'll be careful."

I picked up the portable ramps and stowed them beside the bureau. The contents of the bucket lay in mud covered lumps on the ground. "Nora, do you have a dumpster where we can dispose of this junk?"

Nora gestured behind the house. "Sure, over there. What is all that mess?"

"It was clogging the storm drain in front of the Queen Anne. I scooped it off but forgot to dump it."

Nora looked at the debris spread out on the sidewalk. She stepped closer to the pile and kicked at an object half caked with mud.

"Franklin, what is that?"

I picked up the tan lump and banged it on the curb. The dried mud cracked off in big chunks like a mold sections peeling away from a casting. I handed the object that had been inside the mud to Nora. She rolled it over in her hands and polished it on her apron. Except for a few stains it looked in excellent condition.

"Oh my God!" she exclaimed. "Do you know what this is? It's a man's Forzieri shoe."

It was a little weird to find an almost new shoe in the mud, but the significance of the find didn't register on my fashion-impaired mind.

Ginny was not similarly handicapped. She looked at Nora intently. "Mrs. Simpson, that's a five-hundred-dollar handmade Italian leather shoe. How did you recognize it? They aren't that common."

"After Robert Caspar disappeared with everyone's money his extravagant wardrobe was the talk of the town. The press showed a picture of him wearing these fancy shoes. I've never seen them anywhere else."

I thought about that shoe all the way to Ledyard. Had Robert Caspar returned to the Queen Anne? If so, was he alive or dead?

Chapter 24

The Sunday morning traffic to Ledyard wasn't too bad. On the trip Ginny and I talked about the reactions of the three partners to my bluff that I had Joe's files.

Ginny was concerned "Be careful. Blackmail is a dangerous game. Victor and Steve said they didn't kill Joe over his secrets, but someone did. As word gets around that you have Joe's files, you could be next."

On that note we arrived at our destination. Nora's sister directed us to a first-floor bedroom, the dresser's new home. In short order we had delivered the piece, rearranged the room, and were on our way back to Groton City.

I pulled the truck to a stop in my driveway. Ginny's sun fusion yellow FJ Cruiser was glowing in the sun. "So what is this idea you have for the afternoon?"

Ginny hopped out of my truck and opened the rear hatch of her SUV. "I thought we might head to Rhode Island and do the Cliff Walk in Newport. We can discuss the new developments in our mystery along the way. Maybe the ocean will inspire us." She withdrew a small bag. "Come on, let's go downstairs and get on some bathing suits so we don't need to change at our destination."

A few minutes later she emerged from my bathroom. She was wearing white cotton pants, white sneakers and a long-sleeve peasant blouse. If the suit was underneath, it wasn't showing.

She approached me, noticed my disappointment, stepped up and placed a light kiss on my lips. "Down boy. I had a G-rated adventure in mind."

Ginny insisted that she drive us in the Toyota. I hopped into the passenger seat and soon we were motoring over the back roads of eastern Connecticut on our way to southern Rhode Island.

The interior of the vehicle was immaculate. The leather seats crackled and bathed our noses with new-car smell. Ginny gunned the engine and merged with the traffic on 95 north. "Let's think about what we've learned. Ten years ago Steve Smith, Victor Bennett, Tony Gorky, and Robert Caspar were all involved in a real estate development called Washington Way. The three guys were all engaged in petty theft, but the managing partner, Robert Caspar, double-crossed them and disappeared with all the money."

"And people like my dad lost their retirement savings and the money they were going to use to send their kids to college."

Ginny punched the gas and accelerated around a slow truck. "Right. The police didn't have enough evidence to prosecute Steve, Victor, or Tony, but apparently Joe Simpson discovered evidence that the trio was up to something and used his knowledge to blackmail them into helping him with his neighborhood restoration agenda."

We were flying by traffic like it was standing still. I had one hand on the door handle and the other braced against the dash, imparting a slight wobble to my voice. "I know that Victor Bennett delays demolitions on any historical homes that he is called to knock down until a suitable owner is found. Steve must have been involved in finding preservation-minded buyers. Where do you think Tony Gorky fits in?"

"You told me he is a mortgage broker. Probably his job was to help locate financing for buyers who wanted to renovate." Ginny took her eyes off the road to make contact with mine. It was a sympathetic look. "I also think Steve had another job."

"What's that?"

"Didn't you tell me that you have been getting lots of referrals from Steve to correct problems in houses that are going on the market? It is possible that Joe was pressuring Steve into steering his clients toward you?"

The possibility that my business success was not due to my skills and reputation, but to Joe's manipulations, was insulting. It was like winning a contest and finding out that it was rigged.

Seeing my expression, Ginny hastened to explain. "I think that Steve was glad to do it because you are good at what you do. But tell me, has he ever demanded a kickback or favors from you in return for all the business he sends you?"

"No, he never has."

"Well there were lots of complaints that he did that kind of thing years ago. It's one of the things in Steve's file that led us to suspect unreported income. Steve was not always a nice guy."

"What do we know about Robert Caspar?" I gripped the handle tightly as Ginny powered down an exit ramp.

"He was the senior partner for Washington Way. He may have become greedy, or maybe he was planning a double-cross right from the start."

"So did he die or is he is living it up somewhere?" I breathed easier as Ginny slowed.

"Until you and Albert found the cash up on the Monument Parcel there was no sign of him or the missing money. The appearance of the money now could mean he is back, or someone found were he stashed it and has started laundering it."

"It seems a little odd that the funds were converted to cash. Isn't it difficult to get large sums of stolen cash into circulation without attracting attention?" I asked.

Ginny drove in silence for a couple of minutes. It was late morning and the light traffic suggested that most people were already at their destinations. The scrub pine forests of rural southwestern Rhode Island flowed by, interrupted by the occasional clapboard-sided raised ranch. "Right. Before 9/11 it was easier for someone in the know to launder cash. Things really tightened up after that."

I had a chilling thought. "He disappeared after 9/11. Maybe he died in the Twin Towers."

"Or he could have died before that, or he was out of the country and unable to get back to pick up the money. After 9/11 travel was restricted, it would have been more difficult for him to move around anonymously." "So why did the money appear now?" I asked.

Ginny powered around a rotary. "It could be anything. Maybe the laundering operation was interrupted or the stash was only recently found."

We were on a narrow state road and down to a more comfortable speed. I relaxed my grip on the door handle. "I got the impression from the conversation I overheard when I was hiding up on the Monument Parcel that the hiding place was compromised. Maybe that interfered with the laundering operation."

Ginny nodded in agreement. "Yes, and that makes the old Victorian a good guess as the hiding place. It is nearby, once belonged to Caspar, had been sold recently, and Joe and you had filed for a permit to renovate the place. Anyone with an Internet connection could monitor the sale and permit lists of the town, so it would be easy to keep an eye on the place."

"So if the real reason that Steve and Victor want to keep me out of the Queen Anne was the money hidden there, and they have it now, why are they still trying to stop me from renovating it? They should be spending their time figuring out how they are going to launder several million dollars of cash, not building condominiums."

Ginny's eyes opened wide and slapped her hand on the steering wheel. "That's it. That ties all the pieces together. Remember all those cash deposits listed on the documents in the smart phone? We know that the conspirators are using the Monument Condominium project to get the money back into circulation. But there is no way they can launder all the money by inflating down payments, there's too much. They need to build the development to slip in the rest of the money by mixing it with mortgage payments, material invoices, consulting fees, and all kinds of stuff. "

I was beginning to enjoy the way her clothes pulled as she squirmed against the black leather seats. "So I was wrong about Monument Condominiums. The condos are their laundry."

"Right again. They not only profit from the legitimate sales, but they get to launder all the money from Washington"

"Albert and I saw Victor Bennett and Tony Gorki out by the crates, so they are definitely aware of the money laundering side of the operation, but where do Steve Smith and Bobby Lester fit into in all this?"

Ginny squinted into the sky, waiting for a traffic light to turn green. "It's not clear. I think that Steve is most likely involved in the money laundering too, but we don't have anything to tie him to it yet. Likewise, Bobby may have stolen your girlfriend, but he hasn't done anything illegal that I can determine."

"They need a right of way to keep the laundry going, but why that particular old Victorian? An old house that could have provided a right of way came on the market a week ago. I called the owner and asked if he needed any help getting it ready to sell. He hadn't received an offer yet."

Ginny nodded. "So if the reason people want to keep you out of the Queen Anne is not to preserve the right of way, and not about money hidden there, it must be something else about the Queen Anne that makes it special to the developers."

I was getting overwhelmed with the number of clues and the lack of anything to connect them. "You're right, that's strange. And there are the other unanswered questions. If Joe Simpson was murdered, who did it and why? And what's the significance of the new hundred-dollar bill that Steve found in the old Victorian?"

Ginny took her eyes off the road briefly to make eye contact.

"And, how did Caspar's shoe get in the muck you shoveled off the Queen Anne?"

Suddenly a part of the puzzle fell into place. What if Caspar never left the Queen Anne? The money probably isn't there anymore, but what if his body is? That would provide a good reason to keep me away. Especially from the basement.

Before I could share this theory with Ginny, she hit the brakes, slid into a dirt parking lot, and stopped in front of a small IGA grocery store. As my pulse came down, she explained. "My brain is fried, and I'm hungry. Let's pick up sandwiches and drinks for later, coffee for the rest of the drive, and forget about clues for a while."

The next leg of the trip took us down Rhode Island Route 138, and across the lower Narragansett Bay via the Jamestown and Newport bridges. At the height of the bridge we glimpsed Providence to the north and Aquidneck Island ahead. Ginny navigated the busy streets of Newport with reckless abandon, exited onto Eustace Avenue, and three miles later pulled into the parking lot of First Beach.

We grabbed our supplies and back-tracked to the entrance of the Cliff Walk. The Newport Cliff Walk is three and a half miles of breathtaking views of Easton Bay to the east and lush green lawns of magnificent historic mansions to the west. At places the narrow path is fifty feet above the crashing waves. Numerous side trails lead to small rocky ledges suspended over the waves.

A couple of miles down the trail Ginny took a narrow path between the cliffs. We climbed down, rounded a bend and found a sheltered rock ledge hidden from the hikers above. She took a thick blanket and spread it on the stone. For September it was warm, a seventy-five degree day with a lot of power in the sun.

We undressed and sat on the blanket. The view of Ginny Maxwell in a pale yellow bikini was worth the wait. She wore it with a confident grace that made her as much a work of art as a temptress. She took a bite of her sandwich and lifted her eyes heavenward. "Try the egg salad on rye. You are going to love it."

Ginny ate with her usual gusto, but at a more leisurely pace. She reached gracefully into the sack. I nearly missed the soda she was holding out because my eyes were glued to her bikini top. She shook the can in front of my face. "Franklin?"

I shut my jaw and reeled my eyeballs back in. "I was thinking about dessert."

Ginny smiled, obviously pleased at the effect her outfit was having on me. "Me too, but not here. I have another surprise for you later, if you are game."

She was full of surprises. I hoped that they would continue to be this pleasant.

"I can't wait."

After lunch we cleaned the debris, repacked the bag, added our shorts and shirts on top, and settled in for a brief period of chaste sunbathing. The waves pounded the cliff, occasionally depositing a light salty mist on us. Before I knew it the sun had moved far enough west that we were in the shade, and chilled.

Ginny stared out over Easton Bay. "This is one of my favorite places to think." We hiked up to the cliff walk and followed it back to the First Beach where the sun was still shining brightly. We deposited our bags in the FJ Cruiser and crossed the sand to spend a few minutes strolling in the surf. The water hadn't lost its summer warmth yet and felt good against our bare legs.

Offshore a hundred feet or so, a monstrous machine looking like a combine was combing the shallows. "What is that thing?" I asked.

Ginny laughed. "A sea weed harvester. It's supposed to clean up the beaches to keep the tourists happy but it has been broken all summer. The guy is cleaning up an empty beach."

The water looked clean but the conveyer belt of the behemoth continued scooping its slimy harvest into a hopper. I guess surface appearances are deceiving. "I suppose the state needs to keep the tourists happy. It's probably no different than staging an old home to show buyers the potential."

Ginny looked at me wistfully, like a kid at someone else's

birthday party. "I envy you knowing what you want to do with your life. Renovating old homes and making them snug and beautiful again sounds wonderful. I love your passion."

"You mean you don't love being IRS Barbie?"

Ginny punched me in the arm but she was smiling. "I hate that name. My title is Criminal Investigator. But I'm not sure if that's what I want to do long-term."

"What else would you do?"

"My training is in accounting and business. I'd like to join a small company and produce something of value."

"Maybe you have a hobby or interest you could turn into a business. What do you like when you are outside of work?"

Ginny looked at the mansions up on the cliff. "You and I are not so unalike. I've always loved the beauty of classic old buildings. My Dad used to take me on walks and show me beautiful Victorian mansions. Did I tell you I visited Fort Griswold as a child when we visited Connecticut to see Aunt Julia?"

This I didn't know "So you have roots in Groton City,"

"More than you think. At one point Dad represented some clients in Groton City, but he only practices in Rhode Island now."

We sat on a stone retaining wall allowing our legs to dry in the sun. "Why'd he give up practice in Connecticut?" I asked.

Ginny turned to me with her eyes large and sad. "Franklin, this is something I've never told anyone. He was having an affair with someone in Groton City."

"Wow. That must have been awful for your mom. How did you find out?"

"I heard them fighting about it at the time. They must have worked it out because he stopped working out-of-state and they seem happy together."

When the sun dried us we put on our clothes over the bathing suits and climbed back into the Toyota. I was content as only an afternoon at the beach can produce, slightly sun burnt but relaxed.

Ginny backtracked through Newport and continued west on 138 until we had retraced our route across the bridges. She headed south on route 1 headed for the Rhode Island south shore. We were going in the general direction of Block Island. "I have something else to show you."

I was expecting some tourist destination and was surprised when Ginny pulled up to a three-story stick style Victorian cottage on a salt marsh outside of the quaint little village of Snug Harbor. "Nice house, who does it belong to?" I asked.

"This is my parents' summer home. It's another of my favorite places."

"So I'm going to meet the parents?" I got out of the car, a little self-conscious in my faded jeans, beach shirt, and sneakers.

Ginny grabbed a large bag from the cargo area, threw it to me, and took a second for herself. "Dad wants to meet you, but not today. He and Mom are on their way back from a trip to Europe and won't be home until tomorrow. Tonight we have the place to ourselves."

In hindsight it was the comment about her dad wanting to meet me I should have paid attention to. Instead I focused on the possibilities created by a night alone with Ginny in a romantic beachfront home.

Chapter 25

I stood in front of the French doors leading to the porch and stared at the salt marsh, but my thoughts were on the woman inside. It was a shock to realize how fast my suspicions about Ginny's motives were fading. She was confident and beautiful, but at the same time she was vulnerable, thoughtful and warm. I didn't mind that she was probably smarter than me and definitely into being in charge.

Thinking of smart strong women produced a twinge of guilt over where I'd left things with Linda. I had thought someone as beautiful as Linda falling for me was an inexplicable stroke of good luck that would last forever. Our adolescent lust hadn't been enough to sustain the relationship through the stresses of adult life. That thought was almost sobering enough to make me reconsider what I was planning to do with Ginny but I resolved to start with unbridled lust and work out the rest later.

"I've lost you again, haven't I?" Ginny stood in front of me with her torso wrapped in a bath towel. The top edge was rolled at her chest, leaving her arms and shoulders bare, and a tantalizing slit at her side. "What were you thinking about, our mystery?"

I crossed the few steps between us, put my arms around her and ran my hands over the soft cotton. There was definitely nothing but skin under the towel. "A different mystery, I was thinking about you."

Ginny looked up with a confused expression. She reached up, put her bare arms around my neck and pressed against me. "I know. This is so complicated. There is so much you don't know about me. And I really know so little about you."

"Careful, flattery goes right to my head."

She shook her head pushed me toward the porch. "We need to talk about us, but later. Go work on the other mystery while I shower. There is only one bathroom and you get the second shift. Then I'm going to show you the best seafood on the coast."

Ginny disappeared behind the bathroom door. Soon the sound of running water and soft singing drifted out. To distract myself from a hunger that had nothing to do with food, I grabbed a pad of paper from the counter and headed out to the porch to work out my next moves on the Old Victorian.

First I made a call. "Hi, Dad, how are you?"

"Hi, Frank. I was thinking about you. Where are you?"

"In Rhode Island with Ginny. I won't be home tonight, don't worry."

"I have news for you. I may have solved part of your mystery."

"Great, what part did you solve?"

"Remember you asked me if I knew Miranda Murphy?"

"Yes, so?"

"Well, I figured it out. I knew I had heard that name before."

"So tell me, who is she?"

"The semester you were away at school full-time a local girl ran away to marry some guy who lied to her about his name and a wife back at home. She returned in a few months. She had taken the name Miranda Murphy, but she reverted back to her maiden name after she returned to Groton City. Your Miranda Murphy is Mandy Smith."

That made sense. The bag I found with the envelope addressed to Miranda Murphy was on the ground near where Mandy had been parked. "Who was the guy?"

Dad laughed. "I don't have a name. Rumor has it he was an out-of-state businessman. Apparently he'd been looking for a summer romance with a much younger woman and dumped Mandy in the fall."

We agreed to talk tomorrow and signed off. Thanks to Dad I knew who had ordered the smart phone, but that knowledge didn't move me closer to a solution.

Ginny emerged from the bathroom brushing her hair. "You look like you won a lottery but can't find the ticket. What's up?"

"I talked to Dad. He remembered who Miranda Murphy is. I know her."

Ginny put down the hair brush. "Who is she?"

"Mandy Smith, Steve's daughter." I repeated what Dad told me about her situation.

"So it was her mail you picked up in the parking lot. Isn't Mandy the one Marti described as a notorious flirt who is after you?"

"Marti told you about Mandy's flirting and you remembered?"

"I'm interested in anyone who flirts with my new boyfriend." The words popped out of her lips. From the stricken look on her face, the admission was unplanned.

She considered me a boyfriend. This was far more interesting news than the identity of Miranda Murphy.

"So Mandy or Miranda bought the Smart Phone. She seems an unlikely choice for murderer. What if she bought it for someone else?" she asked.

"Let's get back to the part about me being your boyfriend."

"Focus, Franklin. I'm thinking her sleazy ex-husband bought her the phone. What do you know about him?"

"Not much. He wasn't a local but maybe I can find out from Mandy when we get back to Groton City."

"Shall I interview her?" Ginny offered.

I smiled at the thought of the two pretty women going at it. "No, I'll call. She's more likely to open up to me."

Ginny crinkled her nose. "That's what I'm afraid of."

I had another thought. "Doesn't this move Steve up on the list of people who could be the mastermind behind the Monument

Condominiums project? If Steve had access to the phone, the files we found show that he is up to his neck in another real estate fraud."

Ginny agreed. I headed to the bathroom for my shower. I was behind the frosted glass door when Ginny entered the room with a pile of clothes. "Try these o they're my dad's. You two are about the same size and these are more appropriate for dining out."

After a day out in the sun the shower felt great. I emerged energized and ready to take on what promised to be an interesting evening.

We took a left exit off Route 1 south, doubled back north-bound for about 100 feet, whipped across two lanes and exited onto Succotash Road headed for Jerusalem and Snug harbor. A couple of miles down the fork to Jerusalem a nondescript one-story gray rambling shack was nestled between the two-lane road and a salt marsh. The parking lot was paved with crushed oyster shells.

The Matunuck Fish Factory was still busy even off-season. We were escorted to a table next to the oyster raw bar and on a direct route to the kitchen. A half-dozen skinny waitresses pounded the bouncy floor carrying full platters and drink glasses from the kitchen to the patrons.

At least forty different conversations were in progress around us. Locals talked about what pains tourists were. The few late season tourists talked about food and the deserted beaches. We started with glasses of a sweet Riesling wine from a vineyard in Newport and fresh bread. We followed up with broiled oysters in a peppery, buttery broth.

Ginny and I spent the evening filling in more of the gaps in our stories. I told her how hard things were after Washington Way nearly bankrupted my parents. She described her college life and a little about her parents' careers. She was looking forward to introducing me to them.

The main courses arrived: broiled scallops for Ginny and haddock for me. Both were fresh and cooked to perfection, no longer transparent and not dry. Each was freckled with fresh herbs and a touch of butter and spices.

The coffee and dessert after the meal were as good as the fish. We split a chocolate brownie sundae with whipped cream drizzled with chocolate and Kahlua. We picked at the brownie and dueled with spoons for the last blob of cream and smear of chocolate.

The meal was the perfect prelude to a romantic evening with Ginny. Before hitting the road we ambled through the village, watching fishermen as they unloaded their catch, mended gear, and readied their boats for the night. We finally climbed into Ginny's SUV and drove back to the Maxwell home.

By the time we got back Ginny seemed to have made up her mind about us. She was so filled with pent up sexual tension that we didn't make it into the house before we were wrapped in each other's arms, kissing and groping. I had the car seat reclined and her blouse unbuttoned when a pair of headlights lit up the rear window.

I glanced uncomfortably at the vehicle behind us. "Is there an ordinance against making out in this town?"

Ginny giggled and discreetly buttoned up her blouse before she straightened up. She looked in the mirror. Pink splotches began to appear on her neck and face.

"It's not the police. I think someone wants to park here."

"Who would want to park in your parent's drive?"

I opened the door. The car behind us shut off the engine. The waning daylight was bright enough to illuminate the occupants, a middle aged man and women. Their probable identity slowly came to me.

Ginny's joy overcame her embarrassment. She hopped out, ran to the vehicle and practically jumped into the driver's arms. "Dad, you're back! How was Europe?"

Ginny released her father, ran to the other side of the car and hugged her mother. Max Maxwell climbed out and spotted me. Ginny stopped chattering with her mother long enough to make introductions. Apparently I was her friend.

Max pressed the trunk release and appraised my outfit. "You have good taste in clothes. You don't have a bad back?"

"Back's fine. Can I help you bring anything in?"

Apparently a European vacation required a lot of luggage. Max and I each picked up two bags leaving several behind.

Ginny's mother, Veronica, gestured toward a small guest room. "You can drop the bags in there for now."

I persuaded the family to retire to the living room while I unloaded the rest of the bags. The latch on one bag wouldn't close properly because of a bent hinge. I made a quick repair with the pocket multi-tool I always keep handy. Ginny's Dad crossed the doorway with drinks and noticed my efforts.

"Hey, you're pretty handy. I had no idea where to get that fixed." He flexed the repaired latch. "It looks good as new." He clapped me on the shoulder. "Leave this stuff for now and join us for a drink. You are probably going to hear everything about our trip twice, so you may as well get the first telling out of the way now."

Max and I grabbed glasses and a bottle of wine from the refrigerator and joined the ladies. "Veronica, remember that bag that broke in France? Franklin fixed it."

After expressions of gratitude from Dr. Veronica, and an award-winning smile from Ginny, we settled down to hear about the four-city, four-week vacation. Venice was Veronica's favorite but Max liked Zurich the best. As the session reached the two-hour mark, yawns circulated around the room and Ginny's Mom adjourned the bull session. "Come along, Max, let the young people have some time alone. We need to turn in."

"Mom, we had a pretty full day too, we won't be up long."

Veronica looked at the bags. "If you and Franklin bring the bags upstairs, I'll get the sheets for the pull out bed in the couch."

Ginny and I obediently gathered the bags and made a couple of trips up the stairs distributing them. On our last trip Ginny pointedly took the bag she had carried in from her Toyota and moved it from the master bedroom to a very girlish looking little room with pink print wallpaper and white furniture. Seeing my expression she laughed and gave me a hug and a smile.

"You probably guessed that we won't be sleeping together tonight. I'm so sorry, but my folks are a little old-fashioned and I wouldn't feel right."

Ginny helped me make up the sofa bed downstairs. Her parents had already turned in for the night. She lingered and kissed me softly. I could be wrong, but she seemed conflicted about leaving. When we finally pulled apart she left, trailing her fingers along my hand until she could no longer reach.

Despite my unfulfilled need, the night sounds of the marsh lulled me into a deep sleep. Almost before I knew it, the sun was above the reeds in the salt marsh and my cell phone was ringing. I picked up the persistent device, and took the call. "Hello?"

Albert sounded on the verge of panic. "Franklin, we have big problems."

Chapter 26

The Sunday morning sun painted a silver trail on the marsh as I tried to clear the fog from my brain. Across the water a small boat approached the narrow passage out to Narragansett Bay. I focused on the cell phone in my hand.

"What's up Albert?"

"Mom, Marti, and I had supper at Parthenon Pasta here in Groton City last night. We were on the patio overlooking the river when Linda and Bobby Lester came in."

A sleek boat with enormous motors on the stern crossed the channel in the distance. "I'm not all that happy about her hanging around with Bobby, but it is her business. She made it pretty clear that she is done with me."

"Franklin, will you listen? The problem is not Bobby and Linda, but what we found when we returned home."

Albert loves to stretch out a story, so I waited for him to continue.

"There was a message on our answering machine. The caller demanded that we return the phone and money we took from the Monument Parcel. He threatened Mom and Marti if we didn't comply."

"What's that got to do with Linda and Bobby?"

"I used my tools to trace the call. It came from Linda's phone. Franklin, is she selling us out?"

Whatever was going on between Linda and Bobby, she would never do anything to harm Albert, his family, or me for that matter. Whoever made that call, it was probably without her knowledge. I hoped that was the case.

"Stay cool. There must be an explanation. I'll call Linda, find out what's going on and get back to you."

I dialed Linda's cell phone but the call was forwarded directly to voice-mail. I left a message for her to call.

While I waited for Linda to call back, I staggered into the Maxwell's kitchen looking for a reviving cup of coffee. I primed the coffeemaker and soon the dark liquid dripped into the carafe and the welcome smell of fresh coffee filled the house. I poured the energizing stuff into a brightly colored mug.

It was a cool morning and I was still in sleeping shorts and a tee shirt but I headed out on the screen porch. I sat on the two-person glider and put my feet up to watch the marsh and think about Albert's call. Who cared enough about a hundred dollars and a broken smart phone to threaten Albert's family? These items must be clues to a secret that the owners couldn't risk coming to light. My plan to identify the mastermind was working, but not the way I'd hoped.

A few minutes later Ginny came up behind me, wrapped in a blanket with a steaming cup in her hand. She put the cup on a table, sat next to me on the glider, and wrapped us in the blanket. She gave me the kind of kiss that I would like to begin every day with for the rest of my life.

"How was the sofa? Did you sleep?"

"Better than I expected. The missing dessert aside, I had a great time yesterday."

"Who were you talking to earlier?"

The news from Albert alarmed Ginny. "This could be bad. We hoped to contain our interaction with the mastermind by making him come to the store, but he's taken it out in the open."

"I'm waiting for Linda to call back so I can find out who may have used her phone to leave the message."

"And we'd better figure out who's behind the threats before they act on them."

In the distance a hawk was working the marsh. Ginny was right that using the phone as bait to flush out the mastermind behind the Monument Condominiums development wasn't working. The prey hadn't come to the lure—he was hunting us.

Ginny stared up at the clouds, deep in concentration. "Our problem is that we have multiple crimes and suspects. We're pretty sure that Steve, Victor, Tony, and Robert Caspar were involved in the real estate frauds, but nothing suggests that they're murders. We're still not sure if Caspar is alive or dead. If he is dead, we still don't know if it was natural causes or murder. Joe's dead, but the cause is unclear in his case too. What a mess!"

I agreed. "Let's simplify things. Assume that Joe and Caspar were murdered and that their deaths were related to the two real estate frauds. What big secret is worth killing over, twice, and related to the smart phone and the hundred-dollar bill?"

Ginny looked out over the marsh. "It's the money. That is what it's been from the start."

"The phone is probably the link to the money and the identity of the person who is controlling it. We should get Albert to take a closer look at it."

"Right. Whoever has been laundering the money over the years has gone through a lot of trouble to stay anonymous. His identity might also be worth killing over."

"I could threaten to reveal what's in the files to get Steve and his cronies to help us uncover the mastermind."

"Don't do it, Franklin. Promise you won't use the threat of Joe's files to extort information out of anyone again. Tell them you don't have the files. Someone killed over what was in those files and you could be next."

Veronica Maxwell stepped out onto the porch before I could reply.

"Hi, honey," Veronica said to Ginny. She settled in a wicker chair. The steaming cup in her hand indicated that she too had located the coffee. "Good morning Franklin. Did Ginny tell you we're having an anniversary party at the house tomorrow evening? You'll come, won't you?"

"There is something I need to do back in Groton City, but I'll come back if I can."

Max Maxwell said he had some overdue business to deal with and left before breakfast. I took my phone and wandered along the salt marsh. Gulls were diving on bait fish stranded by the tide as I called Mandy Smith's number.

"Franklin, are you calling to take me up on my offer for some tandem cooking?"

"No. I'm calling because I found a bag you dropped outside the supermarket."

"I wondered where that was. How'd you know it was mine?"

"I found a letter inside addressed to Miranda Murphy. That's you, isn't it?"

"How'd you know? I haven't used that name for a long time."

"Why did you use it in the first place?"

"I was in high school and having a fling with an older guy who was married. We invented Miranda Murphy so no one would find out about us."

"I'm sorry that someone used you like that."

"Are you crazy? I loved him. If Joe hadn't paid me a visit and threatened to destroy the guy I would never have broken up with him."

More of Joe's meddling. "Did your friend give you a phone?"

"That was years ago. I gave it back to him."

"Why are you still getting bills from the phone company?"

"Those are advertisements—once on a mailing list always on the list."

"Mandy, this is really important. Will you tell me the guy's name?"

The line was silent for a long time. "I don't want to make any trouble for him."

"Will you at least tell me when you heard from him last?"

217

"I guess that won't hurt. He called a couple of days ago and asked me to pick up a phone at Silicon Shack. He said something about it being lost and found."

I thought about what I could say to Mandy that wouldn't break any confidences or worse, endanger her. "Don't do it. That phone may be evidence of a crime and you could get caught up in it," I warned.

She argued, but Mandy agreed to keep away from the phone. She didn't promise not to call her former lover right away and alert him, which she probably planned to do.

Linda still hadn't returned my call by the middle of the afternoon. Bright sun had warmed the chilly fall air. The surface of Ninigret Pond sparkled as we packed for the return trip to Groton City. I'd put my phone on the seat of the Toyota while we loaded. It rang. Ginny picked it up and answered.

"Oh Albert, we were expecting a call from Linda. Is everything okay?"

"Ask him if he has he heard from her," I said.

Ginny disregarded my question and listened. "Why would Franklin have checked his mailbox? It's Sunday and he's with me in Rhode Island."

I heard the buzz of Albert's voice but couldn't make out the words. Ginny turned pale. "Oh my God. Your family? And Franklin's too? No? What?" Her eyes opened wide and she put her free hand on my arm in a consoling gesture.

Ginny's reaction made me think something very bad had happened. My heart pounded. "Ginny, put him on speaker."

She ignored me again and continued. "How did they know where you live?"

Something happened at Albert's house. "What happened?" I demanded.

Ginny listened without responding to my question. I threw the last bag into the Toyota. Had the person who left the phone threat yesterday followed through? "Ginny, what's going on?"

She continued speaking into the phone as if I wasn't in front of her having an anxiety attack. "Then someone told them. Could it be Linda?"

"You're right, Bobby Lester is a better guess," she said. "One more thing, check that smart phone for anything like bank codes. I have a hunch."

I thought my head would explode. I was ready to wrestle the phone from her hand when Ginny reacted to the frustration on my face. "Do you want to talk to Franklin? No? Okay. We're on our way. Yes, we'll check on his parents."

Ginny disconnected and handed me the phone. "Albert had to go. He called to say he received another threatening note and pictures of his family entering church today."

"What did the note say?"

"He is to convince you to back off on the investigation of Joe's death, return Joe's files, and give back the cell phone you guys found. Otherwise your families will get hurt."

If their aim was to worry me it worked. "Let's go back to Groton City after I check on my parents."

I called home. "Dad, is anything in the mailbox?"

"On Sunday? Okay, hold on. I'll go and check."

A couple of minutes later Dad reported in from the curbside. "Nope, nothing there. Is there something in particular you're looking for?"

"It's something related to my investigation of Joe's death. Albert and I have tripped into some kind of hornets' nest."

"What do you want me to do?"

"Stay at home and wait for me. I'm coming back and we'll work something out."

Ginny heard the whole conversation. "I'll drive you back to Groton City.

"What about your parents' anniversary party?"

"I'll get you home to keep the families safe. After I drop you off I'll come back to Charlestown. If you work things out in Groton City you can come back for the party."

The familiar feel of my Leatherman's tool on my belt was

missing. I'd left it next to the sofa. I sprinted back inside to retrieve it. While hurrying down narrow hallway decorated with dozens of framed photos, I knocked loose a small picture. I caught the frame before it hit the floor, and stood there gasping. In my hand was the original of the picture I'd found on Joe's roof. The face of the fourth person was clear. It was Ginny's father, Max Maxwell.

Chapter 27

The next hour felt like one of those dreams where something is chasing you and your feet are stuck in quicksand. There was an accident on the highway, so Ginny took coastal Route 1 all the way back Groton City. The little hamlets of Rhode Island's South County whipped by, punctuated by stretches of forests strung out like green dashes.

Ginny respected my silence, probably thinking that worry about the threats had me preoccupied. But it was the photo that was on my mind. What kind of a game was Ginny playing with me? There was proof that her father was present at the dedication of the original Washington Way project. Ginny had to know he was in that picture. That explained why she was so upset when I showed her the copy from Joe's roof. Why hadn't she told me? The obvious answer was that she was collecting anything that would connect her father to my investigation.

I would wait for her to show her hand. In the meantime I would keep her ignorant of my plans to keep the families safe.

We tried the highway again once we were back in Connecticut. Passed the Mystic exits the travel lanes were packed again. We exited at the Clarence B. Sharp highway and drove to my house. When we arrived I knew what to do.

"Ginny, head back to Rhode Island to be with your folks. With luck I'll make the anniversary party."

"Are you sure you don't want me to stay?"

"I need to take care of this alone. I'll call."

She drove off.

Before I entered the house I wandered around the back and made a phone call to the Birchwood Inn Bed and Breakfast in Barnstable, on Cape Cod. I had helped the owners of the romantic 1853 Queen Anne Victorian recreate the original wood molding in the public areas. The owner greeted me fondly and confirmed a reservation for a late arrival tonight at deeply discounted rates. Next I called my friend Eric, the only person I knew who had a van the size of a bus and would be willing to take a trip on short notice.

"Eric, it's Franklin. How's it going?"

"Hey man, great. What's up?"

"I need to get Marti, Albert's mother, and my folks out of town quietly for a week or so. How would you like to take a vacation out on the Cape? All you need to do is chauffeur them around for a week or so."

"I assume you guys don't want the parents' house for a wild party or you would have invited me. What's up?"

"Some very nasty guys are angry with Albert and me. We want the family out of reach in case they decide to make good on threats to hurt them."

"You got it, man. I'll ask Amy to run the gym for the week. How do we slip away without your bad guys noticing?"

"Be parked in the loading zone behind Five Brothers Pizza and Grill on Fort Street at 7:30 tonight. We'll be inside eating. Albert and I'll leave at 8:00 and lure any watchers away. The families will come out to you at 8:30 on the hidden side of the van. My mom will have the instructions, credit cards, and reservations."

"How will we keep in touch?"

"Call me on my cell phone. In case someone is listening in, don't say where you are, and don't leave messages, keep calling until I pick up."

"Okay. See you then. And, Franklin, watch your back."

Albert picked up my call on the second ring. He agreed to get his mom and Marti on board with the plan.

Next I needed to convince my family to go along. That was a job best done in person. I stepped inside and found Mom reading in the living room.

"Mom, how would you and Dad like to get a way for a week or so as an early anniversary gift? This time of year you have the beaches to yourselves, the best seats at movie theatres, and shopping without the crowds. The owners of a nice little bed and breakfast owe me a favor and will be putting you up."

It took a little persuasion but I sealed the deal with Mom as Dad entered the room.

"You two look like that couple who conspired to knock over the casino. What are you up to?"

Mom explained that I was sending them on a mini vacation. "An early anniversary present," she repeated.

Dad could say no to my mother no easier that I could to Linda or Ginny. "We need to be ready by 7:00 tonight? Well, I guess we should get ready, Barbara."

Mom and Dad climbed upstairs to pack. I checked in with Albert. Good news—Mom Henley and Marti agreed to go.

I described a little diversion I had worked out. "Bring the smart phone and I'll bring the hundred. We're going to use the promise of a return of their stuff to lure the crooks away while the folks leave for their vacation."

"We aren't going to give the phone back are we?"

"Why not? We have all the information we need, and it is their stuff technically."

I didn't know how to reach the persons making the threat but I had an idea. I used 411 connect to get the number for Bennett Demolition. A machine picked up. I left a message.

"This is Franklin Breault. Look, Albert and I don't want any more trouble. Tell whoever wants the stuff we found in the woods to meet us at the Bowling Center in Groton City at 9:00 p.m.

tonight and we'll give it all back." I tried to sound scared, which wasn't difficult under the circumstances.

Minutes later Bennett called back.

"The boss says I should pick up the stuff tonight at 9:00. No Cops, no funny business. He says screw this up and someone is going to get hurt."

I called Albert. "The mastermind is sending Bennett to meet us tonight. See you at the restaurant at 7:00."

I spent the next hour trying to figure out how Ginny and Max could fit into Joe's death. He must have uncovered a connection between Max and the real estate scams. Ginny was too young to have participated in the earlier fraud, so it was more likely that she was helping her dad cover his tracks.

"Dad, Mom, come on! We need to be going." It was only 6:30 but their dawdling was driving me crazy.

Dad motioned toward two old-fashioned suitcases. "Relax son, we're almost ready. Why don't you bring these bags out while I see what is holding up your mother?"

Judging from the weight of the suitcases, my parents were prepared for any weather conditions. I loaded the bags and closed the trunk while the car was still in the garage.

"Dad, I'm going to drive over in my truck. See you there."

I pulled out on the street, backed in front of the next house, and waited. The garage door rose. Mom was in the driver's seat. Dad was riding shotgun beside her. She backed into the driveway and stopped. She juggled her keys, adjusted every mirror on the vehicle although they were exactly where she left them. She checked her makeup in the visor mirror.

I banged the steering wheel of my truck. "Come on!"

Mom pressed the remote and sat there watching until the door was fully closed.

By the time Mom started down the street I was so agitated that I nearly ran into her back bumper at the stop sign at the end of the street. I couldn't shake the feeling that bad guys with baseball bats were hiding around every corner.

I took three deep breaths and gave Mom a half block head start while watching to see if anyone followed her. I drove toward Main Street checking my mirror every thirty seconds. The traffic was light—there were no vehicles between us. When we reached the restaurant, I drove by, continued about a half mile up the street, and pulled into the Quick Mart. I swiped my credit card, pumped some gas, and watched for anyone taking an interest in me or the truck. The pump dispensed slowly, but eventually it clicked off. I hung up the pump, took my receipt and climbed back in the cab. My cell phone rang.

"It's Eric. I got here early. Your folks are in the restaurant. No sign of any followers."

With phase one complete, I drove down the street toward the Henleys'. Albert met me at the curb and quickly hopped inside. As we pulled away, I checked the rear view mirror and saw Mom Henley and Marti pull out and head in the opposite direction. Albert and I cruised up toward the Queen Anne and parked in front of the old building, waiting for Eric to give us the all clear.

Eric called. "Everyone is inside." We headed for the restaurant.

We pushed a couple of tables together to accommodate the families.

"Hi. I'm Suzy, your server. Welcome to Five Brothers Pizza. Can I get drinks for anyone?"

It is not like we don't know Suzy, she attended school with us, but the owner makes her go through the whole script with every customer. Suzy started to chat up the parents. She complimented Mom and Mrs. Henley on their dresses. She flirted shamelessly with Dad, incorrectly assuming that he would decide on her tip tonight. I looked around the restaurant; we were the only customers, not a surprise for a Sunday evening. Finally the drink orders were collected and Suzy took her irritatingly cheerful self back behind the bar.

Marti put her hand on my arm. "Franklin, relax. I've never seen the two of you so wired up for a night out." Knowing Albert, he had probably filled Marti in about the true nature of the evening.

"Thanks Marti, but it is not the night out that has me worried."

My mood was not merely showing, but contagious. I had feared that the enthusiasm of Dad and Mrs. Henley for this vacation would spill over into a loud celebration that would call unnecessary attention to us. Instead, everyone was sitting around looking like they were at a funeral.

Dad leaned across the table toward me. "So Frank, tell us about this fantastic place we're going,"

I nearly choked on my soda.

Albert recovered first. "Mr. Breault, it's kind of a secret and we don't want to talk about this in public. Tonight we're a group of friends having dinner."

Dad looked bewildered and hurt. He scanned the empty restaurant, catching Suzy's eye. "Who is going to overhear us, Suzy? Who is she going to tell? No one even knows we're here."

Half an hour later a pizza and platters of French fries arrived. The parents dug in with gusto. Marti, Albert and I were too agitated to eat.

By 8:30 I couldn't stand the wait any longer. "You guys take your time and finish up. Look for Eric's van when you leave, and for God's sake get into the van quickly and go. I'm going to pay for the meal before we leave. Albert and I have a place to be in a couple of minutes." I pushed my chair back and started to stand.

Bam! crash! Albert and I dove in front of our families. *Gunshots!*

"Oh I'm so sorry," squeaked a contrite voice behind me. Suzy was standing in a puddle and dripping with diet soda. I had backed my chair into her. The pitcher and soda were scattered around the floor. Another time I might have enjoyed the wet t-shirt effect, but at that moment my heart was pounding in my ears so loudly that I could hardly hear her stammered apology. "I didn't mean to startle you."

So much for a quiet exit. I apologized for knocking the pitcher out of Suzy's hands and asked her to get the bill for me. She kept saying she was sorry. Probably she was mostly sorry that the only job she could get after high school involved being drenched with diet soda by jumpy customers.

Suzy left to find the bill. Albert stared at me. "Man, you are wired. Are you sure you don't want me to drive?"

Dad looked concerned. "Frank, the way you are acting makes me think that there's more to this than an anniversary trip. What's really going on?"

Everyone was looking at me. They deserved an explanation. I explained that the crooks behind Washington Way were at it again, and they had made threats to protect their secret. "We're going to try to work things out, or get them all locked up and the money back. It'll be easier to resolve this if we know all of you are safe."

Dad, mom, and Mrs. Henley all started talking at once. "What about you and Albert, will you be safe?" asked Mom.

I explained that Albert and I planned to leave the family with their meal and drive off toward the bowling alley and return some things to the bad guys. "We'll straighten everything out while you are having a nice mini vacation."

The storm door creaked as we stepped outside. Eric was sitting in the van. We made eye contact and he nodded. My cell phone rang shortly after Albert and I got into my truck.

"All is quiet out here. I haven't seen anyone who looks out of place," said Eric.

We didn't spot anyone following us on the ten-minute drive to the bowling alley either. Maybe all the precautions were unnecessary. Albert checked that the cell phone was still in his pocket and I fingered the hundred-dollar bill that Nora gave me. Ginny still had the bill Albert removed from the briefcase so I planned to give Nora's hundred to Bennett.

We climbed out, approached the neon-trimmed entrance, and pushed through the glass doors into the foyer. The place smelled of dust, talcum powder, and beer in the carpeted areas around the bar. We trudged toward the registration desk at the far end beyond the pro shop.

Behind the counter a bored looking middle-aged man, with a two bowling ball sized gut, was spraying a pair of shoes with deodorant. We didn't expect Bennett for at least forty-five minutes so we decided to bowl a string to kill time. We rented shoes and signed up for a lane.

Anyone looking would have been able to tell that we don't spend a lot of time doing this sort of thing. Albert quickly figured out the electronic scoring program and typed us into the system. When the game started our amateur status showed. For a sport that looked so easy, we left lots of pins standing after our allotted rolls.

Albert made a particularly bad roll and left half the pins standing. "Bowling is so much easier on an electronic game."

Still, tossing sixteen-pound bowling balls and knocking down pins calmed us. As we were discussing a second game my cell phone rang.

"Everyone is on board and accounted for. We're on the interstate and there are no bad guys in sight. Our ETA on the Cape is 11:45 p.m. Do you want me to call you when we get there or in the morning?"

"Thanks, Eric. We're okay too. Call me in the morning."

We decided to have mercy on the equipment and skipped the second game. We returned the shoes, paid for the games, and headed for the side door. It was quiet at this end of the lanes, with all the bowling taking place at the far end.

Albert pulled open the door to the breezeway that separated the lanes from the outside. Bennett stepped into the foyer from the outside. In the little room he looked even bigger and more muscular than I remembered. "How come your boss didn't come himself?" I asked.

"He sent me. You're not the only one twisting my arm these days, so give me what you have and be quick about it."

I studied Bennett carefully. For a big guy he looked scared. It wasn't us he was afraid of, so what? "The police are looking for you. You nearly ran us and a cop down a few days ago."

Bennett scowled. "I was doing my job. I didn't know anyone was on that road until the cops stopped by my place."

"What about now? Is your new job threatening our families?" I knew provoking him was risky, but I needed to know how much he knew.

Bennett looked from Albert to me and back. His expression was genuine surprise. "What are you talking about? After you called I passed your message along to my project manager and I got a text that said to pick up whatever stuff you had. That's all."

"Who is the project manager?" Albert asked.

"The big money guy behind Monument Condominiums. I've never met him. He sent Steve, Tony, and me special phones that he uses to send text messages and e-mail."

Albert took one look at Bennett's expression and whipped the phone out of his pocket and handed it over. "We found this one. Sorry, it's broken. We were looking for the owner."

Bennett turned it over in his hand. He pressed the power button. Nothing.

Bennett looked at Albert and scowled. "Where did you get this?"

"In the woods up behind the old Queen Anne. Someone must have dropped it and it got wet."

Bennett dropped the phone in his pocket with a quizzical expression like this isn't what he expected. He turned to me. "I warned you to keep out of the Monument Parcel."

"Look, let's get this done. Here. We found a hundred-dollar bill up there too."

Bennett took the bill and held it up to the light. "Is that it? What about the files?"

"What part about broken don't you understand? If there are files on this phone I haven't seen them," I said. It was a bit of a shock how easy the lie came out.

In a change that would have done a chameleon proud, the blood drained from Victor's normally florid skin. In a quick motion he grabbed my collar and lifted me toward the ceiling.

Albert sprang forward and received a blow from a massive fist. As my friend fell like a stone, Bennett banged me against the wall. "The boss said if I got his stuff you'd give me Joe's files."

He shook me like an empty box of cereal with one hand and waved the hundred in the other. "I want an end to the blackmail."

With a bone-jarring thump he slammed me into the wall again. I felt every bump and angle in the woodwork, as he knocked the breath out of me. He did it effortlessly. I understood why he hadn't hit me earlier. I wasn't worth the trouble to him.

"I don't know what you think you know, but you are not going to shake me down like Joe did. I want all the files."

I tried to tell Bennett that I really didn't have anything to blackmail him with, but he had knocked the wind out of me, and I only managed a croak. He released my shirt and I fell to the floor next to Albert. There was a tone of desperation in Bennett's voice as he strode out the door. "I can't have the money man and you blackmailing me. I'll go crazy."

Albert was groaning and holding his stomach. I had a lump the size of a golf ball on the back of my head.

"Are you okay?" I asked.

"It only hurts when I breathe."

"I'm sorry, Albert. I thought the money and the phone were what he wanted."

"What was that about blackmail?"

"Joe was shaking him and Tony and Steve down over some scam they pulled a while back. He thinks I have the files."

Albert let out a croak that sounded like a laugh. "I wonder how he got that idea."

"I'm sorry, man."

"Why can't you use what's in the files to protect us?"

"I know that they exist, but I don't have them."

We staggered back to the truck and climbed in. I had a pretty bad case of the shakes as I drove us back to my place. Albert still looked a little green around the edges. I didn't want him staying alone in the empty bungalow. "Why don't you stay at my place tonight? You can have the couch."

As we descended the steps toward my kitchen, Albert looked more thoughtful than scared, which under the circumstances was impressive. "Bennett is really going to be mad when he finds out about the smart phone."

"What about the smart phone?"

"The one I gave him is a dud I took back under the warranty. Theirs is still in the shop."

Save me from clever friends.

Chapter 28

Muted sunlight, aching muscles and heavy traffic filled with drivers on their way to work signaled the arrival of Monday morning. Aspirin dulled the pain but nothing seemed to mute the anger Albert and I felt as a consequence of being beat up by Victor. We were determined to make the bastard pay next time we met.

At first I was furious that Albert substituted another cell phone, but he was right. There was something on the phone we hadn't found that they were after. The leverage that information provided may be the only thing keeping us alive.

I had a second thought. The information in Joe's files could also provide us with protection. I needed to find them and use the contents to keep the crooks in line.

The first time I thought of using Joe's files it had shocked me. I had a relatively simple take on secrets, lies, deception, and blackmail. None of them was worth the effort. Own up to what you'd done and fix it if you could, otherwise take your lumps. Unless they directly affected me, other people's secrets were of no interest. It wasn't that I was an ethical purist; but keeping track of my own lies seemed like a daunting task and blackmailing someone over their lies seemed like a first step down a slippery slope I wanted no part of. That was until Joe's victims decided to make their pursuit of his files a personal feud with me.

I had promised Eric that I would call Amy first thing Monday morning to make sure she was okay. I reached her at the gym.

"Hi, Franklin. Yeah, I miss him but everything is fine. There was one thing. Linda called this morning."

Cold chills ran down my spine. "What did she want?"

"She asked if I knew where Marti is."

The hair on my neck stiffened. "What did you tell her?"

"I told her she is with your folks and Eric on the Cape. I know it is a secret but I can tell Linda, right?"

The pencil I'd been holding broke in two pieces. Amy may as well have put it on a billboard. "Did you tell her where on the Cape?"

"I couldn't, Eric didn't tell me."

Thank God I asked Eric not to mention the name of the B&B. After I signed off with Amy I was still uneasy.

Minutes later Eric verified that everything was quiet in vacation land.

"Eric, stay alert. Linda is looking for Marti, and a call to Linda is a call to Bobby."

"Right. I'll tell everyone to be careful with the phones."

By noon Albert and I were feeling well enough to be hungry. We treated ourselves to lunch by the harbor. The Sea Skate Bar and Grill is located in a shack down by the marina. It is a utilitarian building with no recognizable style except weathered New England coastal shack. The place was noisy and cramped but the food was good and cheap. The waitress placed a couple of beers and two giant plates of fish and chips on the table. Soon we were feeling better inside and out.

After lunch we decided to collect the family cars we left at Family Pizza last night. Albert drove Mom and Dad's car back to our house while I followed in the pickup. I drove us back to the restaurant to pick up Mom Henley's car but Albert realized that his mother had taken the keys with her.

"No problem. Drive me home I'll pick up an extra set."

As soon as we turned on Hamilton something felt wrong.

Albert pointed toward his driveway. "What's that white pickup doing there?" As we got closer, the front door looked slightly ajar. "Bennett is in my house!"

Albert had the door of my truck open before we stopped.

"Wait," I grabbed Albert's arm. We needed help and I knew who could make things happen fast. I called 911 and reported the intruders. The dispatcher put me through to the local cops.

"Whatever you do, don't go inside," the operator said.

Albert and I were still furious about being sucker punched by Victor Bennett yesterday. Albert twisted out of my grip. "I'm not going to wait with some creep in my home."

My angry electronics geek friend started toward the house.

I reach behind the seat for a weapon. "Here take this." I tossed him a three-foot section of iron pipe. I grabbed a pipe for myself and followed Albert inside.

The house was a mess. The living room furniture was slashed. Albert spotted Mom Henley's favorite vase reduced to a glittering heap of shattered crystal. He let out a low guttural sound.

I motioned toward the back of the house. We held the pipes like war clubs.

The mess in the kitchen was as bad. The contents of the cupboards and canisters were piled in a heap in the middle of the floor. "Listen," I hissed.

The sound of more destruction came from the upstairs bedrooms. Quivering with rage Albert led the silent charge up the stairs. At the top of the landing he turned left and I turned right. I continued down the hall and checked his room. It was empty, so I turned back toward the stairs.

"Take this, you son of a bitch," I heard Albert shout from the other end of the hall.

The dull thud of the pipe on flesh was followed by a howl of pain and a crash. I was hoping that my friend was enjoying his revenge when Albert flew face first through the door. He hit the opposite side of the hallway with enough force to send particles of plaster raining down on the hardwood floor.

A stout man with his back toward me stepped through the doorway and stood over Albert.

The man didn't hear my approach. I swung my pipe like a golf club. The heavy metal hit the side of his ribs with a sickening crunch.

The blow took all the fight out of the intruder. He grabbed his chest, dropped to one knee, and hit the floor like a bag of wet cement.

Albert was sitting slumped against the wall with a dazed expression on his face.

He looked hurt. I dropped down on one knee and grabbed his shoulder. "Albert, are you hurt?"

"What happened?" His eyes focused on the still form next to him. "Bet I don't feel as bad as he does. I vote for kicking his ass down the stairs."

I'm about to explain the line between self-defense and manslaughter, when a flicker of light and the smells of combustion registered on my brain.

In the bedroom flames were jumping up from a heap of papers on the nightstand.

The flames licked at the curtains and sheers, took hold, and raced toward the ceiling. The heat was enough to blister the wall covering. Bits of ancient wallpaper ignited and floated across the room like a meteor shower.

"Albert, we need to get out of here. Get up and head down the stairs."

Albert tripped over the fallen intruder. I picked Albert up in a fireman's carry and staggered down the staircase and through the front door with him over my shoulder.

I sat him on the lawn, his back against a retaining wall. I called 911 again, this time to report the fire.

I was grateful to be out of the building, but dreaded what was to come next. "Stay here. I have got to get that guy out."

One of the cardinal rules about burning buildings is to not go back into them if you are lucky enough to get out the first time.

But leaving the guy I hit to an almost certain death wasn't something I could live with.

Smoke filled the upstairs hall and the high ceilings over the stairs. I reached the second floor in three jumps. My first step in the hall landed on something hard and brittle. Whatever it was crushed under my foot and sent me crashing to the floor. For a moment the wind was knocked out of me. The fall turned out to be a good thing as smoke rolled over me in angry billows.

I looked around but the intruder wasn't in the hall. Thinking that he had regained consciousness and escaped, I was about to rush back outside when I saw a hand and an arm. The guy was inside the doorway of Mom Henley's room. With no time to wonder why he would go back in there, I pulled on the hand.

The guy was limp and incredibly heavy. The smoke was now about three feet from the floor. With no way to breathe if I stood and no time for finesse, I crouched and dragged him into the hall and down the stairs. At the bottom I kept sliding him over the hardwood floor until we reached the front door. Cradling his head I rolled the unconscious man down the concrete front steps and dragged him onto the lawn before I stopped.

I coughed my way through a third 911 call to ask for an ambulance. Alerted by the smoke, a crowd gathered on the sidewalk. During the eternity it took for the fire trucks and ambulance to arrive, the flames and smoke spread until they engulfed the whole second story. The first EMT on the scene attempted to revive the guy I dragged out. His face was dirty and bloodstained from a broken nose. I hadn't taken a good look at him before but as the medic worked on him I did. To my surprise the injured man was not Victor Bennett. The bloody face on the stretcher was that of Tony Gorky, one of the original Washington Way partners and partner in the new Monument Condominium development. He was going to be out of commission for a while. He had a large lump on the side of his forehead, which seemed a little strange since I had only hit him in the ribs.

Behind the medical drama firemen methodically stretched

hoses and began to spray the flames. Two firemen used streams of water to keep the flames away from neighboring homes a mere fifty feet from each side of Albert's. A trio of firemen came from the back of the home. One had lost his helmet and his face was contorted by pain. I recognized the injured man—Steve Smith. The EMT hustled Tony into the waiting ambulance, signaled the driver to wait, and rushed over to Steve. After a quick check, he loaded Steve in the ambulance with Tony.

A second ambulance arrived. The EMT came back to check on Albert and me.

"The fireman who was injured, was that Steve?"

"You know Steve? He's a volunteer firefighter. He should have known better than to enter a burning building without gear. He fell trying to check the back stair. He lost his glasses, took in some smoke, and banged his ribs, but he'll be okay."

The EMT checked out Albert, who was still a little groggy. Something he saw in Albert's eyes worried the medic. He insisted on a trip to the hospital and called for another ambulance.

About that point I was really feeling like crap. Thanks to my investigation my best friend may have been seriously injured and his mother's house was roasting behind me. And none of this was their fight. Worse, the investigation really wasn't about avenging Joe's death, but a way for me to get the Queen Anne and my architectural license.

"So you did find another way to get me beat up after all," Albert joked weakly while the medic waited for someone to help with a stretcher.

While Albert was prepared for transport Officer Williams came over. He took a statement from Albert. "Gorky is going to be arrested," the policeman said. "We'll hold him for assault and arson. I know you're working with Ms. Maxwell and the IRS so I called her about the fire. She's on her way."

I looked at the devastation. The EMTs loaded Albert into an ambulance. "I'm sorry you got mixed up in this. We'll figure out how to fix your house."

Albert looked at the flames and smoke that were still pouring from the windows. "I think the house is too far gone, even for you. I'll be fine. Go back home and keep an eye on your parents' place. Bennett is still out there somewhere."

"Okay, Albert. Call when you're settled in." We bumped fists and they closed the ambulance doors.

The fire company did a valiant job of fighting the flames but after an hour or so it was clear they couldn't save the house. The roof collapsed, destroying anything inside that had not been broken up by Gorky. All that remained of the second floor were a few beams that looked like they were wrapped in black alligator hide.

Ginny's flashy Toyota pulled up at the end of the block. She jumped out and rushed over. On the way Officer Williams intercepted her. They talked briefly, but she only seemed to have eyes for me. She glanced at the ruin and rushed over.

I was sitting on the curb with my lungs still protesting the smoke. She knelt, hugged me, and brushed soot off my face.

"Franklin, I'm so glad you're not hurt." She held on hard for a long time.

Given what I'd discovered at her parents' house, it was difficult for me to be as spontaneously affectionate as before. If she noticed the difference, she seemed to attribute it to the shock of the fire.

"You must have broken all the speed limits between Rhode Island and Connecticut to get here so fast."

Ginny pulled back, took a deep breath. "I do that for fun. On rescue missions I can make that Toyota fly."

"I'm feeling better, and grateful that I wasn't in the car with you."

Ginny's next breath ended in a fit of coughing as a cloud of smoke drifted over us.

"Why did you go in there? You and Albert could have been killed."

"You're right. I never should have involved my friends in this.

Albert is hurt. His mother's home is destroyed. What's worse, this isn't done."

Ginny studied me. "Come on. Let's go to your place. We need to talk."

Chapter 29

Ginny followed me home and parked on the street. She was subdued as we descended to my apartment. If she was faking her concern for me, it was an Oscar-worthy performance. I had the goods on her for her deception but I still wanted to believe that her interest in me was about more than Joe's files.

What did it mean that her father was the fourth man in the picture I found on Joe's roof? Her reaction when I showed her the picture originally made it clear that she'd recognized the photo. Why hadn't she told me? If she was really playing me, why the pretext of being upset that I'd nearly been barbequed in the fire at Albert's house?

"Where are your parents?" she asked.

"They're away again for a few days." I didn't trust her enough to share the details of my protection plan.

"Franklin, I have something to tell you." We were seated in the living room. "I haven't been entirely honest with you about the reasons why I'm interested in Joe's death."

"I've known that for quite a while. I wondered how long it would take for you to tell me what is going on."

Ginny dropped her eyes to the floor. "Before my parents left for Europe, Dad had a conversation with me. He said that Joe had been blackmailing him over that affair he'd had years ago. He said it was an underage girl who threw herself at him. He knew it was

240

wrong and he broke it off. He didn't want to hurt Mom. He asked me to try to find where Joe kept his files and destroy anything Joe had that named him."

"So you were using me to get to the files. All that flirting was nothing more than manipulation."

"Oh, Franklin, it's not that simple. Yes, at first I was friendly to gain your cooperation, but then everything changed. I really fell for you."

I wondered how many times a pretty girl can dangle the same bait in front of a guy before he stops striking like a crazed bluefish. All I knew was that I had reached my limit. "Since you've been lying all along, why should I believe anything you say now? You knew that the picture from Joe's roof showed your dad. I saw the original in his house. I'll bet you removed the copy from the Library to protect him."

Ginny was crying openly now. Despite the fact that she had been manipulating and lying to me since I met her, I desperately wanted to take her in my arms. My wounded pride won the emotional tug of war. "That picture implicated your dad in Washington Way, not an affair. Either you're still playing me, or he lied to you too."

For a second Ginny looked confused. Then the revelation hit her. She stiffened. "You're right. Dad's explanations don't make sense. If I'd been thinking more like a criminal investigator and less as a daughter I would have figured that out. I'm going back to Rhode Island to confront him. I'm sorry for everything."

I didn't bother to follow her out.

Chapter 30

Ginny's FJ Cruiser was barely out of sight when my cell phone rang. The ringtone identified the caller as Linda.

"Frankie, listen. The people who own the smart phone want the real one back. And they want Joe's files. They'll hurt me if you don't give them what they want." There was the sound of Linda coughing.

"Linda, where are you? Are you hurt?" When she ignored my question and continued talking in the same dull tone I realized that I was listening to a recording. "Bring the phone and the files to the train station in Mystic and put them in the bathroom in the Visitor Center at 7:00 p.m. today. Don't bring the police or try another substitution or they will hurt me." Linda's voice was interrupted by another fit of coughing. "Go home after you drop it off. When they're sure you haven't switched phones again they will call and tell you where I'm."

At first I was too stunned for constructive action. This kind of thing didn't happen to people like me. I was still stiff and sore from being beat up by Bennett. The destruction of Albert's mother's house was all my fault for dragging him into the investigation. Worse, I'd left Linda at risk. Without Joe's files I didn't know how to save her. My guts were a tangled mix of anger and guilt.

It didn't take long to figure out what to do. First I called Julia

242

and explained about Linda. "Will you put all the files we printed from the phone in a box and bring them to the Visitor's Center? Maybe those will buy us some time."

She agreed. "I'll set up nearby and see who picks it up," she promised. "Can I give you some advice?" It was hardly a necessary question.

"Yes."

"You're going to need some help. Word has reached me that you have been using the threat of Joe's files to gain the cooperation of some of his victims. You might want to consider using the same tactic to get a posse looking for Linda."

Victor was my next call. It's not socially acceptable to start a conversation with a threat, but I was worked up way beyond polite. "Victor, Linda has been kidnapped. If you have had anything to do with this, I'll see to it that enough information on you leaks to put you in jail."

Victor issued a rapid denial, which sounded sincere. "I'd never hurt Linda. I don't want to hurt anyone. It must be the money man behind the Monument Condominiums. What do you need me to do?"

"Call in a few favors. Get your guys to check any vacant buildings. Have someone check up on the Monument Parcel. I want her found."

Next I called Steve's cell phone. He picked up on the third ring and sounded groggy. "Steve, Linda's been kidnapped. If you had anything to do with it you are going to regret it for the rest of your miserable life."

Steve groaned a reply. "Franklin, you know how I feel about Linda. It's not me. Besides, I'm sitting here with two cracked ribs and a couple of pain killers in me."

I suddenly figured out something. The guy I had hauled out from the fire at Albert's house was much bigger than the guy I'd hit. Tony Gorky hadn't crawled back into the burning room. There had been two people in the house. I'd brought out Tony, the person Albert knocked out. The guy I'd hit, the second person, was the one who hit Albert. He'd escaped, but now I knew who he was. "I guess a whack with a length of water pipe can mess you up pretty painfully."

"It sure can. I lost my glasses and you bruised a couple of my ribs..." Steve's voice trailed off realizing that he'd said too much. "Franklin, you've got to believe me. We got a call that Albert still had the phone. The guy said the house was vacant and we had to find the phone or certain information we wished to keep private was going to come out. The fire was an accident. One of the drapes fell over an old torchier lamp and caught fire."

If Steve's ribs were broken it was unlikely that he had the strength to abduct Linda. "Steve, I'm giving you one chance to save yourself. Use your lowlife contacts and find out who has Linda and where she is being kept or you're through working in this town. Call me when you have answers."

I put down the phone, consumed with guilt. I hadn't trusted Linda and left her unprotected when I sent the family off. I called the hospital where Albert was resting.

"I've got to get out of here. The bed's too short and I'm so bored I'm ready to climb the walls."

"Good. I need your help." I explained again about Linda. "You can be information central. I can't afford to have my phone going off while I'm searching so I'll block everyone except you."

"They're ready to discharge me. Pick me up and take me to Silicon Shack. I've got some equipment that may help us."

Before I made it to the car the phone rang again.

"Franklin, this is Bobby Lester."

"What do you want, Bobby?"

"The money guy behind the Monument Condominiums has Linda."

"Bobby, you are so full of crap. You're in this up to your eyeballs. If anyone has hurt her, it's you."

"You really are a dope, Franklin. Linda's only involvement was to try to make a living and to protect you. That's why they snatched her. They know she is your girl."

244

"I have never known you to stick your neck out except when it profits you. Why do you care?"

"Whatever you may think, I do care about her. I would never let anything happen to Linda."

Despite my intense dislike for Bobby, I knew he was speaking the truth. He had always wanted her. Based on my last conversation with Linda, the feeling may have become mutual. I swallowed my pride and dislike and agreed to a temporary truce.

"Okay, on this one we're on the same side. What do you suggest?"

"Let's start looking at her office. Last time I saw her that's where she was."

"We'll start there. I'll meet you about 5:00. Bring a flashlight and wear something good for crawling around in the dark." I had a few ideas where Linda might be and an extra pair of hands and eyes could be helpful.

I picked up Albert and dropped him at the store with his electronic toys. When I left, he was attempting to track Linda's cell phone.

I drove to Linda's office, and let myself in through the rear door. The place was a mess. File drawers were open and the contents strewn on the floor. A couple of chairs were overturned and the displays were in heaps.

I spotted Bobby's BMW pulling in out front. I crossed to the front door, unlocked it and motioned him inside.

My first response was an overwhelming urge to use him for a punching bag. He had dragged the woman I loved into this mess while trying to break us up. One look at his face revealed that someone had beaten me to my fantasy.

"I caught Bennett ransacking this place. I tried to tell him that she had nothing to do with Joe's missing files, but he said he had his orders. He punched me and told me to stay out of it or it was going to cost me more than a few legal fees," Bobby explained.

"When did this happen?" I asked.

"Earlier today. I have been trying to contact the other partners to get them to intervene, but no one answers my calls."

"You mean Steve and Tony?"

"Right."

"I'm surprised that you don't know that Tony is in jail for breaking into the Henley home, assaulting Albert and torching the house. Steve is recovering from the injuries he got at the fire but hasn't been arrested yet."

"I was hired only to represent them in the condominium development application. I don't do criminal law anyway."

I filled him in on the demands.

"I had someone drop off some files at the station. That should tie up one more of the henchmen. Albert is back at the store trying to get a fix on where Linda is being held."

"Franklin, they aren't going to let Linda go. We have to find her."

"Without violating your professional ethics, you must have some idea of the places that they would take Linda. We need to get out there and start looking for her."

"The Monument Condominiums LLC has holdings all over town. I'll get the addresses. We should start with the vacant houses they have optioned. There are at least two dozen vacant buildings to check." Bobby located the list on his phone and sent a copy to mine. I released the blocking to receive it.

I thought back to the phone call from Linda. In a flash it came to me. I didn't know if that was where she is being held, but I knew where that recording was made. I didn't want Bobby riding to the rescue and decided to check this hunch out myself.

"You start with the properties south of Arnold and east of Thames Street. I'll start at Smith Street and work north. If you see anything suspicious, call Officer Williams."

After Bobby and I split up I used the landline in Linda's office and called Albert.

Albert didn't waste any time giving me the news. "Steve Smith called. One of his guys found Linda's car. It's pulled into the brush along Arnold Street. The last call from Linda's phone was from that neighborhood. Steve's going to check it out personally. He said I should tell you if you called in."

"I'm pretty sure that Linda was in the basement of the Queen Anne when she made the ransom tape. She might still be there. I'm going to check there first. Anything else?"

"Ginny called. She's on her way back from Rhode Island. She left a message for you. She said the guy you're after isn't in Charlestown. He is somewhere in Groton City."

Chapter 31

My heart was pounding as I drove toward the intersection of Mitchell and Arnold. I shut off the headlights and coasted the last half block.

I stepped out and looked up the hill toward the Queen Anne. Fog had rolled in off the ocean. A faintly iridescent mist hung about roof height, blocking the moon and stars but providing enough light to navigate. Several vehicles were parked along Arnold Street. I slipped along the line using the vehicles to shield me from anyone watching. I passed a Jeep with Rhode Island plates but ignored it when I saw Linda's Miata partially hidden in the shade. Its engine was cold, but the third vehicle, Steve's Hummer, was still warm. I slipped in and out of the shadows with an unlit flashlight in one hand. The damp, cool mist wrapped around me like a bad memory. I shivered and ran quietly up the hill until I reached the driveway of the Queen Anne.

I climbed up on the porch listening for signs of human presence. I gently pulled on the remains of a storm door and pushed on the inner door. The wooden slab opened and I slipped into the house. It was much darker inside than on the street. What light penetrated the fog did little more than brighten the window panes. I navigated around piles of debris trying to remember the floor plan.

I tripped on something the size and texture of a small sofa.

My knees plunged into the soft mass, prompting a grunt from the heap.

I risked giving away my presence by turning on the flashlight. The beam revealed that I had fallen on the body of a large man. I shut off the flashlight and knelt beside the still form. The guy groaned again, so I rolled him onto his back. Steve Smith was slowly regaining consciousness.

Steve's eyes focused and darted around the darkened room. "I think she is here but someone hit me from behind."

"Do you think you can walk?" I asked. Steve's reply wasn't reassuring so I helped him up and supported him as we quietly slipped out onto the porch. I set Steve on the front steps and gave him the only weapon I could find, a three foot length of two by two lumber. "Call 911. I'm going for Linda."

I slipped into the house and as quietly as the creaking floors would allow moved toward the back of the kitchen. I inched toward the basement stairs, pulled the door open and crept down the steps.

I must have made some noise, or probably it was the draft from opening the door. A flashlight began to swivel in my direction. I remembered from my earlier visits that the back of the basement, adjacent to the stairs, had a small room that in years past was used to store coal. I slipped into the opening and crouched behind a counter-high stone wall separating the coal bin from the rest of the basement.

The beam of a flashlight speared the air, swept across the wall behind me, and came to rest on the stairway. The footsteps were nearly silent on the sandy floor except for a soft scrape. The stairs creaked and heavy footsteps faded toward the kitchen above. I cautiously turned on my flashlight, holding it down low and against my hand.

In the dim light I saw a partially exhumed skeleton. Most of the body was still buried but the water that had been undermining the foundation had washed away one side revealing a hand, forearm, and shoeless foot. In the damp, not much was left but bones and a few pieces of jewelry. I choked down the vomit in my throat and picked up a watch bearing the initials RC. Toward the center of the grave was another shiny object. This wasn't jewelry but a tool. It was a rusty, long-bladed, quarter-inch antique chisel. I picked it up and placed it in my pocket.

Linda whimpered. I aimed my light across the room and illuminated her, sitting on the sand, her hands tied behind her, and secured to a support column. I sprinted toward her and knelt down with the light on my face. "Shh! It's me. I'm going to get you out of here." I reached for the tape over Linda's mouth. Her eyes were as large as saucers and focused over my shoulder.

I assumed it was the whole kidnapping ordeal that had her so fearful and was about to tell her to be quiet when the blow came.

When I came to, I was sitting on wet sand in much the same position I'd found Linda. My arms were pulled behind me and tied behind a steel column. My vision cleared enough to reveal Linda similarly trussed a few feet away.

"Frankie, are you okay?" She sobbed. When I didn't reply she cursed someone behind me. "Damn you, if you have killed him I'll ..."

"He is not dead," interrupted a vaguely familiar voice. "See, your boyfriend is rejoining us, but that condition is only temporary for both of you."

The speaker stayed out of sight, but I knew who it was. Of the faces in the picture, Tony Gorky was in jail for torching Albert's home, Victor Bennett was enjoying the hospitality of the Groton City Police while he explained why he nearly ran over Officer Williams, and Steve Smith was keeping up his post as a sentry on the front porch. Robert Caspar was almost certainly dead in the coal bin. That only left the fifth partner, the faded face in the photo. Thanks to the picture at Ginny's parents' home I knew who he was. The man's voice confirmed my guess.

"So you decided to do your own dirty work today. What's the matter, couldn't you persuade Ginny to do it for you?" I asked.

My captor let out a disgusted grunt. "You couldn't leave it

alone, could you? In a few weeks all the money would have been gone and I would have destroyed the last link between me and this place. I'd have been rich enough to give you and my daughter a bang-up wedding."

"That's not going to happen. I know too much and so do other people. You are through, so don't make it worse."

Max Maxwell lifted the shovel that he had used to knock me out. He entered the coal bin and was gone for a few minutes. I could hear the shovel biting the sand. *He's reburying the corpse,* I thought. Max returned. "That bastard Caspar needs to stay missing a bit longer to keep anyone for looking for the money."

"So you're the one who has been laundering the money. What I can't figure out is why it took someone with your skills so long to process it all."

"That moron Caspar converted everything we stole to cash, thinking it would be easier to fence. He hid the stuff in the furnace without telling anyone. He hadn't figured on first the war on drugs, and then the crackdown on terrorists following 9/11. By the time I found the money, it was nearly impossible to move that much cash."

"You killed Joe when he figured out that you were laundering it through construction projects and threatened to expose you."

"He contacted me in RI and said he had traced millions in deposits to me. He offered a deal to let me avoid prosecution. Turn over the codes to the accounts and help him with some scheme of his." Max shook his head in disgust. "How could an over-the-hill old-house-nut have figured that out?"

"So you paid him a visit and tossed him off the roof."

"I hadn't planned on that, but it worked out pretty well for me. He would have blackmailed me for the rest of my life. All it took was a little shove. I flew to Europe the next day with all my problems solved, until you stuck your nose in."

"It's over now. Leave us and run. You have the money and a head start. Use them."

"Great idea. But there is the issue of whatever evidence Joe had. You really don't have it, do you?" When I didn't reply he continued. "You're a pretty smart guy. In time you probably would find the stuff. I think that Joe meant you to. That's a chance I don't plan to take. You two are going to die tonight. Steve is going to kill you. Unfortunately he's going to fall trying to make his escape and die in the fire he started. I've been doing the books for Steve, Victor, and Tony for years. It won't surprise you that they appear to have been laundering the money. Having them take the fall for your murders as well as fraud will make this more convincing."

That confirmed my earlier guess. The information in Joe's files that Max feared was not about some extramarital affair he was hiding from Veronica, but his role in the Washington Way fraud. I suspected that Max Maxwell was the ringleader, the one who put Robert Caspar up to the theft in the first place. Later Max had found the cash hidden in the Queen Anne and used Steve, Tony, and Victor to clear it, planning all along to double-cross the trio once again.

"And that smart phone had the information necessary to put you away. I wouldn't be surprised if one of those strings of numbers were bank accounts and passwords. If you kill us you'll never get the phone back."

"With you dead I won't need it. The money will be transferred out before the police have identified the bodies. Enough talk, I'm out of here."

The longer I could keep him talking the longer we had to live. "Max, I don't understand why you would kill Robert Caspar before he told you where the money was hidden."

"I don't know who killed Caspar, but they saved me the trouble."

With that, Max Maxwell climbed the stair. A few minutes later we heard him clumping around the kitchen over our heads.

"Oh Frankie, I'm so sorry. I came here looking for my bracelet. The guy you called Max was in the basement."

"It's okay. We need to get out of here."

"How can we do that? We're tied up."

We heard our captor lugging heavy objects around upstairs. The exertion had him coughing and swearing. He was blocking the exits.

It was time to get creative. Knowing a thing or two about old houses I had an idea. "Linda, look behind me. What am I tied to?"

Linda looked over my head. "It's one of those adjustable jack posts, you know, the kind of hollow pipe they use to lift sagging floors—the ones in two pieces with pins in the middle and a screw jack at the top."

Thank goodness Linda is a designer who knows building techniques.

"Look carefully at the beam the post is holding up. Is the beam above the post in two pieces or continuous?"

"It stretches from wall to wall."

That was what I needed to hear. If I could get the post loose I could slip my arms free and untie us without the floor above us falling in.

I struggled to my feet. I fingered the fat steel pins that held the telescoping sections of the post together. If the pins as big around as my thumb had been placed loosely I might have been able to pop them out and collapse the post. No way. The weight of the beam pressed so hard that the pins may as well have been welded.

I flopped back to the floor and felt the antique chisel in my pocket jab my leg. With a little twisting I managed to get my fingers around and extract it. I got to my feet and probed the steel tube looking for the empty adjustment holes. I found one, inserted the chisel through, locked my fingers around it like the jaws of a pipe wrench, and twisted. Upstairs we heard the sounds of more debris being piled against the cellar door.

The entire column twisted slightly. "Linda, look at the screw on the top of the column. Does it move when I turn the column?"

If the screw was rusted to the top plate a counterclockwise twisting motion should loosen the column.

I locked my hands and scooted around in a large circle twisting the column. The threads were rusty and resisted.

"The pipe is moving but the screw isn't. The column is riding up on the screw!" She knew how these posts work and realized that in a couple of circuits the post might be loose enough for me to yank it off its base. "Keep going!"

By the second circuit around the post, the metal plate at the top had started to slip. The column was shortening!

As I finished hopping around for the third turn, I heard the thump of rapid footsteps above my head, moving toward the front of the house. Smoke began to filter through cracks around the basement door and I heard the crackle of a fire.

The events that came next happened in a matter of seconds, but the intervals seemed much longer.

"Damn you!" roared a voice. "You're not burning me." I heard the sound of a struggle on the front porch. "Steve, we're down here," I called.

I didn't wait for a reply but continued to work on the column.

Linda squirmed against her bonds. "Hurry."

Above us the fire crackled with more intensity. The smoke poured through cracks in the floor, drawn down by the drafty cellar. In the next instant headlights flashed across the cellar windows. Brakes squealed and seconds later I felt the jolt of something crashing into the house.

A voice that sounded like Bobby filtered down. "Oh my God, I've killed him."

Linda and I screamed to be heard over the sound of the fire above us. I made one more hopping circuit around the post. At last the top plate slipped, the column loosened and tipped away from the ceiling. The beam holding the floor over our heads groaned and sagged, but held.

I bent at the waist and tipped the hollow metal tube onto my back. Grasping it, I leaned forward, tilting it toward the front wall. The top of the post slammed into the little window high on the basement wall, breaking the glass. Groggy from exertion and breathing smoke, I leaned against the cool stones and shouted toward the opening.

"Bobby, we're in the basement."

Seconds later Bobby poked in his head through the opening.

"Franklin. The upstairs is in flames. You have to get out of there."

"We're tied and the exits are blocked," Linda said.

"This window is too small for me to get to you," Bobby said.

"Come to the basement window on the Monument side," I said. "The wall is about to fall in anyway."

"Right." Bobby's head disappeared. An eternity later his face emerged in the back window. "The hatchway is locked from inside. Stand back," he said.

A leather-soled two-hundred-dollar Cole-Han shoe smashed into the frame sending the window crashing into the basement. "The opening is still too small."

"Sit down on the ground and push against that stone block under the window," I ordered, remembering the flaw in the construction Steve had pointed out.

Bobby slammed his heels into the stone and the block slid in an inch. He bent his legs and pushed again. The massive rock tipped forward, rocked and fell inward, taking a large section of wall with it.

Bobby slid down into the basement riding on the crude ramp of heavy stones. He slammed down on the wet sandy floor, and crawled toward Linda. He picked unsuccessfully at the knots binding her hands. He ran to the window I'd broken, picked up a piece of glass, raced back to Linda, and slashed at the cords binding her. The ropes frayed. He removed them, pulled Linda up and pushed her in the direction of the collapsed stone foundation wall. "Climb out. I'll get Franklin," he ordered.

Bits of flaming wreckage were beginning to filter through openings in the floor above, creating nightmare shadows as they flickered in the semi-darkness.

Bobby approached me wild-eyed. His clothes and face and

arms were covered with mud. Flaming cinders sprinkled down on him and extinguished with a sizzle when they touched his wet clothes. Blood from cuts on his palms dripped from the makeshift blade. "Turn around," he ordered.

I felt the glass shard slashing at the cords around my wrists. The column clattered to the ground as my arms came free. Bobby finished off the cords around my legs with one firm stroke and grabbed my arm. "Come on. We need to get out of here before everything falls into the basement."

As we scrambled toward the collapsed wall I scooped up the chisel that had saved my life and followed Linda and Bobby through the opening. Behind me the main beam from which I removed the jack post sagged, splintered, and crashed into the basement. Most of the kitchen floor followed. The draft coming from the opening in the foundation caused burning wallpaper pieces to swirl around the room.

Bobby and I burst onto the lawn as a shower of sparks hissed overhead. Without a second thought, Bobby and I jumped on Linda, smothering the sparks on her clothes and hair with our mud-caked hands. She sputtered, pushed us off and helped extinguish the burning cinders on us.

Flames were shooting overhead from the fire not twenty feet away. We rolled a little further to the safety of a drainage ditch and watched the spectacular fire from the slime-covered swale. Despite the heat Linda shivered and huddled between Bobby and me. I appreciated the familiar feel of her body against mine and wrapped an arm around her. I noticed that Bobby had done the same.

In time the flashes of police and fire vehicles appeared on the street on the front side of the building. Several firemen worked around to the rear of the house, pulling a large hose, attempting to keep the flames from spreading to the brush.

"Over here!" I called.

The firemen helped the three of us crawl up out of the ditch and to the street where Steve Smith was already sitting behind an ambulance. Two EMTs had a gurney on the lawn near where Bobby's Beemer was buried into the porch. "I hit some guy running out of the house," Bobby explained.

A neighbor brought over lawn chairs and we sat on the sidewalk along Arnold Street. The three of us were cold, shivering, and filthy, but very grateful to be alive.

Blood was gushing from Bobby Lester's hand. He took one look at the blood and fainted away. I caught his arms as he fell and Linda cradled his head. An EMT rushed over and applied a dressing to the cut. Bobby stirred and opened his eyes. Linda stroked the head of my archrival. "You saved us Bobby."

I took some solace when her attempt at a kiss was interrupted by a fit of coughing.

"Best save that for later," said the EMT. "You breathed in too much smoke."

A car door slammed and the prettiest IRS agent on the east coast sprinted across and into my arms. Ignoring the mud, Ginny pressed against me. The EMTs shook their heads. "Kids."

"Oh, Franklin, I never meant for any of this to happen," Ginny whispered.

"Why are you here?"

"Aunt Julia called and told me Linda had been kidnapped. The police told me about the fire."

"Your father is over there. He was running out of the burning house when Bobby hit him with his car."

Ginny followed my gaze to where the EMTs were loading Max Maxwell onto a gurney. She seemed relieved to see that he was alive. She turned to me with tear-filled eyes. "Franklin, you have to believe me. I didn't know about any of this."

I studied the face of the woman I thought I might grow to love. "You've known all along that Max was after Joe's files. You used me to get to them."

"Franklin, I believed Dad when he said that he was being blackmailed over a silly affair. I wanted to help spare Mother the hurt of finding out."

I might have cut her some slack if I hadn't been so completely taken in by her earlier deception. I was sure that she didn't believe that her father was capable of such evil. But she had played me like the con artist she was. I gestured toward Max. "Go to him, he needs you more than I do."

Ginny lowered her head, turned, and trudged back to her FJ Cruiser. She looked at the EMTs working on Max. Her expression hardened. She climbed in and slowly drove off. She was distancing herself from Max, probably to avoid prosecution as an accessory to fraud and murder. It occurred to me that Max and I were the only ones who knew of her efforts to remove Max's secret from Joe's files.

The police were talking to Steve Smith who had apparently recovered from the bang on the head. He was gesturing angrily toward Max Maxwell telling anyone who would listen that Max intended to leave Steve to burn in the fire. The details he was giving the police were likely to place the icing on the government's case when they charged Max with fraud and attempted murder.

I was relieved that no one had been killed. My stubbornness had gotten enough people hurt already. I was grateful not to have a death on my conscience.

Linda came over. "I'm going with Bobby to the hospital."

As it sunk in that I'd finally lost her, the firemen let up a shout for everyone to get back further. Seconds later the upper stories collapsed into the basement with a roar and a shower of sparks. The Queen Anne was gone. It was a small consolation that it took Bobby's car with it.

Chapter 32

It was the pre-dawn hours of Tuesday morning before the police and medics finally got everyone sorted out. The EMTs strongly suggested another scan of my head at the hospital, but I passed. All I wanted was to point my trusty pickup toward home and curl up in my own bed.

Albert had called Eric to bring my parents home. They made the three hour drive and were back at Mom and Dad's house when I pulled in. We settled in the living room where I told the story of what happened and as much as I knew about Joe's death and Washington Way. As I had with the police, I left out finding Robert Caspar's body in the coal bin. The sun was nearly up before we headed toward the bedrooms.

Sleep didn't come easily. I was through with Ginny. She had manipulated me, conspired to obstruct justice, made false statements to the local police, and endangered my family. The secrets I had on her were enough to get her fired and probably do time in jail as well. She probably had noticed a couple of transgressions that could get me in trouble too. Those offsetting secrets might produce a standoff, but couldn't nurture a romance. I wasn't sure what to do about her.

The fiery collapse of the Queen Anne was a good metaphor for my life, equally in ruins. My world was filled with dishonest people with deep secrets and people like Joe willing to use blackmail to keep them in line. The most frightening thing was that I had begun to enjoy the power behind the extortion. I had found Linda in time because I'd used blackmail on Steve. But maybe the worst discovery of all was the tool in my pocket. I had formed an idea how it came to be in Robert Caspar's grave in the Queen Anne, but wasn't sure I had the courage to follow up on that theory.

Linda hadn't said anything about Caspar's body, so she probably hadn't been in the coal bin the night of the fire. Max and I were the only ones who had seen the body. Unless Max told Ginny she didn't know about the body. Assuming that Max was telling the truth, that he hadn't killed Caspar, only three of us knew he was buried in the dirt basement: Max, me and the killer. Max was in enough trouble already and probably wasn't going to talk. Caspar's killer had no motivation to mention the corpse. That left me with a difficult decision.

Around mid morning I wandered upstairs into my parents' kitchen. I started a pot of coffee. I must not have been the only one who couldn't sleep because as I sat down to my first cup, Dad shuffled into the kitchen. He yawned and rubbed the white stubble on his chin. He poured himself a cup and sat opposite me.

"How's the head?"

"The head's okay. It's the thoughts that keep me up."

"I warned you that things could turn messy if you started digging around the Washington Way disaster. That whole mess ruined everyone who touched it and still hasn't lost its power to destroy."

"Well, at least we can get some of your money back. Albert cracked the codes on some files that seem to have offshore bank account information. It's a matter of time until the money is collected and returned."

"I suspect that the government will take a big bite out of that for unpaid taxes. Still, we could come up with a decent return." Dad paused to take a sip of coffee. "You should have a sizeable reward coming too."

Dad and I needed to talk, but not about reward money. "Dad, how do you think Robert Caspar died? Max Maxwell admitted to a lot of stuff, but he denied killing him."

Dad stared into his coffee cup. He looked up with an expression a poker champion would have admired. "Without a body the police are going to have a tough time pinning murder on someone, assuming that Caspar really is dead."

I looked at Dad carefully. He didn't have the distracted expression I'd seen when he was wandering around Groton Bank. "I might be able to help the police find the body, but I wonder if it's worth all the trouble it will cause."

Dad took a while to reply. He looked me in the eyes. "Do what you have to do, but what's the point? If Caspar's dead, he's beyond punishment. Thanks to you and Albert the money's been found and the guy who put Caspar up to the theft is under arrest in the hospital."

"Wouldn't the body provide closure for Bobby and his mom?"

"I doubt that confirming that Caspar was a thief is going to give them closure, more likely it'll open old wounds."

I couldn't bring myself to ask the direct question on my mind. "Dad, is there anything more I should know about Washington Way and Robert Caspar?"

"Nothing that wouldn't put you in a worse spot than you already are."

We sat in silence for a while and then spent another hour together discussing a plan Dad was working out to sell the house to Albert's family and move to the Florida condo with mom.

I was stiff and sore from the previous day and knew from experience that moving was the best cure for me. "I'm going to spend some time in the shop. There is a pretty coffee table I want to restore the old way. Do you still have the set of woodworking tools you inherited from Grandpa?"

Dad gave me a penetrating stare. He seemed lost in thought. He could have been trying to remember where his tools were, or he could have been reliving some past event. When his eyes focused he cut me a sharp look. "Sure. All my hand tools are in the tool cabinet in the garage. I'm not likely to do any more woodwork, and I don't want to ship all that stuff to Florida. Take anything you want."

I swung by the garage on the way to my shop. Dad valued tools for their function not their beauty, so all the hand tools were heaped in a drawer together. I removed chisels belonging to a set I remembered being displayed in an old rosewood box in Grandpa's shop. I sorted through the drawer until I had extracted as many as I could find. They were one-of-a-kind tools that a blacksmith had made for Grandpa.

I carried them to my shop. The empty display box was sitting on a high shelf. I took it down, sorted the chisels by size and placed them in the slots cut in the box insert. When the seven were all in place one slot remained open.

I reached in my coat pocket, removed the rusty, quarter inch chisel I'd found in the basement of the Queen Anne. It fit in the open slot.

The thirteen inch steel shaft had a wicked point that had at one time been razor sharp, but now the piece was covered with a decade of grime and rust-colored stains. I soaked it in a container of industrial solvent and scrubbed the stains lightly with steel wool. I honed the edge on a bench grinder, and polished the metal shaft on a buffing wheel until it shone like new. A good rubbing with oil restored the luster to the wooden handle. I placed it in the box. One by one I extracted the other seven pieces, and cleaned, polished, and sharpened each one. As I worked, I reflected with surprise how easily I had reached the decision to keep the circumstances in which I'd found the eighth chisel a secret.

Chapter 33

Two weeks following my decision not to ask Dad what he knew about the body in the basement of the Queen Anne, Nora signed what was left of the old Victorian to me. The City gave permission to demolish the place.

I had been waiting for the other shoe to drop in the form of a search for a body, but it never came. The cops found the briefcases of money in Max's car. They wanted to question him, but Max was in a coma and not expected to wake, which might be the best for him. Joe's blood and hair and Max Maxwell's prints were on the paint can removed from Joe's attic. If he woke up, Max would go on trial for murder.

Victor Bennett had been eager to comply with my request to clean up the debris. I ordered him to leave the basement floor undisturbed. I told him we were trying to avoid uncovering a spring and incurring the objections of the wetlands people. Steve, Tony, and Victor planned to take over the Monument Condominium development under a new LLC, and they still needed a road. The trio had bought the lot from me, and an access road into the monument parcel was already under construction over the old footprint of the house.

It's surprising what you can hide under six feet of compressed gravel.

Shortly after the demolition was completed, Ginny asked for a face-to-face meeting. "To clear the air."

I knew what she wanted and suggested a public place, one away from inquisitive ears. We met in the parking lot next to the monument. Ginny placed her cell phone on the seat of her car. I did the same.

We marched to the hillside overlooking New London Harbor. So much wickedness and betrayal had occurred here. Ginny and I weren't here to discuss something as tragic as the surrender and then slaughter of the colonial defenders by their British oppressors. The crimes which Ginny and I were here to discuss weren't as serious as the revolution, but also involved betrayal and murder.

Ginny didn't waste any time getting to the point. "The police don't know that I was looking for information about Dad in Joe Simpson's files. Are you planning to tell them?"

I studied her familiar face and form. She was a beauty. I'd fallen for her when her only interest was in using me. Now it was my turn to use her. "I'm not going to say anything to the police. I need you close to the investigation. You're going to do a couple of things for me."

Ginny's hopeful expression hardened into resentment as the threat registered. "So that's how it's going to be. What do you want me to do?"

"Nothing much. First you are going to expedite the return of Dad's investment from Washington Way. He's sick and needs the money. Second, you are going to see that the IRS expresses no further interest in locating Robert Caspar."

I could almost see Ginny's computer-like brain leaping ahead. "You know where he is or you know who killed him. The question is why you don't want that to come out."

"It would be better for you not to think that way."

"Because the answer would make what you asked a crime."

"Clever girl."

Ginny looked out over the water. "Funny about us. We started out as basically honest people and look at us now, conspiring to suppress information about crimes." Ginny stepped closer and put her hand on mine. "We're really not bad people. Is there any chance for us?"

I ached to take her in my arms and tell her we could give it a try. Instead, I mentally kicked my hopeful heart back into a dark corner. "How could we, with what we know about each other? How could I ever truly believe you?"

I returned to my old truck, climbed inside, and drove slowly away. I'd learned enough about blackmail to know that one-sided love was the ultimate formula for extortion. I didn't trust myself to look at her a moment more.

Once Ginny was out of sight, I turned into the library parking lot and stopped behind a row of holly bushes. I could see Meridian Street, but passing traffic couldn't see me. Minutes later Ginny's Sun Fusion FJ cruiser drove by. At slow speed I could see her makeup had run and tears coursed down her cheeks.

Finally an honest reaction. It was a pity that I couldn't tell if she was grieving for lost love or angry about being blackmailed.

Right then I decided to leave Groton City. My much-loved home town had turned out to be a sewer of deceit and threats. I didn't want to be part of it anymore. Maybe I'd head down to Florida like Mom and Dad. Florida had an unsavory reputation of its own, but at least my expectations were lower. Construction was slow in the south right now, but it was bound to pick up soon.

The old granite library lurked behind a screen of yellow and orange leaves. I climbed out of the truck and headed inside to say goodbye to Julia. Kristi, the student intern I'd met earlier, was behind the massive reception desk. Her long, straight hair was glistening and as dark as the grain pattern of the oak paneling. Her olive skin glowed. She treated me to the kind of expression usually reserved for celebrities. I looked around the room for a famous author doing a reading, but the tables and chairs held only local characters. "Hi, Mr. Breault. Wow, everyone is talking about how you caught that murderer. All my friends want to hear what it's like to know a famous private investigator."

'You can call me Franklin. I'm a handyman. Is Julia in?"

Kristi picked up the phone, punched in Julia's code, and hung up. She was still smiling when the phone rang. She nodded to the caller. "I'll tell him." She focused her smoky eyes on mine. "Mrs. Judge will meet you in Storage Room E."

Storage room E was a space in the far recesses of the basement that I had never heard of. I descended a stairway so old it was made of stone blocks. At the base of the stair was a long, dark corridor. The ceiling was formed by unadorned floor joists punctuated by light sockets filled with fluorescent bulbs resembling pigs' tails. The walls were covered with rough, unfinished wood stained dark by a century of mildew. My boots scuffed across a rough concrete floor.

The hall ended against a door that to the untrained eye appeared to be of rough boards. However, I noticed the absence of hinge pins, suggesting a more sophisticated barrier. The door opened smoothly and noiselessly, revealing a modern steel core that could have heralded the presence of a bank vault.

Storage Room E was about twenty feet square. Every inch of wall space from floor to ceiling was covered with shelves. The shelves contained hundreds of file boxes, yellowed with age and squatting from their own weight. In the center of the room was a rough pine table containing a flat screen monitor, wireless keyboard, and a note.

The note said "Log in. I'll be along in a minute." Below the signature was a password. I tapped the keyboard, entered the character string at the prompt and waited. A program took over and activated a cartoon version of the room I was in. The walls were covered with the faces of file boxes.

When I ran the cursor over a box, a title describing the contents displayed. In a dialog box below the picture of the room was the invitation to: "Type a name, or ask a question."

I typed in the name of a plumber I disliked.

An avatar that looked like a cartoon version of Joe appeared on the screen, approached a wall of file folders, pulled out a ladder, climbed up and took the box down.

David Edgar Cournoyer

The cover lifted and a cursor was placed on a folder. I clicked. The top document was a Best Business Bureau rating sheet listing a C grade. I clicked and an arrest record for robbery appeared. Each click produced another document revealing the poor character of the tradesman.

The final document was a complaint from a customer who found a hidden camera in her renovated bathroom.

A row of option buttons appeared. I clicked on 'violence potential'. "Don't leave this guy alone with your wife," it said.

"Pretty scary isn't it?" said a voice behind me. I hadn't heard Julia enter.

"Is there more like this?"

"There is something on everyone who has ever lived or worked in this town. Maybe more than anyone should know."

"These are Joe's files. How did you get them?"

"Joe and I've been working on this for years. We started after a leak in the roof over his archive gave him a scare. Most of the original documents are here, and the files are growing all the time. The program adds material in public records on a regular basis. I add my personal notes on sensitive stuff."

I considered what she could do with such a tool. "So you knew Ginny was probably using me."

"No. The relational data base and artificial intelligence tools track facts and rumors, but only on locals. Ginny is not from here so she isn't in the system. I didn't even guess her agenda because her behavior was out of character. I'm very sorry how things turned out between you two."

"Why are you showing this to me? I'm not a blackmailer."

Julia gave a crooked smile. "Aren't you? I think Steve, Victor, and Tony would disagree. Think of it this way. This is information. Everything in these files is available to anyone willing to do some digging. The files are a tool to do the digging faster."

"More like picking up a hot tool left too long in the sun."

She ignored my sarcasm. "The system requires two people to

267

work. I'm the analyst and stay in the background. The data would be too vulnerable if anyone knew I had it. Joe was the front man. I'm offering Joe's position to you. Together we could head off the people who are destroying our architectural heritage for profit."

There they were, the keys to success, mine for the asking. Julia was offering me enough power to make my dream of turning Groton City into a model of historic preservation. It was tempting. However, even my limited access to the files had started to corrupt me. Active participation would likely finish the job. Then what would I become?

"Whether it is used for good or evil is up to whoever has access. I'm going to find someone to work with me on this, and it might as well be you. You can head off any abuse of Joe's legacy."

"I'll think about it."

Chapter 34

"Bro, you finished the condo," said Albert.

"Thanks for everything, Albert, especially having my back."

We were in my parents' home where the Henleys had been living since theirs burned. Albert and Marti planned to buy the place when my parents moved to Florida. They'd live upstairs and Barbara Henley planned to settle in my mid century modern basement apartment. Knowing my friends would live there made leaving my home easier.

The family and friends milling around were celebrating the certificate of occupancy I'd earned for my new place. I hadn't moved into it yet, but I'd bought the Simpson's home with the money I got from selling the land under the Queen Anne. I'd split the Greek Revival into two condos, and funded the project by selling the first floor unit to Eric and Amy.

Eric and Amy were telling Mom about their new condo. Not one to let his disability stop him, Eric had worked right along with me, as had Amy. They were as capable as they were loyal.

"Victor Bennett has offered a truck and crew to move you when you're ready," I said. Victor was one of several people grateful for what I hadn't said about his role in the Washington Way and Monument Condominium scams. He was eager to please me. I felt like a character out of the *Godfather*, but I felt good. I guess power does corrupt.

Nora Simpson had come to the party with the sister with

whom she now lived. Nora was still grieving, but the closure provided by the investigation had helped. She looked happy in a blue suit and curled hair. She hugged me. "Well done on the condo conversion, and you've earned your license too."

Nora had persuaded an architect to supervise the renovation of the Greek Revival, giving me the internship I needed. I was please to have my license, but I still felt bad about how much the Simpsons had suffered because of their support. "I'll never forget all that you and Joe did for me."

I wandered around greeting guests and sampling the snacks for a while. Julia Judge found me on my way to the kitchen. "So how does it feel to finally be an up-and-coming architect?"

I poured a glass of beer and offered the first one to her. The work was pouring in too, especially renovations of Victorians. The publicity over my role unmasking the two real estate frauds, and rumors about my link to Joe's files had certainly helped. "Busy. How's 'Joe's List' doing?"

I had accepted Julia's invitation to continue Joe's work protecting architecture, but with a twist. We'd launched a website that helped homeowners locate reputable tradesmen. At last something positive was growing in all that dirt.

"We had our thousandth hit last week. Our other project is doing well too," she said of an old home we'd saved.

As Julia exited the kitchen, Dad came in, wearing his best gray suit. We hadn't seen much of each other lately. He began stacking appetizers on a dish. I could feel the awkwardness in the room. "Did you hear that the Henleys are going to close on this house next week?" he said.

We had a lot to say, to each other but hadn't yet found a way to say it. "I heard. So you're ready to move to Florida?"

Dad seemed lost in thought. I wondered if his illness was progressing. "It's the right thing to do and easier now that you're settled. I'll miss our little talks, though."

I already missed them, but it wasn't renovating the Greek Revival that kept me away. Discovering Caspar's body and evidence that Dad had murdered him had undermined our relationship. I was running out of time to ask the question smoldering in my mind since the night of the fire. I led him to the back porch were no one could overhear. "About Robert Caspar, why did you do it?"

"It wasn't planned. He'd been a friend until he stole grandpa's house and your college fund. When I caught up with him, I lost control. It's over, can't you forget it?"

"Dad you're a murderer. What's worse every time I see you I'm reminded that I covered up the murder."

"I warned you not to dig into Washington Way. But you and your sense of responsibility, you couldn't let go. What do you want me to do? Confess and go to jail?"

I couldn't imagine him going to prison. I didn't want to do jail time either. If we talked to the police now, it would come out that I'd altered the crime scene. Surely obstruction of justice carried a jail sentence. "It's too late for that."

Before we could say more Linda opened the door and straddled the threshold. She slid one arm around my neck and pulled my head down for a kiss. "Too late for what? For me to see the new place today?"

Mrs. Henley and Marti passed near the open door and overheard Linda. Marti put a hand on her best friend's arm. "Go ahead you two. Mom and I'll help with the cleanup."

Marti had been a good friend to us. Whatever Linda's dalliance with Bobby had been, it was short lived. Marti found out her fling was over and passed the good news to me via Albert. It took a while but Linda and I were back together.

Linda and I had rekindled our relationship, but I detected a mutual caution that hadn't been there before. Our relationship had never been easy, but I missed the complete trust.

Linda and I parked in the driveway of the Greek Revival and stepped out onto the entry path. The evening air was crisp and cool with a sea breeze and a hint of spring. Linda twirled in a circle, breathing deeply. "I love this time of year."

The bolts on the front door slid open with a smooth click, revealing a foyer smelling of fresh paint and new lumber. The shiny banister along the stair to the second floor glistened with varnish. The high ceilings, white fluted trim and complex crown moldings of the entry took my breath away.

I finally owned a Victorian home but I was disappointed. To keep costs down and to meet building codes, I'd used so many modern materials and methods that the home was no longer genuine. But it wasn't only the old home I'd corrupted. I too was an imitation of my former, more principled, self.

Linda put down the bottle of sparkling wine and glasses she'd been carrying, stepped up, and kissed me. "I love the way you have modernized the place. It's brilliant."

We drank a toast as lighthouse beacons swept by the widows and lights from boats glowed like giant fireflies.

Later we climbed the steep stair to the attic to reclaim bundles of cotton drop cloths left by the painters.

A black snake undulated across the wide board floor and disappeared into a hole in the wall.

Linda shrieked, and wrapped her arms around me.

"Don't worry, that's Bobby the snake." I'd renamed Harvey and let him stay as a reminder to let old boyfriends lie.

Linda frowned. "You didn't! There was never anything between me and Bobby. He was ..."

"What was he to you, Linda?"

"I thought he'd love me more than you. I know you're more passionate about your work than me. But Bobby loves the law the way you love Victorians, so I was second again."

"Do you still love him?"

"No. Even if I'm second in your life, you have more passion for me than Bobby is capable of."

"Work and romance are different. I can be passionate about work and love you without one taking from the other."

"What about other women? I saw the way Ginny looked at you. Are you passionate about her?"

"There is nothing between us either." That wasn't full disclosure, but complete honesty was proving to be costly.

We made a bed of drop cloths, undressed and slipped in.

Later as we lay exhausted and content, I pushed the hair away from Linda's face. I hoped that my recent financial success, the new home, and the romantic evening might change her mind about us. I was still hurting over the last time she'd refused, but I had more to offer this time.

"Isn't it time we took our relationship to the next level?"

Linda ruffled the hair on my neck and giggled. "We've only been dating since high school. What's the rush?"

"Come on, I'm serious. I want to marry you."

She freed a bare arm from the cloths and touched my face. "Wow. I've loved you forever, but marriage is a big step.

"Haven't we run out of reasons not to?" I kissed her lips.

Linda furrowed her brow, looking troubled. She modestly wrapped a sheet around her torso and sat up.

"Being together day and night could be weird."

"Perfect was the word I had in mind."

Linda looked around the empty room, as if desperate for a reason to object. "We don't even have a proper bed."

I laughed. "I'll build you one, whatever style you want."

Linda twisted her hair thoughtfully, and stared out the window at the Block Island Ferry, silently cruising out to sea.

"Okay, a compromise. I'll move in with you. If everything is still going well in a year, then we'll talk about a wedding."

My new powers of persuasion had landed me a small victory over Linda's resistance to matrimony. All it took to get her to commit to one year of cohabitation was to risk my life and become a blackmailer.

Did I mention that Linda is high maintenance?

David Edgar Cournoyer is an anthropologist and do-it-yourself fanatic. He lives in Connecticut in a house built by his own hands. He has restored several homes including a hundred-year-old Victorian-inspired bungalow in the seaside community that inspired *On the Level*.

Made in United States
North Haven, CT
24 March 2023

34503744R00153